**Logan fell on**  **there, motion** **d** **him upright a** **railing.**

And that was it. He was gone.

She stopped struggling. Tears blurred her vision, and her mind went blank. She didn't understand what was happening, but resistance seemed futile. There were too many hands on her. One of the assailants gagged her and bound her wrists with rope. He tied her ankles, too. Some kind of bag went over her head. Then she was lifted and carried onto the balcony. Although she couldn't see anything, she could feel her body being lowered over the railing. She sobbed into the gag, frozen with terror.

Cady went down and down and down. She didn't hit the water. There was someone waiting for her on a raft below. The other assailants joined them. After they started moving it dawned on her.

She was being kidnapped.

\* \* \*

**If you're on Twitter, tell us what you think of Harlequin Romantic Suspense! #harlequinromsuspense**

Dear Reader,

I'm so excited to introduce my first novel as Susan Cliff! I've always wanted to write a romance about castaways. This fantasy scenario has all my favorite ingredients: exotic location, danger, forced proximity, outdoor survival...and sex on the beach, naturally!

I grew up watching Brooke Shields in *The Blue Lagoon*. I adored Scott O'Dell's *Island of the Blue Dolphins*. I was mesmerized by the ferocity of *Lord of the Flies*, and enthralled by the gender dynamics in *Swept Away* (the Italian version). My formative years were filled with stranded-on-an-island stories, in books and film.

Fast-forward to 2016. When the election cycle was in full swing, I really needed a break from reality. So I went to my happy place, far, far away. I dived into a tale of love and hope and survival. I wrote about two people overcoming impossible odds and learning how to thrive in a beautiful, dangerous place. I wrote about the good guys winning and love conquering all.

I hope this story brings you the same comfort and joy it brought me.

Happy reading!

*Susan Cliff*

# STRANDED WITH THE NAVY SEAL

Susan Cliff

**H** **HARLEQUIN**® ROMANTIC SUSPENSE

Recycling programs
for this product may
not exist in your area.

ISBN-13: 978-0-373-40234-2

Stranded with the Navy SEAL

Copyright © 2017 by Susan Cliff

Printed in U.S.A.

**Susan Cliff** is the pen name of a longtime romance reader and professional writer from Southern California. She has a degree in literature and writing, a job in health and fitness and a happy home with two wonderful daughters. She loves outdoor-survival stories and sexy romance, so she decided to write both. Her Team Twelve series features men to die for—hot navy SEALs who live on the edge and fall hard for their heroines. Visit her at www.susancliff.com.

## *Chapter 1*

His gaze kept returning to the beauty at the bar.

Logan had noticed her as soon as he'd entered the nightclub. Sexy red dress, dark hair, rocking body. She'd have caught his attention in any situation. Tonight he did a triple take, because she resembled the woman he'd been hired to protect for the next three weeks on this Tahitian cruise.

Unfortunately, the bodyguard detail had fallen through, leaving him stranded on the high seas with nothing to do.

He took another pull of his fancy microbrew and scanned the rest of the room. It had been months since he'd been in a club. Longer still since he'd enjoyed the comforts of female company. He shifted his sore knee, blaming the injury for the drought he'd been experiencing. Never mind the real culprit.

*Telskuf.*

Instead of dwelling on a mission gone wrong, he focused on a woman made right. Slender, with smooth brown skin and a lot of curly hair. She sat poised on a bar stool, sipping a fruity cocktail. She looked fantastic in red. He'd read somewhere that men couldn't resist the color. It triggered an uncontrollable response, like a biological urge to mate. He'd dismissed the notion as pseudoscientific foolishness then.

He believed it now.

It was an eye-catching shade, bright and hot, like fireworks. Most of her back was bare. The straps of her dress crossed prettily between her shoulder blades. He wondered how easy it would be to take off.

She glanced over her shoulder at him as if she could sense his attention. When her gaze connected with his, something strange happened. His breath caught in his throat, and every muscle in his body tightened with awareness. It was almost as if he knew her, but he didn't know her. He'd have remembered meeting this woman. She was fashion-model beautiful. She didn't smile or invite him over. Seeming flustered, she swiveled back toward the bar and picked up her drink.

He was captivated in an instant, and he couldn't even tell if she was interested in him. She might be shy. She might be unavailable. Either way, he had to find out who she was, because all of his senses had come alive. The contrast between her demure demeanor and that sexy dress fascinated him.

Most of the women he hooked up with made it clear they were into him. They approached him first, and he liked that. He could get lucky in any of the San Diego bars that catered to military men. He was young, single and in top condition. He hadn't become a Navy SEAL by sitting on the couch.

Lately, however, he'd lost his taste for one-night stands. He'd just turned thirty, and he was tired of going out. Tired of being single. It would be nice to have someone to come home to after a grueling assignment, but his work schedule didn't leave much room for dating. He had to be ready to leave the country at the drop of a hat. He was overseas a lot, and long-distance relationships were hard to maintain.

He was kind of stuck. He didn't have a steady girlfriend, but he needed companionship, even if it was only for a few hours. He needed a woman's touch. That was why he'd wandered into this bar. He'd come in last night, too, and gone back to his room alone. Although there was no possibility of a meaningful connection here, he couldn't leave the ship. He'd spent three days prowling around the decks, swimming in the lap pool and working out in the gym until sweat poured down his body.

He was bored. He was...keyed up.

He'd always been a type-A personality, restless and overactive. Since his surgery, he'd been incapable of relaxing. He hadn't slept well. He'd been plagued by nightmares. Maybe a pretty face could help chase away the demons.

He left his table and approached the bar, bringing his bottle with him. The woman in the red dress was studying her phone. Not a good sign. He figured his chances of striking out with her were about fifty/fifty. She was drop-dead gorgeous. He was no slouch, but he might not be her type.

She glanced up as he leaned his forearm against the bar. Her expression was expectant, and a bit wary.

"Hey," he said.

She smiled politely. "Hey."

"I'm Logan."

"Cadence."

He definitely didn't know her. He'd never heard the name before. She didn't look that much like the former president's daughter, upon closer inspection. "Can I buy you a drink?"

She lifted her tumbler, which was half-full. "One's my limit."

Damn. He wasn't sure if she was rejecting him or just the drink offer. "Are you the designated driver?"

"I work here."

"In this bar?"

"On the ship."

He didn't want to make her uncomfortable by hanging around, but he also didn't want to give up too soon. He waited a few seconds, hoping for some encouragement. She set her phone aside and gestured for him to sit down.

Score.

He tried not to get too excited about the courtesy, even though she was offering him the opportunity to advance. Maybe she was interested, just not easy. He could handle that. The idea of spending more time than usual, and working harder to win her over, appealed to him. He didn't mind a challenge.

As he settled in the empty bar stool next to her, he found himself tongue-tied. She was hot, and his game was rusty. It took a few seconds before his brain started functioning again. "What do you do?"

"I'm a chef," she said, sipping her drink. "At Fillet of Soul."

He liked that. He liked food. He liked her mouth. Her lips were nicely shaped, closed around a thin black straw. The cocktail in her hand looked like a combination of fruit and mint. "I ate dinner there tonight. The halibut was delicious."

"I prepared that."

"I almost licked the plate."

She laughed at the compliment. "What do you do?"

"I'm in the navy."

"My dad was in the navy."

He was glad to hear it. Navy girls were among his favorites. They were well traveled, well brought up and appreciative of military men. "What division?"

She told him about her dad's service in Kuwait, before she was born. Logan had been to Kuwait, and plenty of other war-torn places. He lifted his beer in respect. She clinked her glass against his.

"Hooyah," he said.

"Hooyah," she repeated, smiling.

So far, so good. He was trying not to ogle her like a snack he wanted to gobble up, but it was difficult. The front of her dress was even sexier than the back. Her breasts plumped against the bodice. His eyes slid down and veered back up.

Too late. She caught him looking.

*Focus, Starke. Focus on the conversation.* "What does he do now?"

"He's a police officer."

Logan raised his bottle again.

She moved her straw around in a mix of ice cubes and crushed mint. "So you like ships?"

He shrugged, because he'd never been on a cruise ship before. After spending so much time in tight quarters on military barges, he wouldn't have chosen this for a vacation. "I was supposed to be working."

"Doing what?"

Logan couldn't disclose the specific details. "Guarding someone."

"A celebrity?"

He made a noncommittal sound. "My client canceled her trip at the last minute, and I was already onboard, all expenses paid."

"So you decided to stay."

"Yes."

Logan had been a Navy SEAL for six years, five of them under President O'Brien. Now O'Brien was a UN dignitary. Secret Service usually provided security to former presidents and their children for a lifetime, so Logan wasn't sure why SS wasn't guarding Maya O'Brien. There was some speculation, behind closed doors, that the current POTUS hadn't signed the protection order for O'Brien's family.

Either way, Logan had been happy to step in. It was an opportunity to serve a man he respected, and to make a few extra bucks during his time off. Cruising to Tahiti was no hardship. He was still recovering from knee surgery. He'd completed his physical therapy sessions, but he couldn't return to regular duty for another six weeks. Inactivity drove him crazy. He'd needed a change of scenery.

His current view was spectacular.

Cadence's phone vibrated on the bar's surface, indicating a new text. Logan could read the name of the sender: Andrew. She frowned in irritation and turned off the notifications. His protective instincts stirred.

"Someone bothering you?" he asked.

"No one important."

"Your ex?"

It was a personal question, but she didn't seem to mind. After a short hesitation, she showed him the conversation. The photo next to the text bubble showed an Asian guy in a pretentious-looking black uniform.

Him: You took a job on a cruise ship? That's beneath you
Her: You're beneath me
Him: I wish
Him: I miss you

"He's a chef, too?" Logan asked.

"A celebrity chef," she said, rolling her eyes. "Andrew Yu."

Logan wasn't impressed. "Sounds like he can't let go."

"Well, he's going to have to, because he cheated. On TV. With his costar."

"Ouch."

"Yeah."

He could tell she wasn't giving Andrew any second chances. She wasn't a pushover. He liked that. Maybe she was looking for a rebound, a diversion, or a little revenge sex. Logan was happy to be in the right place at the right time. "You should take a picture of us and tell him you're already on top of someone else."

She laughed at this suggestion, as if it really appealed to her. She had a sexy laugh, throaty and uninhibited. But she didn't pose for a photo with him. She tucked her phone into a little black purse and finished her drink in silence.

He hoped he hadn't blown his chances by being too aggressive. Subtlety wasn't his strong suit. When he wanted something, he went for it, and he wanted her. He didn't see any reason to pretend otherwise.

The club's reggae band launched into a popular Bob

Marley song, interrupting the awkward moment. She perked up at the sound.

His knee told him not to, but his mouth said, "Want to dance?"

# *Chapter 2*

She'd seen him at the restaurant.

And on the Lido deck. And in the pool, doing laps.

Every woman onboard had seen him. You couldn't *not* see a man like that. He was built like a god, with a sculpted physique that made her mouth water. He had broad shoulders and powerful thighs. Abs from a fitness magazine. Even his face looked strong. The female employees already had a nickname for him: Adonis.

Cady had admired his form just this morning, during her workout. The gym's treadmills overlooked the pool. He swam like a gold medalist. She'd watched his muscles ripple in the glistening water. When he climbed out, she'd studied every inch of his body, including the brace around his knee. The injury didn't appear to slow him down.

Rumor had it that he'd been cruising the bar last night—and he'd left alone. She hadn't come here with a specific plan to catch his attention, but she'd mentioned him to her best friend, Deborah, over the phone. Deb had insisted that she put on a sexy dress and try to "look available, but not thirsty."

Too late. One glance at him and her throat went dry.

Apparently the dress was working its magic, because he'd been staring at her. She'd picked up her phone to play it cool. Which was the opposite of looking available, but she'd been nervous. Andrew's annoying texts hadn't helped.

Months after the fallout, his betrayal still stung.

It stung a little less now, in Logan's company. She couldn't even feel it, to be honest. She couldn't feel anything except the heat of his gaze.

He wasn't handsome like a movie star. Not quite. His nose appeared to have been broken a few times. His jaw was square, and his smile was charmingly off center. He had the outdoorsy look of a football player or a mountain climber. He was at least six feet tall. She marveled at his size as they faced each other on the dance floor. His shoulders took up a lot of space. He was very solid, and…not very graceful.

She smothered a giggle while he shuffled back and forth to the music. She didn't mind his stiffness. She loved to dance, with or without a good partner. He was fine as hell, just standing there. The way he watched her, as if her simple moves were mesmerizing, made her want to rock with him all night long.

He was wearing tan pants and a white safari-style shirt. Nothing fancy, but his clothes fit well. He had close-cropped brown hair and a clean-cut, no-nonsense vibe. Underneath that tight control was a hint of raw sexuality.

He wasn't shy.

When the band switched to a slow song, his hands

went straight to her hips. She shivered at the contact. She could feel the warm press of his fingertips through the thin fabric of her dress. She could feel his boldness. Their gazes met and held. He had great eyes. Bedroom eyes that traveled up and down her body in a slow caress. They drifted from her mouth to her breasts, as if these were his two favorite places to look. She didn't blame him for looking. She wanted him to do more than look.

He drew her closer, aligning their lower bodies. Although he was at least six inches taller than her, she was wearing heels, so it wasn't a mismatch. She twined her arms around his neck. Her breasts met the hard wall of his chest. His hands flexed at her hips, and his arousal swelled against her belly.

Cady had been around this block before. There were always men who got too excited on the dance floor, or those who felt entitled to come up behind her and grind on her without asking. She'd shaken off her share of losers. It was tiresome. Never once had she encountered a stranger's erection and become weak-kneed with lust.

Until now.

Logan wasn't exactly a stranger, but they'd met ten minutes ago. They'd shared one conversation and two dances. They were also in public, on the cruise ship where she worked. None of that seemed to matter to her body, which all but melted in his arms. It didn't matter to her mouth, which let out a soft moan. Her nipples tightened, and her skin tingled with awareness. A greedy pulse throbbed between her legs. She rocked her hips back and forth against him. He groaned in response.

He didn't grind on her. He gripped her hips as if he wanted to slow her rhythm, or maybe move her up and down on him. But he didn't actually move her. He continued to sway to the music, holding her close. She traced his shirt collar and felt the warm skin underneath. Then she threaded her fingers through his short hair. Putting her hands on him felt like heaven. She wanted to touch him all over.

Then the song ended.

People clapped.

The band started playing a lively dance hall tune, totally killing the vibe. She felt like she'd been doused with cold water. Logan narrowed his gaze at the stage, as if the musicians had broken some secret guy code.

Cady wasn't sure what to do. She could either stay on the dance floor, sandwiched against him, or break apart and reveal his very obvious arousal. "Maybe I should turn around," she said in his ear.

He let out a pained laugh. "I don't think that will help."

She did it anyway, twisting in his arms. There was a door nearby that led to the outside deck. He stayed close behind her as she walked toward it. His erection nudged her bottom with every step. It was an awkward exit, but seconds later they were gazing at the dark ocean, sucking in the cool night air.

Then they were both laughing. She collapsed against the rail, giggling. She laughed until her cheeks hurt and her eyes were wet with tears. When she regained control of herself, she hazarded a glance at him. He was staring at her like she was a starry sky, infinite with possibility. Her heart skipped a beat, and her breath hitched in her throat. She adjusted her bodice, which had slipped down an inch. He watched her movements with interest.

"It's the dress, isn't it?" she asked.

The corner of his mouth tipped up. "It's not the dress. It's what's underneath the dress."

"Very little," she admitted.

He groaned, tearing his gaze away. "You're killing me."

She grasped the cool aluminum, feeling giddy. She might fly away from happiness and excitement.

Andrew who?

She gave Logan a minute to collect himself. She needed a minute, too. She stared at the moonlit sea, in awe of its immensity. This was her first cruise, her first trip to Tahiti. She'd lived along the coast for years and never seen this much ocean. After a few deep breaths, she turned to face him. He looked calm and in control.

"Better?"

"Yes."

"You want to go back in?"

He arched a brow. "The problem will surely arise again."

She laughed at his wry expression. "We can avoid the slow dances."

He glanced toward the bar. The music sounded too loud now, the lights too bright. Although he didn't reply, she could read his thoughts. He didn't want to dance. He wanted to take her to his room. She leaned against the railing, tempted.

"Do you do this a lot?" she asked.

"Do what? Get hard in public?"

She flushed at the blunt words. "Pick up women in bars."

"I've done it before," he admitted. "You?"

"No." She wasn't that kind of girl…or she hadn't been in the past. But she'd never felt this kind of chemistry before, either. "My friends keep telling me to try new things. Live a little. I always play it safe."

"Taking a job on a cruise ship isn't playing it safe. Is it?"

"I guess not." She didn't tell him that she'd done it to run away from Andrew, not to embrace adventure.

"You don't dance like someone who plays it safe."

She smiled in agreement. Dancing was her escape. It was the only time she felt totally free and uninhibited. When he smiled back at her, her stomach fluttered with awareness. He was incredibly attractive, and clearly into her. His admiration was like a shining beacon, lighting her up from the inside out.

She was tempted to leave with him. Her gaze lowered to his hands, which were wrapped around the railing next to her. He had nice hands, with wide palms and long fingers. No ring. "Are you married?"

He gave her an incredulous look. "No," he said. "Hell no."

She flushed at his response, aware that her question revealed a distrust of men. He pulled his phone out of his pocket and brought up his Facebook page. It showed a picture of him in combat gear. Relationship status: single.

"You said you were in the navy."

"That's right."

"Are you a sailor?"

"I'm a SEAL."

It was her turn to gape at him. "You're a Navy SEAL?"

He put his phone away, shrugging. "I'm on injury leave right now, but yeah."

"How did you get injured?"

His eyes became shuttered. "I tore a ligament in my knee."

She was curious about the details, but his expression told her not to press. He probably couldn't share confidential information. He hadn't told her who he was supposed to be guarding on this cruise. The fact that he was a Navy SEAL set off major warning bells for her. His job was the epitome of danger.

Cady was risk-averse, for good reason. She was the daughter of a police officer. Her grandfather had died in a tragic accident right before her eyes. She'd developed a strong sense of caution as a child, and it seemed to grow stronger every year. She liked to feel secure at all times. She never drank to excess. She always wore her seat belt.

Logan wasn't the kind of man she would normally choose to date. He was too intense. He did terrifying things in the name of their country. Things she didn't want to imagine. On the other hand, this wasn't a date. This was a chance encounter. After the cruise was over, she'd never see him again. He might not be steady boyfriend material, but he was an excellent candidate for a night of pleasure.

"We don't have to go anywhere," he said. "If you want to stay and dance, I'm game."

"No."

His face fell. "No?"

"I don't want to hurt your knee."

"Screw my knee."

She laughed at this, moving closer to him. Maybe she was drunk. Drunk off one smashed-peach mojito, a boatload of sexual chemistry and one devastatingly dirty dance. "What are my other options?"

His gaze darkened with interest. "Anything you like."

"Let's go."

He grasped her hand and walked back through the bar. She picked up her purse on the way out. Despite his injury, she had to hurry to match his stride. Which was fine by her. Now that she'd decided to "live a little," she couldn't wait to get started.

His room was only two levels down, so they took the stairs. Her heart pounded in her chest, and her knees felt weak. His grip was strong and reassuring, his hands wonderfully large. When they reached the landing, her heel got caught on the carpet and she stumbled against him. His arms went around her waist to steady her. She felt secure and exhilarated at the same time. It was an intoxicating sensation.

"Thanks," she said, breathless.

His gaze locked on hers. They were alone in a quiet hallway. She didn't know where his room was, but she needed to touch him right here and now. His mouth descended, as if he'd read her signals and shared her impatience. She twined her fingers through his hair. Then they were kissing like crazy.

There was no tentative warm-up. No gentle brush of lips or soft, hesitant petting. He buried his tongue in her mouth and thrust his hands beneath her skirt—both hands! With a possessive grunt, he lifted her against him. He had her back to the wall and her legs around his waist in the blink of an eye.

Lord. It was glorious.

He was like a caveman. His mouth was hot and delicious, his tongue bold. She kissed him back with equal enthusiasm, squirming against him. His erection jutted at the apex of her thighs, and his big hands splayed over her bottom.

She whimpered into his mouth, already lost. She was on fire for him. If he ripped off her panties and took her right here against the wall, she wouldn't protest. She'd sob his name and sing Glory, Glory Hallelujah.

He didn't rip off her panties. He broke the kiss and removed his hands from under her skirt, glancing around to make sure they were still alone. Then he took a step back. "Sorry. I usually have more self-control."

She touched her swollen lips. "So do I."

"I'll try to go slow."

"Okay," she said, swallowing hard.

After that was settled, they both rushed down the hallway toward his room. She burst out laughing at their lack of decorum. He laughed along with her. His hair was mussed, his collar askew. She'd never felt like this before, awash with joy and arousal. He pushed her up against the door and kissed her breath away. All of her senses were heightened. They were standing on the threshold of ecstasy.

But she didn't get in.

There was a sudden flash of movement behind Logan. He was yanked backward and thrown into the opposite wall. She counted three figures in black masks, circling like sharks. She shrank against the door, but one of them grabbed her and clamped a hand over her mouth. Her scream was muffled by a leather-covered palm. She was shoved into the room next to Logan's. It was dark. Thin curtains fluttered by the open balcony entrance. Her knees met the edge of the bed and she fell across it with her captor. She kicked her legs wildly and bit at the gloved hand. He didn't let go.

Logan crashed into the room and got immediately wrapped up by two assailants. They wrestled him onto the balcony. He managed to jerk his arm free and throw a brutal punch, staggering one of the masked men.

Cady watched in horror as the second man swung a blunt object at Logan, hitting him in the temple. Logan dropped to his knees. Blood streamed down his forehead. Strangled sounds emerged from her throat. Logan fell onto his stomach and stayed there, motionless. The two men hauled him upright and pitched him over the railing.

And that was it. He was gone.

She stopped struggling. Tears blurred her vision, and her mind went blank. She didn't understand what was happening, but resistance seemed futile. There were too many hands on her. One of the assailants gagged her and bound her wrists with rope. He tied her ankles, too. Some kind of bag went over her head. Then she was lifted and carried onto the balcony. Although she couldn't see anything, she could feel her body being lowered over the railing. She sobbed into the gag, frozen with terror.

She went down and down and down. She didn't hit the water. There was someone waiting for her on a raft below. The other assailants joined them. After they started moving it dawned on her.

She was being kidnapped.

## Chapter 3

Logan hit the water like a ton of bricks.

He was still reeling from the blow to the head. The hard slap against the surface didn't help him regain his senses. He plummeted into the dark abyss, blood streaming from his scalp. Although he was an expert swimmer, among the best in his BUD/S class, he faltered. He was disoriented. He couldn't tell up from down.

Panic gripped him, and he let out a silent scream. Bubbles emerged from his mouth. Bubbles that led him toward the surface.

He swam hard and broke through, gasping for breath.

Good God. He'd almost drowned like a rookie. Worse, he'd been easily overpowered by a couple of light-weights—after almost banging a woman in the hallway outside his room. How embarrassing. He wasn't even drunk. Extreme lust wasn't an excuse. Neither was his injury. He'd let three unarmed men get the drop on him.

He was lucky to be alive.

He touched his brow, wincing. He felt nauseous. His vision sucked. He had a concussion, no doubt about it.

He spent the next few minutes treading water, waiting for his thoughts to clear. He couldn't seem to focus.

Damn. He might still drown yet.

While he struggled to stay alert, he became aware of a raft in the vicinity. It was dark, and he couldn't see anything but vague shapes. The black expanse of the cruise ship hull loomed against the foamy breakwater. There was a figure sliding down a rope from the balcony of Logan's cabin to the raft below.

The raft had a motor, but they didn't engage it. Maybe it made too much noise for a stealthy getaway. Two men used paddles instead, cutting quickly through the chop. Logan counted four heads on the raft. One was lumpy, as if wearing a hood.

Cadence.

They'd taken her. She was the target of this raid, not him. He didn't know why…and now he was faced with a tough decision. He could follow the raft and try to rescue her, or stay here and save himself.

SEALs were taught to put the team above themselves, but they were also taught that dead men couldn't help anyone. Sometimes self-rescue had to be the top priority. Logan knew he couldn't keep pace with the swift-moving cruise ship. There was no way to climb aboard. These vessels were built to discourage pirates, not give them a convenient ladder. The only way to get rescued was to shout for help and hope someone heard him.

But down here at sea level, no one would hear him. Except the kidnappers.

While he waited for the raft to move out of range, he considered his only other option. The mother ship would be nearby, probably less than a mile away. He could swim a mile in his sleep. If they didn't fire up the engine, following them would be easy. Climbing aboard the mother ship and fighting off multiple assailants would *not* be easy, but screw it. If he was going to die anyway, he might as well choose the nobler cause.

So he started swimming.

His mind was fuzzy, but his body worked fine. He swam after the raft until it disappeared in the dark night. The sound of the motor made his spirits plummet. His chances of catching up to the raft narrowed. Even so, he kept swimming. He didn't look back at the cruise ship, because it was too late to change course. He was committed.

It occurred to him that the kidnappers had mistaken Cadence for Maya O'Brien. They'd broken into the room adjacent to his, which had been reserved for Maya. The two women were about the same size. They had similar coloring.

Logan's gut clenched with unease. If this was a targeted attack on a former president's daughter, ransom might not be their endgame. Either way, Cadence was in extreme danger. Because she wouldn't pass for Maya O'Brien up close, and as soon as they discovered their mistake, they'd kill her.

He swam harder, galvanized to action. It was one of the most grueling swims of his life. Top five for sure. He surged forward, his arms pumping. He'd done a six-mile in Santa Cruz during storm swells. He'd crossed the Persian Gulf in the dead of night. He'd made the trip from Coronado to the San Diego Bay in a flak jacket.

But he'd accomplished all of these feats as a team. He'd never been in the middle of the ocean alone, with a bum knee and a head injury. He had no support, no intel and no visuals. If he reached the ship, which seemed more unlikely now that he'd lost sight of it, he'd be out-numbered by at least three to one.

The stakes were high. The chances of survival were low.

On the plus side, he was making great time. He also had the element of surprise. The kidnappers shouldn't have been so careless in disposing of his body. They clearly expected him to drown, not give chase.

He was Logan Nathaniel Starke. He didn't quit. He didn't sink. He didn't *die*. He protected his assets, and he was going to make those bastards sorry they hadn't finished him off before throwing him overboard.

His perseverance was rewarded by a dim light ahead. He'd found the mother ship, and by some miracle of fate, it wasn't even moving. He closed the distance as quickly as possible, his muscles burning from exertion. They were pulling up the anchor. The raft had been stowed. He switched to a modified breaststroke on the last stretch, which kept everything from his nose down under the surface. He didn't want to be spotted.

The ship was a forty-foot deep-sea cruiser with a protected wheelhouse in front. The galley and cabins were in the back. There was a transom door and a convenient swim step. It was an ideal setup for an ambush. He assumed Cadence would be inside a cabin. She'd be guarded by at least one man, although there was nowhere for her to go. The ocean was a death sentence, not an escape route.

As he reached the swim step, the engine turned on. He scrambled aboard and crouched by the transom door, water streaming down his body. His weak knee throbbed in protest, and his stomach roiled with nausea. He struggled to catch his breath. He'd made it here, against all odds, and now the real danger would begin. This was no time to surrender to exhaustion.

He waited for the cruiser to gain momentum. His scalp had stopped bleeding, and his vision was clearer. He counted two men in the wheelhouse. That was good. He didn't see any blunt objects lying around. That was bad. He needed something to strike with, or this rescue operation would be short-lived.

The transom door was unlocked, so he slipped inside. The galley was empty. He grabbed the only weapon he could find—a mop handle. Unscrewing the top, he set it aside and crept down the steps to the cabin.

Again, he found an open doorway. These pirates were completely unprepared for a hostile takeover, which was kind of ironic, like thieves who left their loot in full view. Logan listened at the entrance for a few seconds. He heard two men arguing in French. Logan didn't speak French, so he had no idea what they were saying.

One of the men walked out of the cabin, still muttering under his breath. Logan said hello with a sharp blow to the head. The man crumpled to the ground quietly. He was of European descent, midthirties, dressed in black. Logan stepped over him and entered the cabin. Cadence was sitting on the floor. Her wrists and ankles were tied. There was a gag in her mouth and mascara tracks on her face.

Logan didn't dwell on these details. He had to focus on the guard, who appeared to be the muscle of the operation. Logan guessed he was Polynesian, from one of the local islands. When Logan swung the mop handle, the man blocked it easily. Then he brandished a wicked-looking knife and went on the offense. Logan leaped backward, avoiding a series of wide arcs. His back hit the wall, and he ducked down to avoid the blade. After it missed him, Logan jabbed the end of his stick against the man's rib cage. The knife tumbled out of his hand. The man staggered sideways and bent to retrieve his weapon.

Logan couldn't wait for a better opening. He leaped on his opponent's back and held the mop handle across his throat, cutting off his airway. The man slammed Logan into the wall in an attempt to dislodge him, but Logan didn't budge. They both went down to the floor. It took every ounce of Logan's strength to maintain his grip on the stick.

The man struggled to break free. He reached for his knife, which was sitting right there on the ground. Cadence kicked it away.

That little bit of help made all the difference. The man finally passed out. Logan almost did the same. He let go of the mop handle and shoved his limp body aside. Black spots danced across his vision. His head felt like it might explode. Sweat trickled down his temple. Or maybe it was blood.

He couldn't afford to rest, so he took a few deep breaths and pulled himself together. He rolled over, picked up the knife and cut the ropes that bound her. She untied the gag with trembling hands. Her mouth was raw, her eyes wary. She didn't seem relieved by his rescue. She looked terrified.

Of him.

This wasn't an unusual reaction to trauma, but it still unsettled him. He expected her to trust him, not shrink away in horror.

Unfortunately, he couldn't say anything to put her mind at ease. He touched a finger to his lips in warning. Then he lifted her to her feet, giving her a cursory inspection. She appeared unharmed. Even if she wasn't, they had to get off this boat immediately. He didn't have the strength to overpower the rest of the crew. His energy was spent. He pulled her through the door, stepping over the bodies that were piling up. The guy outside was regaining consciousness. Logan hoped he'd lie there for a few more minutes.

They crept up the stairs, through the galley and out the transom door. The raft was hanging from a pulley system on the starboard side. He used the knife to cut it loose, praying they wouldn't be seen by the men in the wheelhouse. As the raft fell against the railing, his European friend staggered into the galley.

Damn it.

Logan couldn't let the man reach the wheelhouse and alert the others. He passed Cadence the rope that was still attached to the raft. "Hold this," he said, because he wanted her to stay put. Then he barged through the galley to take his opponent down. His knee buckled on the first step, which threw off his attack. The European noted this weakness and seized the opportunity to launch his own assault. He tackled Logan around the waist and pushed him backward. They burst through the transom doors and fell right off the stern, into the dark sea.

The man didn't let go underwater. He clung to Logan like a goddamned octopus. He was trying to drown Logan, and it was working. As soon as Logan broke through the surface, the European dunked him again. Logan's movements were clumsy from fatigue, but his instincts were still sharp. So was the knife in his right hand. Making a strangled sound, he buried the blade in the man's belly. Then he twisted it.

The arms around him loosened, and the weight fell

away. Logan treaded water, gasping for breath. Cadence was there, in the raft. She'd managed to push it overboard and get inside. He swam toward her and handed her the knife before hauling himself out of the water. Once he was safely inside, he rested on his back for a moment, one hand over his thundering heart. He was nauseous and light-headed. As soon as his stomach settled, he straightened and searched the water for a body.

He didn't see one.

The cabin cruiser continued on its journey, oblivious. Their escape would be noticed at some point, but now they had a chance. They had to put as much distance between the raft and the cruiser as possible.

The paddles weren't inside the raft. They must have been left on the deck. He explored the motor with wet hands, looking for a pull cord. What he discovered made his blood run cold. There was a key ignition.

Without a motor or paddles, they were sitting ducks. The kidnappers would circle back and recapture them.

Or recapture her, rather. He had no value to them. If they knew she wasn't Maya O'Brien, she was equally worthless. Logan didn't doubt that these men had firearms at their disposal. They hadn't used them on the cruise ship in the interest of stealth. There was no reason to be quiet now.

"Can you start it?" she asked.

"Not without a key."

She stared at him in dismay.

"I might be able to hot-wire it at first light."

"What do we do until then?"

"We wait," he said grimly. "And hope they don't come back for us."

# Chapter 4

One of the best nights of her life turned into the worst.

The absolute worst.

She survived it, somehow. So did Logan. They waited in silence for the boat to double back for them, but it never did. Logan said the kidnappers must not have realized they were gone right away. He also said the raft would be difficult to spot in the dark, like a needle in a haystack. The ocean was immense, and frightening. The raft rose and fell with every swell, traveling on a swift current.

What followed them wasn't a boat. It was the body of the man Logan had killed. He floated on the surface, facedown, his white T-shirt bobbing. It was almost as if the corpse was swimming after them. She watched in horror as his body jerked suddenly. He flailed back and forth, reanimated. Tail fins thrashed on the surface as sharks tore him apart. First one, then two, then a half dozen.

Cady threw up over the side of the raft.

When she leaned too far out, Logan grabbed her by

the arm and yanked her back. She wiped her mouth, shuddering.

The night dragged on, never ending. She was cold and miserable. Logan stripped off his wet clothes and wrapped his arms around her, but she didn't stop shivering. Her mind replayed violent images. Black masks. Glinting knives. Sharks circling.

She couldn't believe they were in this situation. She couldn't believe they'd escaped. When Logan had entered the doorway, his face pale and his clothes wet, she'd screamed into her gag. She'd thought he was a ghost, for good reason. She'd seen him get knocked unconscious and thrown overboard. No normal person could survive that. He'd appeared out of nowhere and fought like a man possessed.

One minute, she'd been weeping silently, frozen with fear. The next, she was watching Jason Bourne attack his enemies.

She didn't understand why she'd been targeted, or how Logan had arrived on the scene. The whole thing was surreal. And sinister. He'd incapacitated one of her captors and gutted another like a fish. She knew he was a Navy SEAL, trained to kill. She also knew he'd acted in self-defense, and he wasn't a danger to her. Even so, her first reaction to his daring rescue wasn't relief. It was terror.

The brutality of his actions, and the ease with which he'd executed them, still disturbed her. She hadn't signed on for this. She wasn't equipped for it. She was a chef on a cruise ship, sailing toward an uncertain future. She'd been in a slump, personally and professionally. Her idea of adventure was using new spices in a recipe. Leaving the bar with Logan was the wildest thing she'd ever done.

Now she was stranded on a raft in the middle of the ocean.

She shouldn't have gone back to his cabin. She should have listened to her instincts, instead of her hormones. She couldn't have predicted this outcome, of course, but she'd known what kind of man he was. He was an elite soldier. He had hero written all over him, along with heartbreaker and risk taker.

She'd only wanted a single night of excitement with a man whose gaze had warmed her from the inside out. Instead she got this stone-cold warrior who watched sharks feed on a corpse without flinching.

Her stomach lurched at the memory. She rolled over and dry-heaved quietly.

Logan kept his hand on her back like an anchor. His touch felt reassuring, despite the fraught circumstances. She didn't want to be here, but she was glad she wasn't alone. She was glad they were alive, and relatively unharmed. When her stomach settled, he pulled her into his arms and held her close. Little by little, her tremors subsided.

At dawn, he put on his damp clothes. She sat up and stared at the rising sun. Its reflection glinted across the ocean, illuminating their plight. There was no pirate boat on the horizon. There was nothing. No cruise ship, no commercial barges, no airplanes, no islands. No drinking water. It might as well have been the Sahara Desert.

Her gaze met his. His features were rough-hewn in the harsh daylight. There was a big lump on his temple, and dried blood clumped to his eyebrow.

"Are you hurt?" he asked.

She didn't think she was, but she felt numb. She slowly took stock of her condition. Her mouth was still sore from the gag. She rubbed her wrists, which bore rope burns. Other than those minor discomforts, she was fine. "I'm okay."

"Did you understand what they were saying?"

Cady spoke a smattering of French. She hadn't caught every word. "They thought I was someone else."

"Maya O'Brien."

"The president's daughter?"

"I was supposed to be guarding her."

Now it made sense. The kidnappers had made a mistake. They weren't targeting her. Cadence Crenshaw was nobody. Maya O'Brien was America's daughter, rich and famous. "Were they terrorists?"

"I don't know," he said, frowning. "French Polynesia isn't a hot spot for terrorism. Their motivations might have been financial."

"When will they start looking for us?"

"The kidnappers?"

"The rescuers."

He studied the clear blue sky above them. "Today, with any luck. They'll know something is wrong when you don't show up to work. Employees will see the signs of a struggle in the cabin next to mine. Then they'll launch a search party with air support."

"Do you think they'll find us?"

"Yes."

She hoped he was telling the truth. His expression revealed nothing, and she didn't know him well enough to judge. Maybe he was honest to a fault. Maybe he was a strategic liar. Maybe that head injury had rattled his brain. He'd already said that the raft would be difficult to spot on the open sea.

"I thought you were dead," she said in a hushed voice. She still couldn't quite believe he was real.

"Nah," he said. "I don't die that easy." His smile was wan, belying the boast.

"What did you do?"

"I swam."

She gaped at him in wonder. Her head had been covered during the kidnapping, so she'd been disoriented. She'd assumed the men had pulled him out of the water for some reason, or he'd grabbed a tow rope. "You swam from the cruise ship?"

He nodded.

"How?"

"It wasn't that far."

Her next question was more important. "Why?"

"Why what?"

"Why did you risk your life like that? You hardly know me."

His gaze darkened. "I know you well enough," he said, squinting at the horizon. "Even if I didn't, I'd have done the same thing. There was nothing else to do. Staying near the cruise ship wasn't an option. My chances of getting rescued there were very low."

She studied his battered face, trying to gauge his sincerity. He might have had no other choice, but he was also downplaying an incredible act of heroism. He'd swum after a motorized raft and overpowered two men—after sustaining a concussion. It was an amazing feat, almost superhuman. Most people couldn't save themselves, let alone others. They froze in the face of danger. Cady had experienced this phenomenon firsthand as a child. She'd watched her grandfather die and been paralyzed, unable to help him.

It was the most traumatic moment of her life. Until now.

Logan removed his cell phone from his pocket. He took it apart, piece by piece, and set the components out to dry. It didn't take long; the sun was brutal. Light reflected off the ocean, magnifying the effect. Within an hour, everything was bone dry, including her throat.

He had no service, of course. He couldn't even send a text. He turned off the phone and tucked it away. "I'll try again later."

Cady stayed quiet. She doubted they'd drift into a better service area anytime soon. They were several days' travel from Tahiti by cruise ship. She didn't know of any other islands between here and there. She closed her eyes, swallowing hard. Maybe they'd arrive on the shore of a private resort and sip fruity cocktails at noon.

She mixed a fantasy drink with her favorite ingredients. Crushed ice. Fresh fruit. Something really bougie, like a strawberry-basil bourbon spritzer.

Logan emptied his pockets to study the contents. In addition to his cell phone, he had a wallet with cash and credit cards. She had nothing but the dress on her back. Her purse had been lost in the melee. Her shoes had fallen off. So had his.

His next project was hot-wiring the engine. He used his knife to disable the ignition and open the casing. He spent the better part of the morning with his head down, cursing. It reminded her of her father doing auto repairs. He flinched when one of the live wires singed his fingertips. After some trial and error, he twisted two wires together and the engine turned over. He flashed her a victorious grin. Then he disconnected it, killing the motor.

Her spirits fell. "We're not going anywhere?"

"I have to save fuel," he said. "We can't travel far on a gas tank this size."

"Why did you hot-wire it?"

"Because being able to move a short distance will help us get rescued. If we see a ship in the distance, we can approach it. If a plane goes by, I can fire it up and do some circles to get their attention."

She searched the horizon for signs of an airplane or a ship, with no luck. The glare of sunlight on the water burned her corneas, and constantly scanning the area exhausted her eye muscles. When she couldn't continue, he took over. She curled up in a ball, her stomach roiling. She wondered how long it took to die from thirst. She didn't ask Logan, because she was afraid the answer might be one day.

The afternoon sun was brutal. He removed his shirt and dipped it in the water. Then he wrapped the wet cloth around his head, turban-style. The hunting knife he'd taken from one of the kidnappers was tucked into his belt. He looked like a storybook pirate, with perfectly defined abs and a tantalizing strip of hair below his navel.

She remembered how his body had felt against hers on the dance floor, and how eager she'd been to touch him. Their brief, lust-drenched interlude didn't seem real. She'd never experienced such a powerful rush of attraction before. Who meets someone at a bar and wants to tear their clothes off after ten minutes? In what alternate dimension do two mature, *sober* people fall into a sexual trance and make out in public? She might have been embarrassed if she wasn't so worried about dying.

"You need protection from the sun," he said, drawing his knife. He motioned for her to move closer.

"What are you doing?"

"Cutting off this extra fabric."

She held still while he sliced through her tulle over-skirt. The serrated blade was sharp, with a wicked point at the tip. She tried not to think about where else it had been. She couldn't afford to throw up again.

When he was finished, she used the fabric like a veil, covering her head and shoulders. It was blisteringly hot. Her lips were dry. His were already cracked.

They didn't speak, because it hurt to talk.

After what seemed like ten or twelve hours, clouds gathered in the sky. There was a sudden, intense down-pour. She closed her eyes and opened her mouth, des-perate for moisture. The raindrops didn't quench her thirst, but the cool water felt like heaven against her skin. When she opened her eyes again, he was watching her. She wondered if he was thinking about the kisses they'd shared. Was it a strange, distant memory for him, too? A moment of passion that had slipped between his fingers?

He pulled his gaze away, flushing. She doubted he felt any embarrassment or shame about his behavior. Men never did. Maybe he was just sunburned, or he couldn't figure out why he'd been so enthralled with her. She probably looked like a bedraggled sea witch. Humidity wasn't kind to her hair.

When puddles gathered on the bottom of the raft, they both drank their fill. With the sun behind the clouds, the temperature was pleasant. For a short time, she almost felt comfortable, and hopeful about getting rescued. Then the temperature dropped and darkness fell. They spent another night shivering, huddled for warmth.

In the dead of night, she was awoken by a bump against the side of the boat. She sprang upright, clutching Logan's arm. He was alert beside her, his muscles tense. It was very dark. There was a sliver of moon, high in the sky.

The bump came again, on the opposite side. A fin skimmed the surface of the water.

Shark.

She let out a terrified scream.

He clamped his hand over her mouth, which only increased her panic. It reminded her of the kidnapping. She'd been silenced with a rough slap during the attack, and she still had a tender spot on her cheek. His fingertips pressed into it, adding to her discomfort. She pushed his hand away, incensed.

"Shh," Logan warned. He studied the surface of the water intently. She crossed her arms over her chest, her throat tight. She supposed that screaming wasn't helpful, but it was a normal reaction. There were freaking *sharks* circling!

"Can they puncture the raft?" she asked.

"Maybe."

His answer chilled her to the bone. She scooted closer to him.

"They won't do it as a strategy. But if they decide to take an exploratory bite…"

She gripped the crook of his arm. "What should we do?"

"Stay calm and quiet."

Although she wasn't calm by any stretch, she didn't make a sound. Neither did he. After a few tense moments, his shoulders relaxed. The sharks didn't bump the raft or flash fins again. Hopefully they'd lost interest.

"I'm sorry," he murmured. "I didn't mean to hurt you."

"You didn't. One of the kidnappers did."

His eyes glinted in the dark. "He hit you?"

"Yes."

"Which one?"

"The one you killed."

He nodded, as if the man had gotten what he deserved. "Go back to sleep. I'll keep watch."

She curled up in the raft and closed her eyes, but she didn't sleep. She was cold and hungry and sick with fear. She'd applied for a job on a cruise ship because she'd wanted to get away from it all. Her longtime boyfriend had become enamored with another woman on reality TV. She'd watched every episode, just to torture herself. Their breakup had turned her entire life upside down. She'd left San Francisco and moved back home with her parents.

It was a low point, to say the least.

She'd needed an escape. Well, she got one. Now Andrew seemed like a blip of the radar, tiny and insignificant. She didn't miss him.

She spent most of the night praying for day, and most of the next day praying for night. The heat was unbearable. The sun sucked the life out of her, beating down in relentless waves. There were no ships, no planes, no clouds, no rain.

Logan stripped down to his boxers and used his pants to shade different parts of his body. He gave her his shirt to wear. The fabric kept the sun off her back. She leaned over the side of the raft and trailed her fingers through the water. So much water. Clear, blue, deadly water. She made a cup with her hands.

"Don't even think about it," he said.

She splayed her fingers, letting the liquid fall out.

She knew they couldn't drink salt water. "Why can't we swim?"

"With the sharks?"

"They only come at night."

"Salt water robs moisture from your skin. You'll dehydrate faster."

"What about urine?"

"What about it?"

She'd watched him pee over the side of the raft this morning. "Should we...drink it?"

"Hell no."

"Is it toxic?"

"Not as toxic as salt water, but it won't help you rehydrate. It will just get your mouth wet and taste bad."

"How do you know?"

"I'm a SEAL. I've had extensive survival training."

She dug her fingernails into her palms. "What if it doesn't rain again?"

He took his pants off his head, scowling.

"What if we don't see a plane, or a ship?"

"You want to drink pee, is that it?"

"No, that's not it," she said, raising her voice. "I'm just scared. I don't want to die, okay? Maybe you can take all of this in stride and go thirty days without water and fly around the world like a superhero, but I can't."

He draped his pants across his broad shoulders. "We're not going to die today, Cadence. Is that clear?"

"It's Cady."

"What?"

"No one calls me Cadence except my grandfather. And he's dead now."

His expression softened. "Was he a military man?"

"Army. Drill sergeant."

He nodded his approval. "The most important element of survival isn't strength or intelligence. It's tenacity."

She didn't argue, because that sounded legit.

"People with quick minds and vivid imaginations can struggle in situations like this. Sometimes creative thinkers are their own worst enemies, believe it or not. It's healthy to be afraid, but you can't let your fear take over. What you need to do is focus on simple tasks. Keep your thoughts occupied."

"How?"

"For now, you can be my lookout. If you put that extra fabric over your eyes, it will reduce the glare. Then you can scan the horizon and the sky in sections."

She did what he suggested, for as long as she could. Even with the tulle shade, it was hard on her eyes, and there was nothing to see. While she kept watch, he used his knife to remove the lining from his wallet. He made something similar to a Zorro mask, with narrow eye slits, and tied it to his face with a piece of fabric from his pants pocket. Then he fooled around with the engine again. Birds circled overhead, waiting to feed.

On them.

When he told her to take a break, she tucked her body into a tiny bit of shade along the side of the raft and pulled his shirt over her head. The task had worked to blank her mind, but it had also exhausted her. Without food and water, she had no energy.

It didn't rain that afternoon.

She slept.

The next thing she knew, it was full dark, and the raft pitched beneath her. Waves sprayed over the side and threatened to dump them into the sea. She bolted upright, sensing a large presence.

There was an island! That was the good news. The bad news was that it didn't look hospitable. It looked like a giant cliff in the middle of the ocean. Instead of washing up on a breezy, white-sand beach, they were about to get dashed against some jagged rocks—and there was no way to avoid the impact.

Logan shouted over the din of the crashing waves. "Hold on!"

She gripped the rope on her side of the raft just in time. The raft flipped over, rolling in the breakwater like a surfboard after a spectacular wipeout. She didn't let go of the rope, and that probably saved her. The raft buoyed upward. She broke the surface with it and managed to take a quick gasp of breath before the next wave hit. Then she was caught inside again, tumbling around in the giant saltwater washing machine.

She endured several more cycles of this before the real danger presented itself. There was an underwater fortress of razor-sharp rocks. The raft got shredded against it. So did her skin. Her legs scraped over a surface that felt like a cheese grater. She cried out in pain, struggling to swim. The raft was snagged on something. She had to let go of the rope, but she didn't know if she could make it to the shore.

Luckily, Logan was right there. He grabbed her from behind and shoved his forearm under her chin, urging her into a reclined position. She didn't fight him. With swift, sure strokes, he towed her to safety.

Well, relative safety. There was no safe space here, no easy escape from the wicked rocks and relentless waves. He deposited her at a granite outcropping near the base of the cliffs. She clung there, breathing hard.

Then he left her.

"I have to get the raft," he shouted. As if the raft was the more useful item, between the two of them.

She managed to keep her head above water while she waited. It took him several tries to unsnag the raft. She looked around for a way to get out of the water. In the dark, she saw only pounding waves and vertical cliffs. They might have to circumnavigate the island in hopes of finding an access point.

But—at least they had hope. Out adrift, there was nothing. So she held on tight to the volcanic rock, grateful for its presence. Grateful for its gritty, porous surface. She'd been terrified that she'd never see land again, let alone touch it. She thought she'd never see anything but endless ocean and the inside of a raft.

As the waves kept rolling in, she rested her cheek against the rock and wept. Because they were here, and they were alive.

# Chapter 5

Logan woke up on the beach at dawn.

He had sand all over his face. Lukewarm surf tickled his feet. His mouth was dry, his head pounding. With a low groan, he rolled onto his back and wiped his eyes. A tiny crab scuttled away from his ankle. He was lucky it hadn't crawled up the leg of his pants.

Cady was lying next to him on top of the deflated raft. It was flat from the impact with the rocky shore. She had her hands tucked under her cheek. The extra material from her dress covered her head like a red wedding veil. Her skirt was twisted around her upper thighs. Her feet were bare and pretty, with unpainted toes.

The crab that had been investigating him touched the heel of her foot. She let out a startled shriek, kicking it away. Then she sat upright and pulled the veil off her face. She looked a little worse for the wear. Still beautiful, because her features were lovely. But dehydrated, with chapped lips and bloodshot eyes. Her hair was a natural style, not straightened. Now it was a wild tangle of curls.

They'd been forced to swim around the island last night after getting slammed into the rocks. She was a strong swimmer, thank God. He couldn't have saved the raft and her. They'd slogged through at least a mile of rough water before this cove appeared. As soon as their feet had hit the sand, they'd dropped.

"Are you okay?" he asked. His voice sounded like crushed gravel.

"Thirsty," she said.

"We have to find water."

She glanced at the high cliffs behind them. "Up there?"

"Yes."

"I can't move."

He knew she didn't mean it. She didn't want to move, but she could do it. She only needed a bit of encouragement. He spotted some coconut trees along the edge of the beach, and a couple of fresh green fruits sitting on the sand. A mature coconut rolled in the surf. He went to retrieve both kinds. The green ones had more juice, so he used his knife to chop off the end and bore a hole. Then he gave it to her. She took an experimental sip.

"Oh my God," she said, gulping more.

"Good?"

"So good."

He'd learned about coconuts in his survival class, but he'd never actually had a fresh one. When she passed it back, he drank his share. The flavor was mild, like vitamin water with a hint of sweetness. Although he wanted to down it all, he restrained himself and let her have the rest. His reward was watching her expression of pleasure as she finished it. She upended the coconut to get the last drops. Juice dribbled down her chin and her smooth brown throat. He imagined putting his mouth there and licking the moisture away.

To distract himself, he took his phone apart again and set it on a leaf to dry. Then he went to work on the older coconut. First he removed the dry husk, which wasn't easy. The nut inside was impenetrable. He couldn't cut it with his knife.

"Let me," Cady said.

He handed it to her, curious. She picked up his knife and chopped one of the empty green coconuts in half, so it worked like a bowl. Then she held the brown nut over the bowl and hit it with the spine of his knife. She whacked it five or six times before it cracked. Milky fluid spilled between her fingers and into the green bowl. Another strike split the nut into two halves. The fruit inside was white as snow and smelled like heaven.

"Nicely done," he said.

She gave him one of the halves and kept working. Apparently there were multiple steps to this process. She had to break the nut into smaller pieces before the fruit could be pried out of the shell. There was also an outer skin to peel away. When she freed the first chunk, she offered it to him. He popped the fruit into his mouth and groaned. Extreme hunger was one hell of an appetizer, because it was the most delicious thing he'd ever tasted. Pleasantly chewy with a mildly sweet, nutty flavor.

"Wow," he said, eager for more.

She pried the rest of the fruit from the shell and used her teeth to remove the skin. They devoured every morsel. After the meat was gone, they shared the milk, which he didn't love. It reminded him of warm goat milk, or camel milk. She laughed at the face he made.

The meal was labor-intensive—and ultimately unsatisfying. He needed more than half a coconut to fill his stomach. His main priority was finding fresh water. "We should get going."

She followed his gaze up the cliffs. "Do you think this island is inhabited?"

He shrugged, evasive. There were thousands of islands like this in the South Pacific, and most of them were deserted, but why burst her bubble? "We won't know until we hike to a higher vantage point. That's next on my to-do list."

She groaned, flopping onto her back. "Has anyone ever told you that you're too industrious?"

He didn't answer, because he was distracted by her short skirt. Getting rehydrated had enlivened his senses. On the raft, his desire for her had been squelched by thirst, hunger and a mild concussion. Now it came roaring back. It urged him to stare at her bare legs and imagine himself between them.

Her dress was wrinkled and torn, with a rip from the hem to the top of her thigh. She had various scrapes and bruises from getting dashed against the rocks. She looked like a scream queen from a horror movie. The one who survived, gore-splattered, after battling the bad guys. She was shell-shocked, but still sexy.

He turned his gaze toward the ocean, frowning at his thoughts. Since when had he found bloody knees and torn fabric attractive? He'd gone off the deep end. Maybe the primitive setting had turned him into an animal. Or maybe it was just her. Their chemistry at the bar had been explosive. It was like a punch in the gut, every time their eyes met.

But they weren't in the bar anymore. They were on an island in the middle of nowhere. Their relationship had changed the moment she'd been attacked. She'd been targeted because she was with him. She'd been taken *from* him. Now she was his responsibility. He couldn't ogle her the way he had on the dance floor. He had a professional obligation to protect her, just as he would have protected Maya O'Brien. He had to act like a proper bodyguard.

She was an asset. Not some piece of ass.

He rose to his feet, determined not to fail her. They needed food, water and shelter ASAP. He doubted they'd find people, based on the size and structure of this island. He had to make a fire or they'd get eaten alive by bugs tonight. He wasn't sure if they'd return to this cove, so he pulled the raft as far away from the shoreline as possible. Then he collected some fire-making materials. The dry husk threads from the coconut were ideal. He dipped some of the longer threads in the gas tank and rolled them up in a palm leaf.

"What's that for?" she asked.

"To help start a fire. Just in case." He put his phone back together and offered her a hand. She winced as she stood up.

"Sore muscles?"

"Sore feet. From the rocks."

He inspected the soles of her feet. She had several shallow cuts. He considered letting her stay on the beach, but that was against survival protocol, and carrying water back for her would be a hassle. What would she do if he got injured or delayed? He also wasn't convinced the kidnappers had given up. Those men had a much better chance of pinpointing their location than the rescuers.

If there *were* rescuers. He wasn't counting on that, either. They'd have no idea where to look. Only the pirates knew they'd stolen a raft. They knew this area, presumably. They could study the currents and wind conditions and estimate a landing zone. They might come back to tie up loose ends.

"I'll make you some shoes," he said.

She sat down in the shade again while he gathered several palm leaves. He folded them into squares and tied them to her feet with a narrow strip of the same material. The "shoes" wouldn't be comfortable to walk in, but they'd protect her from further injury. He didn't bother making a pair for himself. Even though he'd been off-duty for several weeks, his feet were tough and he preferred going bare.

The cliffs along the edge of the beach were slippery and steep, with no discernible path. He found the safest route and climbed behind Cady, giving her support and instructions when she needed it. She only lost her footing once, near the top. Although he was right there to catch her, his bad knee almost buckled under her weight. His heart pounded at the close call. A fall here would be disastrous. It would entail a swift death or prolonged suffering.

He'd seen a lot of dead bodies over the past six years. Most were men that had been killed by the enemy, or fought for the enemy. Women and children were harder to accept. There was a pregnant woman in Syria who would always haunt him.

He pushed the mental picture out of his mind, with some difficulty. He held on to Cady for an extra second to make sure she was steady. She glanced over her shoulder at him, letting out a ragged breath. Then they continued over the edge of the cliff. He didn't relax until they were both on stable ground.

When they entered the rain forest, the lush vegetation became a fortress. He took the lead. It was slow going without a machete, but not impossible, and the leaves were pleasantly free of thorns. Unprotected vegetation indicated that there were no leaf-eating animals on the island. That usually meant no people.

She followed close behind him. He knew she was tired, because he was tired. His knee throbbed with every step and hunger gnawed at his belly. He had to stop to adjust his belt around his waist. He'd already lost weight. She watched with wary eyes, saying nothing. She had a dancer's body, slender and compact. He liked her curves where they were. He needed to provide some sustenance before they both started wasting away.

If this island was deserted, they could be here awhile.

The day wore on, and finding water proved elusive. The rain forest was teeming with life, colorful birds and vibrant greenery. Everything was damp. It was humid as hell. He was soaked in sweat. But a convenient wellspring? Nah.

"I need a break," Cady declared. "If I take another step, I'll drop."

He allowed a short rest, glancing around. He was impatient to reach the summit, wherever that was. He couldn't see more than ten yards in any direction. While she sat with her back propped against a tree trunk, he noticed a liana vine hanging from the canopy above. Liana vines, like green coconuts, were a source of fresh water. He whacked it in half and let the end drip into his palm. The liquid ran clear, so he lifted it to his lips to taste. It was fine. He drank a few mouthfuls and passed the vine to her.

After two days at sea, they couldn't get enough fresh water. He watched her throat work as she swallowed. When she returned the vine, he quenched his thirst in greedy gulps. They drank until there was nothing left.

Logan had been worried that they'd die of dehydration on the raft, despite his assurances to the contrary. He was still worried about it. He'd dismissed her idea to drink urine, but at one point he'd been tempted. Anything to get his mouth wet.

He lifted his gaze to the sun-dappled canopy overhead. He estimated it was early afternoon. They were burning daylight.

She closed her eyes and leaned her head against the tree trunk. He couldn't expect her to hike through the jungle all day without proper shoes, on a mostly empty stomach, after last night's grueling swim. She didn't have his training, his muscle mass, or his stamina. It was a miracle she'd come this far.

Instead of badgering her, he let her rest. He spent the next few minutes exploring their immediate surroundings. The island was a haven for birds and flying insects. Mosquitos were a constant threat. Ferns and elephant plant grew wild.

He stumbled upon a tree with bumpy green fruits, similar to avocados. The branches were too high to reach, but he picked one off the ground and tucked it into his pants pocket. Then he examined the other trees in the area. He didn't see any more fruit. A crow-sized bird kept flitting about overhead, squawking in distress. After a cursory glance upward, he noticed what appeared to be a bird's nest in a crook between two branches.

He climbed the tree and hit the jackpot. Three eggs. He secured them in his shirt pocket before he descended. When he returned, Cady was on her feet. She was hopping around, swatting at her neck and shoulders.

Ants.

That was the problem with taking a break in the jungle: ants. He helped brush the insects off her bare back, hiding a smile.

She bent over to shake out her curls. "I can still feel them in my hair."

"I'm sorry."

"You don't look sorry," she grumbled.

"Only because I found some eggs." He took the green fruit out of his pocket. "And a tree full of these."

She snatched it from him. "This is a breadfruit."

"How do you know?"

"I'm a chef," she said, rolling her eyes. "I've studied the local produce."

"Can we eat it raw?"

"It's not good raw. You cook it like a yam or a potato."

"I'd eat a potato raw."

She handed the breadfruit back to him, shrugging. It was rock hard with a thick skin. He needed to make a fire anyway. It was safer to boil the eggs, if they could. His mouth watered at the thought of a hot meal. Any kind of meal.

"Are you ready?" he asked.

"I guess."

They continued uphill. His injured knee slowed him down considerably, so she kept up with him pretty well. The foliage thinned out as they ascended, which made the hike easier. He increased the pace, sensing they were near the summit. Soon they broke through the canopy and he could see the island's high point.

A quarter of a mile later, they were there. She sat on a flat rock at the peak, trying to catch her breath. He stood and took in the panoramic view.

It was majestic.

Stark, remote, dizzying and majestic.

He couldn't see any other islands nearby, just an endless stretch of calm blue water. They were all alone on a big rock in the middle of the ocean. The summit was at the south end, judging by the position of the sun. They'd landed on the west side, which boasted one small, protected cove. The rest of that coastline was sheer cliffs and crashing waves. It was extremely inhospitable, possibly unapproachable. Sharp points jutted up from the sea around the shore like protective daggers.

The eastern side of the island was less severe, with gentler slopes and softer edges. It had a sprawling white-sand beach, framed by dozens of coconut trees. Beyond that, a sparkling expanse of crystal-blue water, with tide pools and an extensive coral reef system.

It was a fisherman's paradise—but largely inaccessible, even by boat. There was no convenient shoring area. The island was small, only about five miles long and two miles wide. Getting around on foot wouldn't be a problem. He spotted a craggy rock formation to the north, with what appeared to be fresh water cascading down its edge.

Overall, Logan was pleased. This spot was like a private tropical getaway, untouched by human hands. People paid big money to vacation at secluded resorts and nature preserves. He could survive here a few weeks.

The company wasn't bad, either.

He glanced down at Cady, gauging her reaction. She wasn't admiring the view or counting the island's resources. She was weeping. Tears rolled down her pretty face. She wiped them away, sniffling.

"What's wrong?" he asked.

"What's wrong?" she repeated, incredulous. She gestured to the deserted island and the open ocean all around them. "There's nothing here!"

His stomach clenched with regret. Of course she was disappointed; she'd been hoping for a rescue that wouldn't come and inhabitants that didn't exist. She didn't care what the island had to offer, other than a way out. She only saw what it lacked: visitors, conveniences, transportation and neighboring islands.

Logan didn't blame her for being upset. She hadn't signed up for this. She'd been kidnapped, traumatized and lost at sea. Now they were on dry land, but still completely isolated. She didn't want to stay here and battle the elements. She wanted to go home.

Instead of escaping her nightmare, she was stuck in it. With him.

# *Chapter 6*

What was wrong? Was he *serious*?

She couldn't believe he'd asked that. He'd lost his damned mind. He was standing at the summit of this bug-infested hellhole like the lord of his domain. He wore a relaxed expression, as if the gut-wrenching view invigorated him.

"We're stranded on a deserted island. You're not disturbed by that?"

He raked a hand through his hair, scowling. He didn't look tired, even though they'd hiked for miles. Sweat dampened his face and shirt, but he wasn't winded. She felt like she might faint from overexertion. He seemed unaffected by the climb. "I'm trained to stay calm in emergency situations, and to follow a specific survival protocol. You see a deserted island, but I see lifesaving resources."

"I see a jungle fortress surrounded by sharks."

He nodded, as if this was a fair assessment. Then he pulled out his phone and checked for service. Yeah, right.

Shaking his head, he put it away. "I'm sorry. I should have tried to manage your expectations better."

"My expectations?"

"I assumed the island was uninhabited, but I didn't want to demotivate you."

"You didn't want to demotivate me," she repeated dully. She'd turned into a parrot. She was a jungle parrot sidekick in a shredded red dress, with leaves for shoes.

None of this seemed real.

Her stomach dropped as she remembered what he'd said about the possibility of a rescue. She'd been dubious about his claims, but she hadn't pressed him on it. Now she studied him with new suspicion. He stared back at her, cool as ice. "Do you think they're looking for us, or did you lie about that, too?"

He tore his gaze away. "I don't know."

"You don't know if you lied?"

"I don't know if there's a search effort underway," he said in a clipped tone. "They send rescue teams to reported accidents, like plane crashes or shipwrecks. Kidnappings at sea, without a specific location…"

Her spirits plummeted. There was no rescue team. What would they look for, other than the pirates? A man or woman overboard had no chance of surviving in the open ocean. Cady and Logan would be presumed dead.

"Let's focus on the positive," he said.

She threw back her head and laughed.

"We're alive."

She stopped laughing, because she sounded deranged, and he had a point.

"Being on dry land is a vast improvement over the raft. Two or three more days at sea would've killed us."

She let out a ragged breath, fighting tears again.

"As deserted islands go, this one is ideal."

"How?"

"Most uninhabited islands are spits of sand with a few palm trees and no fresh water. They're uninhabited for a reason. There's no way to live off them. This place is different. It has everything we need to survive."

She studied the green landscape with wet eyes.

He crouched down next to her and pointed at the shoreline. "Look there. Tide pools are easy to forage, and full of seafood. Are you allergic to shellfish?"

"No."

"Do you like it?"

She nodded, because she did. She loved it, in fact. Shrimp, crab, fish, sushi…she even liked sea urchin.

"And over here, check it out," he said, moving his finger. "That white line in the rock face is a waterfall."

"It's far away."

"It's close to the beach, which is where I'd build a shelter. I can make an SOS signal right there on the sand that would be visible from the air. There are coconut trees and palm trees. Maybe some more of that breadfruit."

"I've seen taro plants."

"Yeah? They have roots you can eat."

"I know."

He directed his finger at her. "There's something special here, too."

"What?" she asked warily.

"You. You're a great resource. You're a chef. You've studied the local plants. You can cook the hell out of a fish. You're also in excellent shape. You're a strong swimmer. I couldn't ask for a better partner."

"Now you're going overboard."

"I mean it."

"You wouldn't rather have another SEAL with you?"

He held her gaze. "There's no one I'd rather have with me."

She didn't know how to feel about this proclamation. The intensity that had excited her at the bar—and terrified her in the aftermath of the kidnapping—was still there, glittering in his eyes. But his brutal actions were no longer at the forefront of her mind. He'd been kind to her. He'd shared his clothing and his body heat on the raft. He was a good man. Although he hadn't been completely honest with her about their predicament, and she didn't trust him not to bend the truth again, she felt safe with him. She also knew he wanted her. She tried not to be flattered by his desire, and failed.

He was incredibly charismatic. That was why all of the women on the cruise had been agog over him. It wasn't just his face, though he had handsome features. It wasn't just his body, though that was a perfect ten. He radiated strength and confidence. When he focused his attention on her, she turned into mush.

"I'm no survival expert," she said, glancing away.

"Have you ever been camping?"

"In an RV, with my grandpa."

"The drill sergeant?"

"Yes."

"This won't be like that."

She laughed again, wiping the tears from her cheeks. "No kidding."

"How are your feet?"

"Terrible."

"I'll rewrap them before we go."

"Must we?"

"It's all downhill from here."

"Ha."

She spotted an aloe vera plant, so she sent him to pick some for her. While she took care of the cuts on her feet, he applied the slick moisture to his chapped lips and sunburned cheeks. Heavy beard stubble shadowed his jaw. He looked a little rough around the edges, but ruggedly handsome. This environment suited him. It didn't suit her. She felt sweaty and dirty. Her hair was all over the place. There were oily stains on her dress from the coconut milk. *Rugged* wasn't a word used to describe women, so she tried to think of a similar term. *Natural*, maybe. She was at peak natural right now.

When she was finished with the aloe vera, he rewrapped her feet with new leaves. "We'll see if we can make it to that beach before nightfall. Then I'll start a fire. We'll have a cookout, and sleep under the stars."

She arched a brow at his fanciful phrasing.

"Too much?"

"Let's bring it down a notch. You're supposed to be managing my expectations, remember?"

"Right. Okay, here goes. Let's try to get as far from the summit as possible before the afternoon rain hits and makes the terrain even more treacherous."

Well, that wasn't as upbeat, but she'd asked for it. She noted a few dark clouds on the edge of the horizon and figured this was the likelier scenario. With a low groan, she rose to a standing position. After a quick stretch, she followed him down the hillside. Her arms and legs ached from overuse. She felt like a wrung-out dishrag. Logan, on the other hand, appeared hale and hearty as hell. Damn his rugged ass. She stared at his broad shoulders, remembering how his muscles had bunched beneath her fingertips, and how easily he'd lifted her.

It started raining.

He kept going.

She tried to be strong and brave and a team player, but it was just beyond her. She was soaked from head to toe. Her energy was sapped. Hiking uphill while wearing leaves for shoes was difficult. Downhill, on wet ground…it was impossible. She slipped and fell hard, right on her butt. Although she had plenty of padding there, it didn't feel sufficient. She felt like she'd gotten spanked by the island, big-time.

She didn't get up. She rolled onto her side and cried.

He knelt next to her. His hand rested on her waist. Instead of asking questions, he waited for her to compose herself.

"I'm okay," she said finally. "I just fell."

"Where does it hurt?"

She gestured to the general vicinity. The back of her dress had ridden up, exposing her sore, muddy bottom. He swept his palm over her abused flesh, squeezing gently. Then he gave her a soft pat of sympathy.

"I don't think anything's broken," he said.

"Are you a medic, too?"

"No."

She tugged her dress into place, suspecting he'd enjoyed that exam a little too much. He winced as he staggered upright, as if his knee was bothering him. The injury reminded her that he was a human being with real weaknesses. He wasn't impervious to pain. He schooled his expression quickly and helped her to her feet.

"We need to find shelter for the night."

Unfortunately, there were no convenient cabanas to duck into. There wasn't even a dry rock to crawl under. She trudged along behind him, her head down. She was cold and wet and her butt hurt. The only pace she could manage was slow. The rain dissipated. The slope of the hillside became less severe, and the foliage grew thicker.

In the gathering dusk she imagined a lot of creepy crawlers that probably weren't there. Spiders hanging from the trees. Centipedes scuttling through wet leaves on the ground. Poisonous frogs, pit vipers and tiny, flesh-eating parasites.

Then the mosquitos descended, and she wished for anything but them. She waved the buzzing nuisances away from her ears and wrapped the tulle around her head in an attempt to protect her face.

When a mosquito bit the tender flesh behind her knee, she shrieked in protest. "I'm getting eaten alive!"

"So am I," Logan said, slapping his neck. "This sucks."

"Literally!"

He dragged her toward a large rock formation that rose up in the gloom. Its mossy surface was covered in vines, hiding what appeared to be the mouth of a cave. He had to push aside the foliage to gain entry. It was pitch-black inside, and smelled bad. It was the least inviting shelter she could imagine, but she would've gone into Satan's lair at this point. She held his hand in a tight grip as they ducked into the cave.

"I don't know what's in here," he whispered.

"As long as it's not more mosquitos."

He stayed still for several moments, breathing hard in the dark quiet. "We can't explore the interior."

That was fine with her. She had no desire to explore. None whatsoever. Her eyes adjusted to the lack of light in slow increments. He sat down with his back against the cave wall. She wanted to curl up next to him, but she wasn't sure which side of him was safer.

What if a wild animal wandered in?

What if one tried to get out?

"Here," he said, splaying his legs. She settled between them, her back against his front. He put his arms around her. He was wet, but warm. His heartbeat pounded in a strong, steady rhythm. Fast, but not too fast, like hers. He was alert, rather than panicked. That was comforting. She could count on him to stay calm even when she was freaking out.

"What's that smell?" she asked. "Rats?"

"Bats."

Ugh. The hairs at her nape prickled at the thought of them flapping around her curls. Their nasty little teeth and leathery wings. At least the cave was free of mosquitos. She'd die of rabies, instead of malaria. "Can you make a fire?"

"Not without dry wood."

She tried not to squirm around too much, but she was uncomfortable. The ground was hard against her sore bottom. She was hungry and thirsty.

"Tell me about yourself," he said.

"What do you want to know?"

"Where do you live?"

"I lived in San Francisco, until recently. I left a few months after I broke up with Andrew. It seemed better to make a fresh start. Right now I'm staying at my parents' house in Long Beach."

"I still live with my parents."

"You're kidding."

"No. I'm overseas a lot, and they have a guest house. It works out."

"Where is it?"

"Del Mar. It's a suburb of San Diego."

"Is that where you're from?"

"Born and raised."

Her grandparents lived in San Diego. She was stranded on a deserted island with a fellow Southern Californian. What were the odds?

"Did you grow up in Long Beach?" he asked.

"Close. Irvine. My parents moved because my mom got a job offer there. She's a high school principal."

"A principal and a cop for parents?"

"Sounds fun, right?"

"Were you a rebellious teenager?"

"Not really. Were you?"

"Nah. I was a mama's boy. Still am."

"How old are you?"

"Thirty. You?"

"Twenty-seven."

He grunted in response, shifting his injured knee.

"Am I hurting you?"

"You're fine," he said gruffly. "You should try to get some sleep."

"What will we do tomorrow?"

"Find water. Make a fire. Build a shelter."

She groaned at his overzealous to-do list.

"The beach isn't far. Tomorrow will be an easier day."

"I doubt there will be any easy days on this island."

"Maybe not, but we'll live."

"You sound confident."

"I am."

"Have you ever failed at anything?"

He didn't answer. When silence stretched between them, she realized this was a touchy subject. More painful than his busted knee, perhaps. She wondered if he'd failed to complete a mission, or failed to protect someone.

"I should have thanked you for saving me," she said.

His arms tightened around her shoulders. "Don't worry about it."

"It's a big deal," she insisted. "You risked your life."

"It was the least I could do," he said. "You got kidnapped while you were with me. *Because* you were with me."

"That wasn't your fault."

"I convinced you to leave the bar."

She hadn't needed much convincing. She flushed a little, remembering how uninhibited she'd been. How she'd devoured his mouth in the hallway. "I wouldn't have done the same if our situations were reversed. I wouldn't have started swimming after you."

"I'm trained for combat and water rescue. You're not."

She didn't think it was only a matter of training. He was a hero by nature. She wasn't. She'd been frozen with fear during the attack, and for hours after. The same thing had happened when she'd witnessed her grandfather's death. She'd been catatonic, unable to move or speak. Unable to help.

She wasn't calm in emergency situations. She didn't like taking risks, or stepping out of her comfort zone. Whenever she did, she regretted it. This situation was a prime example. Her first attempt at a one-night stand had resulted in her kidnapping. It couldn't get any worse than that! She didn't embrace danger, like Logan. As grateful as she was to be under his protection, his presence set off major emotional warning bells for her.

She had to be careful with him. She was still trying to move on from her last romantic disaster. He was clearly a no-strings type, and a magnet for adoring females. He'd caught the eye of every woman on the cruise. She couldn't afford to get attached.

But keeping her distance wasn't an option, so she pushed aside her misgivings and settled against him. He made a warm, steady wall behind her. She felt safe in his arms. Although the chemistry between them was still there, she wouldn't act on it. They weren't going to finish what they'd started on the dance floor.

That ship had sailed—literally.

Their almost-hookup had been a once-in-a-lifetime thing. A perfect storm of physical attraction and opportunity that couldn't be re-created. Even if she'd wanted to take the risk, there was nothing remotely sexy about their current situation. They were in a bat-infested cave. She was covered in mud. So was he.

She closed her eyes, determined to ignore the exciting male contours of his body, and the dull throb of cuts and bruises on her own. She tried not to worry about what might befall them tomorrow. He'd advised her to focus on the present, and think positive. Tonight they were alive. She was exhausted, but unharmed.

Then a dark blanket of fatigue settled over her, and she drifted off.

# *Chapter 7*

Logan woke in the same condition as the day before, with one exception.

He'd grown accustomed to the dry mouth and nagging headache that had plagued him every morning. He was sore from lying on the hard ground. His stomach ached from emptiness. The only new development was an uncomfortable erection. Maybe he hadn't been hydrated enough to pitch a tent until now. He'd been weak and nauseous from the concussion. Today he was back in full form, so to speak.

Cady's proximity probably had something to do with it. She was curled up on her side next to him with her bottom snuggled against his crotch. There was no denying that she had a world-class ass. It was soft and supple and beautifully shaped. He had a vivid recollection of how those lush curves felt in his hands.

Damn.

Speaking of hands, his right one was cupping her left breast. She was smaller on top, but no less perfect.

*Damn.*

He smothered a groan and rolled onto his back, chagrined. He hadn't meant to grope her in his sleep. His stomach clenched with unease. He waited for her to jump up and slap him silly. She stayed motionless, her chest rising and falling with even breaths.

She didn't stir. She hadn't felt it.

Inching away from her, he studied the interior of the cave with bleary eyes. Last night he'd imagined a gaping cavern of snakes and pitfalls. In reality, it was a shallow, abandoned bat nest. The walls had crumbled, leaving a pile of guano-covered rocks less than five feet from the entrance. There could be an intricate network beyond that, but the path was blocked. That was why this cave was empty, with vines covering the mouth.

Also, it smelled bad.

He rose to his feet with a wince. His knee was stiff, among other things. He lumbered toward the cave's entrance and shoved aside the foliage. Light flooded the interior. Cady sat up and blinked at him owlishly. She looked like a forest sprite. Her hair was a tangled halo of dark curls with leaves in it.

"Sorry," he said. "I was…invading your space."

She rubbed her eyes. "What?"

"Never mind," he muttered, and went out to water the nearest tree. She followed a moment later. He already had his pants unzipped, so he turned his back to obstruct her view. His knee buckled as he sidestepped. Cursing, he regained his balance.

She walked into the jungle and crouched behind a bush to do her own thing. By the time she returned to the front of the cave, he had his body under control. He didn't ask how she'd slept, because he already knew. They'd both been awake half the night. She had dark circles under her eyes. Getting a good rest on hard ground was difficult, even for him. He needed to build a shelter today.

"How are you?" he asked.

She touched her throat. "Thirsty."

"Your feet okay?"

"No, they hurt."

He nodded, unsurprised. All of the hiking they'd done would slow the healing process. He knew she wanted him to be honest with her about the challenges they faced, but he was more concerned about keeping her morale up. There wasn't much he could do for her cuts. With his bad knee, he couldn't carry her.

"Do you want to stay here and rest?"

Her nose wrinkled. "Rest, in that hideous cave? I don't think so."

He smiled at her honesty. "As soon as we get to the beach you can take it easy."

"How far is it?"

"Not far."

"You have no idea, do you?"

"The island is only about five miles long. I think we're close to the coast."

She inclined her head east, toward the sunrise. "That way?"

"Yep."

She gathered the extra fabric from her skirt to use as a shawl. As he collected his eggs and breadfruit and aloe plant, his stomach clenched with a sharp pain that surprised him. He'd been hungry before, but not like this. He'd never felt true hunger pangs.

"My stomach hurts," she said.

"Mine, too. We'll eat some more coconuts at the beach."

They hiked all morning. The waterfall he'd spotted from the summit didn't materialize. Neither did the white-sand beach he'd hoped to see. It was baking hot, with no breeze. The foliage that blocked out the sun also seemed to hold in heat. Sweat slicked his skin and tickled his mosquito bites. His damp shirt clung to his back.

In contrast, his throat felt like sandpaper. He was losing too much fluid to perspiration. Staying hydrated under these conditions was almost impossible.

Cady trudged along with a zombie-like stoicism that concerned him. Although she was stronger than he'd expected, he was afraid to push her too hard. When he found another cluster of liana vines, it was none too soon. She collapsed in the shade, her face pale. They drank until her color returned. Then they drank some more. She used the aloe on her lips, which were healing well. He did the same. His sunburn felt better. This environment was challenging, but it was nowhere near as harsh as the open ocean.

After a short rest, he stood and offered her a hand. She rose to her feet too quickly. Her lashes fluttered, and she swayed backward. He caught her before she fell, holding her upright. She didn't faint, which was a good sign. She stared at him in surprise. His heart pounded against hers, half relieved, half…something else.

"I got light-headed," she said.

"I can see that."

She clung to him for a few seconds. Her fingers were curled around his biceps, her slim body pressed to his. He liked the way she felt in his arms, despite the circumstances. He'd liked the way she'd felt this morning, too.

"Okay now?" he asked.

"Yes."

He released her slowly, struck by a wave of guilt. He was having a hard time keeping his hands off her, and his thoughts were completely inappropriate. She was weak from exhaustion. He should be taking better care of her.

His desire for her was awkward, but manageable. What really bothered him was the sense that he was letting her down. He was failing her, the same way he'd failed his comrade in Telskuf. If Logan hadn't been injured, Hud would still be alive.

The loss of his teammate weighed heavily on Logan, and it made him feel even more protective of Cady. She was his team now, and she needed him to survive. She shouldn't be hiking like this. He cursed himself for not being able to carry her. She could get heat exhaustion, and then they'd really be in trouble. There were a thousand ways to die here. She could contract dengue fever, or pick up a nasty intestinal bug. She could succumb to an infection, just from the cuts on her feet.

"I'm going to scout ahead," he said.

"No," she said, grasping his arm. "I can walk. Take me with you."

He raked a hand through his hair, torn. She was afraid to be alone in the jungle, which was understandable, but he really needed to find the shore. He glanced around and spotted a seagull flying over the tops of the trees. They were close.

He nodded his agreement, and they started walking again. She seemed to have recovered from her dizzy spell. They followed the bird's flight path to a clearing. From there he could see swaying palm trees, loaded with coconuts.

They'd made it. Thank God.

There was no gradual transition from inland to coast.

The foliage just ended where the beach began. He stumbled forward and fell to his knees in the sand, basking in the change of scenery. He hadn't realized how much he'd needed fresh air and sunshine. The thick canopy had felt suffocating and oppressive.

This beach was paradise. Pure paradise.

It was all soft white sand and crystal-blue water. There were coconut palms for days. The tide pools promised a plethora of tasty seafood, and the underwater reef would offer even more. His chest swelled with emotion. He couldn't see the waterfall from here, but a tall rock formation rose up in the distance like a monument of hope.

Cady didn't stop on the dry sand. She raced straight into the surf and collapsed there, letting the gentle waves lap over her. He laughed at her antics, his spirits soaring. They were going to be all right.

He hadn't allowed himself to feel relief until this moment. He also hadn't dwelled on the dangers they'd faced so far. The days at sea had been dark, to say the least. The odds of arriving at an island like this were astronomical. He'd had brushes with death before, but they were the flash-bang kind, over in the blink of an eye. Slow starvation wasn't his cup of tea. They were incredibly lucky to be alive.

He wanted to join her in the waves, fully clothed, but he couldn't afford to get his fire-starting materials wet. So he shucked out of his pants and pulled his shirt over his head before he dove in. The water felt deliciously cool on his overheated skin. He submerged his entire body, getting his hair wet, rinsing away the dirt and sweat and jungle funk.

It was glorious.

She was right there with him, laughing and splashing

around in the waves. He hadn't seen her this happy since the night at the bar. She looked like a tropical goddess in her red dress, eyes dancing.

He drew her into his arms and kissed her. He couldn't help himself. His relief overflowed, and his instincts took over. He pulled her on top of him and kissed her beautiful mouth. Then he rolled on top of her and did it again.

He didn't put much thought into his actions. He just let his impulses take over and went along for the ride. They'd been through a lot together, and he felt a deep connection with her. He told himself it wasn't even sexual—but he wouldn't have done this with anyone else. He didn't kiss his comrades after a successful mission. He didn't grab random women and plant one on them when the mood struck.

She kissed him back with the same joyful ebullience, twisting her arms around his neck. It was all innocent fun, as frothy as the foam-specked surf. She laughed into his mouth as a wave crashed over his back. Then the water around them bloomed bright red.

He lifted his head, his heart pounding. "Are you hurt?"

"No." She studied the cloud of crimson around them. "My dress is bleeding. It's dry-clean only."

He didn't know dresses could bleed. The sight of red dye spreading across the water chilled him to the bone. It was like a portent of doom and a bad flashback rolled into one. He remembered the last time he'd seen a woman in a pool of blood. The interpreter's wife, in Syria. That moment had been difficult for his entire team. They'd failed her.

Logan blinked away the memory, his gut clenched with unease. Cady resembled a shark attack victim, and he was on top of her. He didn't believe in visions or premonitions, but he did believe in gut feelings. His gut told him that he was putting her at risk. He shouldn't be touching her like this. He'd dropped the ball the night they'd met, and now here they were. He couldn't repeat that mistake.

His behavior was also unbecoming of a SEAL. Hunger must have turned his brain into mush. He had to stop acting like a lovesick schoolboy and start acting like a professional. She was depending on him to keep her alive.

"Sorry," he said in a stiff tone. "I got carried away. It won't happen again."

She stared at him in confusion, as if he'd turned into someone she didn't recognize. Another wave struck, swirling her dress around her thighs. The wet fabric clung to her breasts, outlining every curve in exquisite detail.

He disentangled himself from her and rose to his feet, suddenly aware of his own attire. Water streamed down his body. He was soaked to the skin, and half aroused. His hand dropped to the front placket of his boxer shorts to make sure it was closed. Her gaze followed his motion. He adjusted himself and turned away, flushing.

Although the chemistry between them was red-hot, his excitement was more of a byproduct than a driving force. He hadn't kissed her because she was sexy. He'd kissed her because he was overwhelmed with emotion. That had never happened to him before. It was an unexpected complication, but now he'd be on guard. Forewarned was forearmed. He'd squash whatever feelings needed to get squashed.

He waded out of the surf, determined to hold himself in check. He had to stay in control, and concentrate on survival.

His first task was combing the beach for coconuts. There were about a dozen mature ones strewn across the sand. Fresh coconuts were less abundant. They didn't fall off the tree when they were green. They had to be shaken loose or picked by hand, and climbing a coconut tree was a great way to fall and break your neck. After a short search, he found two.

He also gathered several different types of wood. He wasn't familiar with any of them, so he had no idea what would burn well or make the best bow drill, which was his preferred method of starting a fire.

Cady didn't sit idle while he wandered the beach. She explored the area as well, and returned with a nice score: a bunch of ripe bananas. His stomach rumbled with hunger. "Where did you find those?"

"There's a cluster of banana trees right over there."

He followed her gaze to the edge of the beach. There were several banana trees laden with green fruit. Grunting his approval, he directed her toward a shady spot under a palm tree. They sat down and shared the feast. He devoured three bananas, one after the other. When he reached for a fourth, she stopped him.

"You'll get sick if you eat too many."

"Bananas are good for you."

"Only in moderation."

He was still hungry, but he deferred to her greater knowledge of food and nutrition. He couldn't afford to regurgitate his only meal of the day. They switched to coconuts, draining every drop of juice.

He lifted one of the empty shells. "We can use these to collect water."

"Later," she said, leaning her back against the tree trunk. She pressed her palm to her flat belly, as if it was uncomfortably full. "I can't move."

"Fine," he said easily, because he'd promised her a break. The waterfall wasn't going anywhere. There were liana vines in the rain forest, less than a hundred feet away. He had plenty of other tasks to accomplish. "Stay here and rest."

"Where are you going?"

"Not far. I have to collect some materials to start a fire."

"Why do we need fire? It's a million degrees."

"It was cold last night."

"How far will you go?"

"I'll be within shouting distance."

She waved a hand in the air to grant him permission. It was a regal, graceful gesture. Queen of the Island. His lips quirked into a smile. The trauma of the past few days had wrung some of the attitude out of her, but not all. Her resilience was reassuring. He needed a strong partner, and she had a lot of potential.

The best place for a shelter was near the edge of the beach, where the tide wouldn't reach them. He decided on a spot between two massive palm trees. There was plenty of shade, a nice breeze and a natural windbreak. First he dug a shallow depression in the sand. Then he made a fire ring with about a dozen volcanic rocks. He tossed some sticks and branches inside the pit. There was a bench-sized piece of driftwood nearby, so he dragged that over to sit on.

After the stage was set, he worked on a small hut for the fire. He had to keep the pit dry or he'd be starting over from scratch every time it rained. He harvested palm fronds from several different trees, and ventured into the forest to chop down a sapling. Using its slim, sturdy branches, he formed a simple A-frame and covered it with palm fronds. This would protect the fire from the average afternoon shower.

The third step was constructing the bow drill. He needed a flat wooden base, a bow-shaped tree branch, a spindle and some rope or cordage to create friction. If one of the pieces was flawed, there would be no ember, so he chose his materials carefully. He carved the flat base out of driftwood and shaped the spindle from a sturdy stick. When that was done, he went in search of a top rock to hold the spindle in place. He found a flat stone with a curved depression in the center.

The last thing he needed was cordage—and he didn't have any. He'd left their only rope with the deflated raft. That was poor planning. He blamed the flub on dehydration and a concussion. He didn't have any shoelaces; he had no shoes. His belt wouldn't work. Sighing, he ventured into the jungle for more material.

Young liana vines made excellent cordage, so he cut down several. He sliced the vines into long strips and braided them together for extra strength. This process was time-consuming and labor-intensive. When he was finished, he was soaked in sweat again. It was blazing hot, even in the shade.

Cady hadn't moved from her spot under the palm tree. Her dress fluttered around her thighs like a red flag.

He rolled his pants up to the knee and took the fire bundle from his pocket. It was dry, and still smelled like gasoline. He set it next to the pile of kindling in the fire pit. As soon as he had an ember, he'd transfer it to the bundle. When he had a flame, he'd add kindling. He felt confident about executing his plan, but making a primitive fire wasn't an easy task. It required skill, patience, upper body strength and perseverance.

He moved the bow back and forth in a rapid sawing motion, visualizing a hot coal. Waiting for the telltale smoke.

It didn't come.

He continued to work the bow. His foot held the base in place. The vine cordage didn't move as smoothly as rope or a shoestring, but it was all he had. Sweat beaded on his upper lip. He sawed faster. The only thing that started burning was his forearm muscle. His injured knee hurt like a son of a bitch. He gritted his teeth, ignoring the pain.

Was that smoke?

He stopped to check his progress. There was no coal, which was disappointing. Maybe the driftwood wasn't hard enough to generate an ember.

He carved a new base from another piece of wood he'd collected on the beach. Then he tried again, sawing his heart out. His hand ached from the repetition. Blisters formed on the inside of his palm. His knee throbbed in protest. Smoke curled up from the notch where the base met the spindle.

Almost there…almost there…

*Snap.*

The cord broke in half.

He tossed aside the top rock and the bow, swearing. There was a sooty black spot at the notch in the base. It wasn't a coal. It was nowhere near a coal.

Goddamn it.

He leaped to his feet and cursed at the sky. He said things his mother wouldn't be proud of. He threw the wooden base across the beach, calling it every dirty name in his vocabulary. Then he sat down in the shade, seething. He'd learned how to make fire several different ways in an outdoor survival class. He'd practiced this method a dozen times. He'd even taught it to his comrades. But he'd never tested his skills in a tropical setting with unfamiliar materials, or in a real-life emergency. The pressure was getting to him.

If he didn't make fire, they were going to be in serious trouble. Fire was the ultimate morale booster. They needed fire to stay healthy, mentally and physically. Without fire, the nights would be miserable. They couldn't stay warm or fend off mosquitos. They couldn't make use of most of the island's resources. They couldn't cook without fire. They'd probably die without fire.

Logan's gut clenched at the thought. He wasn't prone to mood swings or negativity. He knew better. Focusing on the worst-case scenario could get you killed. But he'd also learned that a positive mind-set wasn't bulletproof armor.

He'd stayed positive in Telskuf, and everything had gone to hell anyway. Months later, he still couldn't come to terms with what had happened. He remembered chaos and confusion. Their communications system had malfunctioned. Then a simple misstep had resulted in his injury. He couldn't complete the mission. He couldn't even walk on his own. Samir had to support him. Instead of retreating with them, Hud had continued into the building.

He'd never gotten out.

Logan felt directly responsible for the loss. He'd agonized over it, second-guessing every action he'd taken that night.

Seeing Cady in a pool of crimson had taken him to the

same dark place. It had affected him on a deeper level than any of the blood he'd shed, on desert sands or in the open water. He'd calmly killed men with a variety of weapons, including his bare hands. He'd watched the corpse of the man he'd gutted get torn apart by sharks with relish.

That was pretty messed up—and he didn't care. He wasn't going to cry over a good kill, done in self-defense. What bothered him more was the idea of failing.

Failing to get a fire started.

Failing to provide for her.

Failing to protect her.

Failing to keep her alive—the same way he'd failed his teammate in Telskuf, and the interpreter in Al-Hasakah, and the interpreter's wife.

Making a sound of frustration, Logan rose to his feet to get more cordage. His knee almost gave out, and black spots danced across his vision. He leaned against the tree to regain his balance. His arms quivered uncontrollably.

This was the price he had to pay for overexerting himself.

He focused on taking deep breaths until his muscles relaxed. Instead of walking into the jungle, he sat down again. There was no sense in continuing to work on the fire right now. His hands ached, his palms were blistered and his biceps felt like jelly. As much as he hated to admit it, he needed a break.

So he stretched out in the shade and closed his eyes for a few minutes, giving his body time to recover.

## Chapter 8

Cady took pity on Logan and brought him a fresh coconut.

It was their last one. There were plenty more on the trees, thirty or forty feet high, but she had no idea how to get them down. The bananas were off-limits until tomorrow. They contained nutrients that were toxic in large amounts.

He was lying on his stomach in the shade with his head in his arms. All of that caveman yelling must have tuckered him out. She understood the reason for his meltdown. They were in an extremely stressful situation. Every basic necessity was difficult, if not impossible, to attain. They hadn't been getting enough food or sleep. Her behavior had been erratic, too. She'd been crying one minute, laughing the next.

Instead of disturbing his slumber, she sat down beneath the opposite tree and studied him. He was facing away from her, unaware of her presence. Something about his state of repose appealed to her. She hadn't seen him resting on his stomach before. He was always on the move, always working hard—and it showed. Every muscle was on point.

His shirt was damp with sweat, his hair mussed. Broad shoulders narrowed to a lean waist and a very cute, very tight butt. His pants were rolled up to the knee. He had nice calves, hairy and suntanned and strong. He even had nice feet. They were big, like the rest of him. She shivered at the memory of his wet boxer shorts clinging to his body.

Lord.

She'd abandoned all of her reservations about hooking up with him the instant his mouth touched hers. She'd forgotten that she was starving and exhausted. She'd forgotten everything but the feel of his hard-muscled body on top of her. Her cheeks heated at the memory. He'd been the one to come to his senses, which was even worse.

She couldn't blame the island for her lack of inhibitions. It was him. He made her throw every rule out the window.

*It won't happen again.*

She puzzled over the strange declaration he'd made. Now that they were stuck together, he'd decided not to pursue her? She didn't know why he'd changed his mind. Some men lost interest quickly. Some only wanted casual relationships, and there was nothing casual about their current predicament. Maybe he'd decided she wasn't his type. Or maybe she just looked like a hot mess with dirty clothes and tangled hair.

She set aside the coconut with a frown. He didn't act disinterested. He still watched her with hungry eyes. His desire hadn't cooled, but his attitude had. He'd been almost formal with her since the kidnapping. He'd kissed her as an impulsive celebration, not because he was trying to get with her.

It didn't really matter what his deal was, because she wasn't trying to get with him, either. Momentary lapse of reason aside, she'd put him on her no-play list. He was too intense, too risky, too big...too everything.

She leaned her back against the palm tree and sifted the fine grains of sand through her fingers. This spot in the shade was pleasant, with a gentle breeze. The view was incredible, but also disconcerting. She'd never been on an empty beach before.

In the jungle, it was easier to forget they were all alone. Out here, the isolation was clear. They were still stranded in the middle of the ocean, countless miles from civilization, with little or no hope of rescue.

Even so, only a fool wouldn't appreciate this place, after what they'd been through. A stunning white-sand beach, lined with fruit trees, was a vast improvement over a stinky bat cave. It was practically a five-star resort.

He mumbled something in his sleep, startling her. It sounded like he was saying "go with thud."

She dusted her hands off and leaned closer to listen.

"Leave me," he said. "Go with Hud!"

Not *thud*. Hud.

She assumed it was a name, though she'd never heard it before. His leg twitched in a restless motion. She stayed quiet, reluctant to wake him. His brow was furrowed in distress. While she watched, his shoulders tensed, and he threw out his arms as if some invisible force had attacked him.

Then he rolled over and stared at her, breathing heavily. He had sand in his hair and eyelashes. Fine grains stuck to his sweaty skin.

"Who's Hud?" she asked.

He groaned, scrubbing the sand from his face. Then he gave her a cautious look. "He was a member of Team Twelve."

"What happened to him?"

"He died."

"Overseas?"

Logan nodded. "Telskuf. Iraq."

"The same place you got injured."

His brows rose. "Did I say that?"

"No. I just guessed. Tell me about him."

He glanced past her, contemplative. "He was funny. We went through BUD/S training together. He'd make everyone laugh, even when it hurt to laugh. No one could beat him at poker. He was a smooth talker."

She smiled at this description. Logan wasn't a smooth talker. He was more of a blunt instrument, quiet and brutally efficient. He used as few words as possible to convey meaning. "Do you miss him?"

"Very much," he said, meeting her gaze.

She didn't ask any more questions. He seemed reluctant to show emotion, and he was still mourning the loss of his friend. Instead of prodding a sore wound, she fell silent, studying his appearance. The bruise on his forehead had faded from dark purple to sickly green. His eyes were puffy from sleep. His shirt was half-buttoned and filthy. He was beyond rugged; he looked like he'd been on a bender, or in a barroom brawl. Despite his rough edges, she found him handsome and endearing. The fear she'd felt after the kidnapping had faded. Every day they were together, her trust in him grew.

"I brought you a coconut," she said.

He picked up the coconut and chopped the end off in

three quick strikes. They passed it back and forth, sharing the juice. It wasn't enough to quench her thirst. She tilted the fruit upside down to get the last few drops. He watched her with a hungry expression. She set aside the empty husk, flushing.

"We need to find water."

She let out a ragged breath. "What about the vines?"

"Those are a finite resource. We should save them for emergencies."

"This isn't an emergency?"

He didn't answer. Apparently, their situation could get worse. They could become gravely ill or sustain serious injuries. Her mind supplied a dozen examples of freak accidents. Broken bones, parasites, snakebite...

"Can you walk?" he asked.

She wiggled her bare feet. They felt fine when she wasn't putting any pressure on them. The soft sand didn't bother her as much as rocky terrain. "I'll try."

"You can always stay here."

"No," she said, stricken. "What if something happens to you?"

"That's why I'd rather go together. It's not far."

She'd heard that lie before. The waterfall he'd pointed out yesterday wasn't even visible from this beach. There was a vague mountainous shape looming in the distance. They'd have to climb uphill or circle around it. The entire island formed a half-moon, with the summit on one end and this smaller peak on the other.

"Let's check out the coastline first," he said. "Water always flows downhill. Maybe there's a runoff."

She hoped so, if that meant they wouldn't have to hike inland. They collected the empty coconuts and headed toward the tide pools. This section of beach was interspersed with slabs of volcanic rock. The perforated surface was sharp on her tender soles, so she stayed on the sand whenever she could.

If Logan felt any pain, he didn't show it. He searched every nook and cranny of the tide pools for sea creatures. He spotted several crabs, which led him to draw his knife, but they scuttled into hiding places the blade couldn't reach.

"Tomorrow I'll make a spear," he called out to her.

Beyond the tide pools lay another stretch of white sand. She continued across the beach while Logan chased crabs. She caught a glimpse of a blue plastic object, half-buried. It looked like a bucket. When she reached it, she fell to her knees and started digging. The treasure she unearthed was a basic utility bucket. The handle had broken off, but the rest was intact. She rinsed the bucket in the surf and held it up in the air, triumphant.

Logan rejoined her, grinning his approval. "That's a great find."

"You think it just washed up?"

"Yeah. There's a ton of trash in the ocean. I'm surprised there isn't more here. We must not be near any major currents."

The beach gave way to a section of rock cliffs that resembled the other side of the island. The sand was wet and flat, as if the tide had just receded. They skirted around the cliffs to a secluded little cove, and found another pleasant surprise. Water rushed down a mossy rock wall and formed a shallow pool in the sand below. It wasn't the waterfall he'd pointed out from the summit, but a smaller runoff.

Logan ran toward it with an eager whoop. She followed at a slower pace. They stood ankle-deep in the pool of water. Behind the falls lay the mouth of a cave. Water rained over the entrance like an outdoor shower. He made a cup with his hands and filled it. She did the same. The water looked clear and felt wonderfully cool.

He took an experimental sip. "It's freshwater."

"Is it safe?"

"I think so. There aren't any large animals or humans here to contaminate the supply. Even if there were, the water is flowing through volcanic rock and moss, two natural filters. It's about as safe as you can get."

That was good enough for her. She brought the water to her lips and drank. It tasted better than the water from the liana vines, which had a gritty, tree-bark flavor. The coconut juice was delicious, but she couldn't drink it all day. It wasn't what she wanted to quench her thirst. There was no substitute for freshwater. She could feel it hydrating her entire body. She drank as much as her stomach could hold.

He set the bucket underneath the steady spray. While it filled with water, he ducked into the cave. She went with him. Unlike the bat cave, this one smelled clean. It was spacious, with a high ceiling. The sand beneath her feet was damp, indicating that the waves lapped inside the cavern at high tide.

Logan pointed to sunlight on the opposite end of the tunnel. "I think this goes through to the other side of the island."

"Great. Let's get out of here."

He laughed at her lack of enthusiasm, wiping the moisture from his face. Her dress was wet from the waterfall. So was his shirt. The fabric clung to the muscles in his chest and arms. "We can explore another day."

She turned around, relieved to leave the dark cavern.

On her way out, she almost stepped on something that looked like striped rope. When it moved, she shrieked and jumped backward, into Logan's arms. He carried her to the mouth of the cave. By the time he put her down, the snake had slithered out of sight.

"What was that?" she asked, still trembling.

"Sea krait."

"Are they poisonous?"

"They're venomous, yes, but they rarely bite. Next time you see one, don't scream and jump around like that. You scared it away."

She couldn't believe he was scolding her for letting a snake get away. She put her hands on her hips and cocked her head to one side. Even from that angle, it didn't make sense.

"It's a food source. We need protein."

She'd eaten some strange delicacies, and she wasn't squeamish about trying another, but the thought of him messing around with a venomous snake sent her stress levels skyrocketing. "What we need is fire," she said, her voice sharp. "Not you risking your life for a snake we can't even cook!"

He flinched as if she'd slapped her. "I'm working on that."

She nodded an acknowledgment, and he dropped the subject. She hadn't meant to criticize his efforts; she just didn't want him to kill any snakes. They were in enough danger without him taking unnecessary risks.

He turned and picked up the bucket, hefting it onto his shoulder. Then he walked back in the direction they'd come. She followed him along the base of the cliffs and across the tide pools. The return trip took about ten minutes. She had to hurry to keep up with him, even though he was carrying an awkward weight.

As soon as they arrived at the beach with the palm trees, he set down the bucket and covered it with a palm frond. Then he disappeared into the jungle for a few minutes. She stayed in the shade, nibbling her lower lip. She could sense his tension. Although she wanted to get along with him, she wasn't interested in tiptoeing around his ego. She'd done that with Andrew, and he'd walked all over her. It occurred to her, in hindsight, that their relationship had never been equal. She'd been the sous chef at a restaurant his uncle owned. Andrew was the manager. When he left to participate in the reality show, Cady hadn't been promoted. They'd hired another man to fill the position.

She didn't expect Logan to defer to her. He was the survival expert, and she was a civilian. He had nerves of steel, and she didn't. She couldn't match him in skill or daring, but she could be his partner.

He brought a length of green vine back with him. He cut it into thirds and braided the strips to make one cord. Then he attached it to a bow-shaped stick.

"Can I help?" she asked.

"Yes," he said, surprising her. "Come here and put your foot on the base."

She knelt where he indicated, with one foot planted on a wooden piece to hold it steady. It wasn't a comfortable pose, and she felt self-conscious about his proximity. She didn't complain, because she was trying to prove herself. He moved the bowstring back and forth in swift, practiced motions. She could tell the task required a lot of upper body strength. Logan was probably the fittest man she'd ever met, and he struggled with it.

She struggled to keep her foot in place. Her calf muscle ached from holding the position. He was breathing hard, his biceps flexing. She worried his hands would slip and he'd stab her bare foot with the stick, or burn her with a hot coal.

Then the cord snapped.

And she was secretly glad, because she needed a break.

Logan wasn't glad. He leaped to his feet, cursing with frustration. She glanced at the horizon and noted it was almost sunset. There were no clouds in the sky, and no mosquitos. They wouldn't die without fire, but she really wanted it. They had eggs and breadfruit to cook, and she was hungry.

She stood and stretched, feeling low.

"I need your straps," he said suddenly.

Her hand rose to the front of her dress. "My straps?"

"The vine cordage isn't going to work. I have some rope, but I left it with the raft, and I'll have to hike back to get it. I don't want to wait that long. It could rain anytime. We don't have a shelter or another way to stay warm."

After a short pause, she nodded her agreement. They needed fire. This was important. If she had to sacrifice a piece of clothing, she would.

She moved closer and turned her back to give him access to the straps. She felt the whisper of the blade as he sliced through the fabric. Then he came around to the front, his expression flat. He cut the straps with brisk efficiency. She clutched the bodice against her chest before it fell away.

After he made a new bowstring, they resumed their efforts. It was difficult to keep her dress in place. The fabric inched down with every little motion. Whenever she let go, it started slipping again.

"Hold still," he said. "Focus on this."

She gritted her teeth and left her dress alone. He reminded her of her drill-sergeant grandfather, who'd died barking orders. She pushed aside that dark memory and concentrated on her foot placement. One of her breasts popped out, but she ignored it. So did Logan. He didn't take his eyes off the tools in his hands. Sweat dotted his forehead.

Finally—finally—the coal formed.

Smoke rose up from the base where her foot was resting. He tossed aside the other tools and gestured for her to move. She did, gladly. He transferred the coal to something that looked like a bird nest. Then he cradled it in his palms and blew gently.

Flames erupted.

She wanted to cheer, or weep, but she was afraid to jinx it. He looked tense, as if the job wasn't done yet. He placed the bundle of fire in the pit, under a teepee of twigs. When those started burning, he added some sticks. Then branches.

Before long, they had a real fire. He'd made fire.

It was great timing, too. Dusk had fallen. The fire was a reason to celebrate, and far more of a relief than finding this beach, but they both stayed silent. There would be no kissing and rolling around in the sand tonight.

He collapsed on his back, eyes closed tight. His chest rose and fell with rapid breaths. He was either emotional, or exhausted.

Exhausted. He didn't get emotional.

She remembered that her breast was out, so she tucked it away. Then she stared at the fire and thought about dinner. She was ravenous, but campfire cooking wasn't her forte. She hadn't been camping since she was twelve. They had no pots, pans or utensils.

"I need to boil water," she said. "The breadfruit can be cooked over an open flame, but the eggs will explode."

"You can boil water in a coconut husk."

"How?"

He stayed stretched out on the sand, unmoving. "Put a few small rocks in the fire, and some water in the husk. When the rocks get hot, I'll transfer them."

There were a couple of golf ball–sized rocks in the fire ring already, so she tossed them on top of the flames. Filling the coconut husk was trickier. She nestled it in the sand and poured water from the bucket carefully. When that was done, she peeled the breadfruit and sliced it. It was difficult without a flat surface, but she managed. She put the slices in another empty husk. Boiling the breadfruit would taste better than charring it on a stick.

He sat upright, groaning a little. She hoped he hadn't reinjured himself with that marathon of physical exertion. She felt a surge of guilt over what she'd said earlier. He'd seemed insulted by her comment, and determined to make fire because of it.

"Are you all right?" she asked.

"I'm fine."

"How's your knee?"

"It hurts."

She heard the strain in his voice, and saw it in the lines of his face. If he admitted to feeling pain, it must be agonizing. "I didn't mean to criticize…about the fire."

"It doesn't matter."

"The thought of you picking up that snake really freaked me out."

"I wouldn't pick it up. I'd just kill it."

She wasn't comforted by the distinction. "I'm not brave, like you."

"What do you mean?"

"I'm just an ordinary person."

"So am I."

"No, you're not. An ordinary person doesn't do combat and water rescue and snake handling."

"That's training, not temperament."

"It's both."

He raked the sand from his hair, shrugging.

"I don't have the temperament for this."

He made a scoffing sound. "Everyone gets scared in emergency situations."

"Yes, but some people can stay calm and take action. They're the rescuers. Others are frozen with terror. I'm that second type."

"How do you figure?"

She was reluctant to tell the story, but it was the best way to get her point across. "Remember how I said I went camping with my grandpa?"

"Yeah."

"I'd go with him and my dad on fishing trips and stuff. I was an only child, and I think my dad wanted a boy."

"I know how that is. I'm an only child, too."

"Really?"

He nodded. "My mom totally wanted a girl. She took me to all of her Charity League meetings and tea lunches."

"Did you like it?"

"Hell no. I was a rowdy kid. She made me wear bow ties. I couldn't even sit still."

She smiled at the mental picture. He couldn't sit still

as an adult, either. "One year my dad got shot in the line of duty."

"By who?"

"Some lowlife. Domestic violence call. Anyway, he fully recovered, but he couldn't go anywhere that summer, so I went with my grandparents. It was an RV trip through the Sierra Nevada."

"Go on."

She forced herself to continue. "I was on a hike with my grandpa when we heard someone calling for help. A man had fallen over the edge of a steep cliff. The earth had eroded under his feet, I guess. He was hanging by a branch, but he couldn't pull himself up. My grandpa yelled at me to stand clear. Then he dropped to his stomach to give the guy a hand."

Logan's brow furrowed with concern. "What happened?"

"They both fell. And died."

"Jesus."

"I didn't move. I was paralyzed with fear."

"How old were you?"

"Twelve."

"You were a kid. You couldn't have done anything."

"I mean that I didn't move for hours. I couldn't bring myself to look down the cliff. Someone came along and found me, and I couldn't even talk."

"You can't blame yourself."

"I didn't help him."

"He'd have taken you down with him."

She wasn't convinced of that, but she'd never know. She hugged her arms around herself, feeling numb.

He poked at the fire with a stick. "Did anyone in your family blame you?"

"No. My parents said they were glad I stood clear. But my cousin called me a coward at the funeral."

"Well, he was wrong. A coward wouldn't have kicked the knife away to help me during that fight. A coward wouldn't have gotten in the raft, or survived the open sea, or swam her heart out in the middle of the night. A coward wouldn't have hiked through the jungle all day or slept in a bat-infested cave. You don't have a cowardly bone in your body."

Her eyes filled with tears. "Then why am I so scared?"

"Fear isn't cowardice. I'm scared, too."

"You don't show it."

He grunted an acknowledgment.

"Is that Navy SEAL training?"

"It's man training. From birth."

She smiled at the joke, a little sadly. "If you kill a snake, I'm not cooking it."

"Fair enough," he said, smiling back at her.

She didn't tell him that her biggest fear wasn't snakes. It was being left alone here. She had no idea what she'd do without him. Temperament aside, she didn't have the training to survive on her own.

"I'm sorry about your grandpa."

She took a deep breath. "It was a long time ago."

"You're doing great, Cady. We're going to get through this. The most important aspect of survival isn't training or temperament. It's tenacity, remember?"

She nodded, comforted by his words. When the rocks were ready, he moved them out of the fire with two sturdy sticks and dropped them into the water. She added the eggs, her stomach growling.

"How long do you boil them?" he asked.

"Only a few minutes. They're small. The breadfruit will take longer."

"You'll have to put more rocks in the fire. The water won't stay hot."

She had to search the beach for a second set of rocks. By the time she returned, the eggs were done. They were about half the size of a chicken egg. She gave him two and kept one for herself.

He popped the first egg into his mouth, shell and all, crunching with relish. She tested her own egg by biting it in half. The shell was thin and nutrient-rich. The egg inside was piping hot and soft. It tasted mildly fishy. It wasn't yummy, but she'd take it.

The hot-rock method wasn't an efficient process for cooking breadfruit. She probably took it off the heat too early, because they were both tired of waiting. She'd never tried breadfruit before. It was kind of like zucchini, with a starchy, gummy texture. They both devoured their share because they were starving.

It was the best meal they'd had yet. Her stomach had shrunk over the past few days, so a small amount was enough to satisfy her. It wasn't enough for Logan. She could tell he was still hungry. He had one of those never-quit metabolisms, along with a never-quit attitude. He needed a ton of calories to maintain his body weight. Two little eggs didn't put a dent in his protein requirement.

She gave him another banana, figuring it was safe. Then she drank water from an empty coconut shell and watched the stars come out. There were more than she'd ever imagined, spread across a monstrous sky.

"I didn't get around to building a shelter," he said. As if he'd been wasting time, lounging.

"It's okay."

He'd chopped down some palm fronds earlier, so he spread them out on the sand. She curled up on one side of the fire. He took the other. She was acutely aware of the distance between them. Their heads were almost touching, but nothing else. He didn't hold her close the way he had last night. Although the fire was warm, she preferred his arms.

"Tomorrow will be better," he said.

"How do you know?"

"Today was a better day than yesterday, and yesterday was better than the day before. We have fire and an excellent water source. Right now we're just surviving, but we can thrive here. We can have good days."

She liked his optimism, but she didn't care about thriving so much as being rescued as soon as possible. Because every day they spent together she felt closer to him—and more afraid of losing him.

# Chapter 9

Logan woke with the sun.

He'd dreamed that he was back in Telskuf, searching for Hud. He didn't know why he was searching. The explosion had left nothing but burning piles of rubble and a huge crater. There was no possibility of survival. No remains to find.

He sat upright, shaking off the remnants of the dream, along with the sand that was always clinging to him. It was in his hair, on his neck, underneath his clothes. It spilled out of the rolled-up cuffs of his pant legs.

The fire was still going. That was a relief, because he hadn't really taken care of it last night. He'd tossed a thick log onto the pile and slept like the dead. Now the log was ash and embers, with one stubby end intact.

Cady was curled up on her side, facing away from the fire. She had that red veil wrapped around her head to protect her from bugs. The mosquitos didn't swarm on the beach like they had inland. There were a few, but the smoke kept them away. It didn't keep away sand flies or crabs or snakes, which was why he needed to build a sleeping platform.

He rolled the log stub into the embers so it would catch. Then he lumbered to his feet and blinked at the sunrise. Just another day in paradise. He walked down the beach, testing his knee. The dull ache was bearable. His stomach rumbled, telling him that the most pressing issue of the moment was food, not shelter.

Last night, after making the fire, he'd been whipped. His hands were sore and his knee had hurt like a son of a bitch, but the real reason he'd stayed off his feet was dizziness. He'd almost passed out. His body had said that's it. No more. You're done.

He hadn't expected his system to shut down like that. He was used to extreme physical challenges and sleep deprivation. He had great stamina. He'd aced every endurance test during BUD/S training. But he'd never gone several days without food and water, after sustaining a head injury. Some ill effects were to be expected under these conditions. He hadn't told Cady about it because he didn't want her to worry.

And maybe he didn't want to admit weakness. Whatever.

He felt better this morning. The eggs had supplied a bit of protein. He was more hydrated and less stressed. Getting fire was a huge weight off his shoulders. He knew he shouldn't overexert himself again—not until he'd eaten a full meal. Once he had some meat in his belly, he could go all out and make this island his bitch.

He was Logan Nathaniel Starke. He didn't quit. He didn't faint. He nodded at the waves. *Let's do this.*

When he turned away from the shore, he saw Cady was awake. She had the veil wrapped around her shoulders, as if she felt a chill. He added some wood to the fire. She tugged at the bodice of her dress, which he'd ruined last night. He remembered how the fabric had slipped down, revealing one dusky-tipped breast. Not that he'd looked. He'd been focused on the fire. Still, the vague impression was enough to get his blood pumping.

He gathered the strap from the sand. "I can reattach this."

She turned around to give him access to the back of her dress. He bored a hole in the fabric with his knife, and tied it with fumbling hands. He had blisters all over his palms, but that wasn't the reason for his clumsiness. It was her silky skin.

The front of the dress posed an even greater challenge. Her face was there, staring right at him. So were her breasts. He had to slide his battered hand into her bodice while he poked a hole in the fabric. When his knuckles grazed her soft flesh, she inhaled a ragged breath. His gaze met hers, and he felt the same pull as always, drawing him in. Then he stabbed the tip of the knife into the center of his palm.

Cursing, he yanked his hand free.

"Did you cut yourself?"

"It's fine."

She grasped his wrist and turned his palm over to examine it. The minor cut was the least of his problems. He had weight-lifting calluses, so his hands were tough, but not tough enough to protect him from the blisters that had formed last night.

Her brow furrowed in concern. "You got these making the fire? They need to be bandaged."

He agreed to the treatment because he couldn't afford to get an infection. He gathered a few elephant plant leaves and the broken cordage. Then he sat down and let her tend to him. She cleaned his skin with cool water from the bucket, and applied some soothing aloe vera. He didn't know where to look while she worked. There was no safe place to put his eyes. Her mouth was lush, her breasts plump against the uneven bodice of her dress. He imagined it slipping down again. The sting of the cut didn't distract him. Warmth pooled to his groin as she wrapped his hands in folded-up leaves and secured them with cordage.

"All done," she said in a husky voice.

He muttered thanks and tore his gaze away from her. He added another branch to the fire, even though it didn't need one. She rose to her feet and filled a coconut shell from the bucket. Instead of drinking it herself, she offered him the cup. He drained it in four or five gulps, grateful for its cooling effect.

When he could stand without embarrassing himself, he ventured into the jungle. His next order of business was making a spear. He needed a sturdy branch with a circumference about the size of his hand grip. Green wood, because it was stronger. After he found a good branch, he started to shape the end with his knife.

She gathered an armful of wood and a bunch of bananas while he worked on the spear. "This is the last of the yellow ones."

"How many green?"

"Dozens."

He ate two. Foraging would become more difficult the longer they were here. The mature coconuts wouldn't last forever. That was why it was so important for him to hunt. He could make a fish basket, and set some traps for birds. He considered the possibilities as he sharpened his spear point. When he was finished, he stood and jabbed the end into the sand. It was a blunt weapon, hastily made, but he had high hopes.

"I have to go hunting," he said. "Can you stay and take care of the fire?"

"What does it need?"

"Just make sure it doesn't go out. Add some wood when it gets low."

"Do we need more wood?"

"Yeah. A lot more."

"What about stuff for the shelter?" She fingered the palm leaves.

"That can wait until I get back."

"How long will you be gone?"

"I don't know. An hour or two."

She didn't look happy about staying here without him. She didn't want to be left behind. After hearing that story about her grandfather, he understood why. He could build up the fire and bring her along, but he'd rather go alone. Hunting required total concentration, and he had trouble focusing around her.

"I'll be right at the tide pools," he said. "It's not far."

"What if a rescue plane comes while you're away?"

He glanced at the deserted sky. A rescue plane was unlikely, and human figures were almost impossible to spot from the air. They needed to make a signal fire at a higher location, which was a major undertaking. He wasn't doing it today. "Do you want to work on an SOS?"

"How?"

"Dark rocks would show up pretty well on this beach."

"Should I spell SOS?"

"You can do that, or make a triangle. Both are universal distress symbols."

"A triangle," she said, moistening her lips. "Right here, by the fire?"

He gathered some stones from the beach and marked three points to get her started. "Don't bother with the sides. Just make three big piles."

"Got it."

Feeling optimistic, he strode toward the tide pools. He was surprised by her willingness to collect wood and help out. She was a beautiful woman, and a city-girl chef. Call him sexist, but he hadn't expected her to work this hard.

Although his instincts toward her were protective, and he liked to be in charge, he needed to remember she could pull her own weight. She also stayed calmer when she had a task to focus on. Most people did.

When he reached the slabs of volcanic rock, he rolled up his sleeves and went to work. He spotted several tiny hermit crabs, but they scuttled out of range as soon as he stepped closer. Before long, he got distracted by the colorful fish in the shallows. They were everywhere, darting in and out of the coral. Blue ones and orange ones and fluorescent yellow. He aimed his spear at everything that moved, but his bandaged hands felt clumsy. He didn't hit any targets.

He tried changing his stance to avoid casting a shadow. He tried adjusting his strike to account for the water's distorting effects. It didn't work. The fish fluttered around like butterflies, taunting him.

Apparently hunting with a primitive spear wasn't any easier than making fire. He might have to rethink his weapon. He studied the nearby seabirds, who picked at the rocks and crevices with pencil-thin beaks. They were having a feast.

As the sun soared higher, the glare off the water

burned his eyes and baked his face. His bad knee felt like rubber. He hobbled inland to take a break in the shade. The optimistic mood he'd started the day with evaporated. He didn't want to quit. He was hungry, damn it. But hunting was an exercise in patience, and he had none.

Experience told him his odds would improve with trial and error. He would learn the best techniques for the setting, the optimal conditions. He couldn't expect success on his first try. The fish weren't going to jump out of the water for him.

While he leaned against the tree trunk, frustrated with his weakness, he caught a glimpse of movement in his peripheral vision. There was something crawling down the side of the tree, like a giant tarantula. He scrambled forward, his heart racing.

It wasn't a tarantula. It was a crab. A big-ass, slow-moving crab.

He sank his spear point into a soft place behind the animal's head. Its legs flexed and relaxed, flexed and relaxed. Then it went still with death. Logan gaped at it for several seconds. The crab was huge, with vivid blue streaks on its legs and body.

He returned to Cady with a fresh kill on the tip of his spear, triumphant. When she saw him, her eyes lit up with delight. "Oh my God," she said, her hands on her cheeks. "That's a coconut crab."

"Yeah? Do they taste good?"

"Let's find out."

She took the crab off the spear, squealing. He built up the fire while she cleaned the meat. He noted that she'd collected wood, and made progress on the triangle symbol. It wasn't big enough to be seen from the air, but it was a start.

"I'm going to cook this between two rocks," she said. "Will that work?"

He shrugged. "I don't see why not."

She placed a flat rock in the center of the fire. The crab went on top. Then she covered it with another flat rock. The process was much faster than boiling water in a coconut husk. He started to smell roasted meat immediately. His stomach growled in anticipation.

When the crab was done, she used two sticks to take it off the fire. They sat on the driftwood log, waiting for the meat to cool. Then they pulled the shell apart and feasted on the tender white flesh.

He groaned at the first taste. With no seasoning, no utensils and no pots or pans, she'd created a masterpiece. The rock technique had sealed in the moisture and prevented the meat from getting charred. She'd cooked it perfectly.

"What do you think?" she asked.

"I think I love you."

She laughed at the compliment. "It's good, right?"

He grunted in agreement and savored every morsel, sucking the meat from the crab legs like straws. She did the same, licking her fingers. He wasn't stuffed when the meat was all gone, but he was satisfied. He'd never enjoyed a meal more.

"Where did you find that crab?"

He told the story, which made her laugh in this beautiful, uninhibited way. Her hair was a mass of ebony curls, her teeth flashing white against her smooth caramel skin. Her laughter might have stung his ego if he hadn't felt so great about providing for them. He also couldn't begrudge such a gorgeous sight.

She caught him staring and went quiet. Maybe he

shouldn't have made that joke about being in love with her. Maybe it wasn't a joke, and he was really starting to feel something he shouldn't be feeling.

He tore his gaze away, frowning. "I need to, uh, get the shelter started."

"What can I do?"

*Stop being so irresistible.* "You can collect palm fronds from the beach. We're going to need a lot of those."

While she went in search of loose fronds, he worked on making a handheld axe. He'd found a piece of quartzite yesterday that was about the size of his fist. He used a chunk of granite to strike the quartzite, causing it to flake. It didn't take long to shape one end into a sharp edge, but it was bloody work. His fingers had multiple cuts when he was finished. His leaf bandages were shredded, and the blisters on his palms were raw.

Cady made him sit down so she could bandage his hands again.

He endured the treatment with impatience. Then he used the axe head to chop down a bunch of bamboo stalks, and some vine for lashing. She helped him carry the building materials back to the beach.

Although his strength and energy had returned to normal levels, time worked against him. By late afternoon, they'd lashed together enough bamboo stalks for a sleeping pallet. He'd formed a simple A-frame over the pallet, and she'd layered palm fronds on top. He wanted to build a platform for the pallet, but that would have to wait. Tomorrow, he'd improve the shelter. Today, they had a floor and a roof.

Good thing, because it started to rain.

He covered the wood pile and made sure the fire was

well protected before they crawled inside the space. It was just long enough for his body, and wide enough for her to lie next to him. The bamboo didn't make a comfortable mattress, but it felt nice to stretch out on his back. His muscles ached from overuse. He stared at the palm frond ceiling and listened to the soft rain. They stayed dry, for the most part.

They didn't stay warm. The heat of the fire didn't reach the shelter. He thought about ways to fix that. After he built a platform, he could make a pit for hot rocks, like a sauna. A better roof would help seal out moisture. He needed some moss or another soft material for padding and to hold in warmth.

Cady shivered beside him. Her smaller frame was more susceptible to cold.

"Do you want my shirt?"

She blinked at him in the dark, seeming hesitant. His shirt probably smelled bad. He shrugged out of the fabric anyway and draped it over her like a blanket. She curled up in the crook of his arm. He could feel her smooth cheek against his pectoral muscle. Her soft hair tickled his biceps.

Getting close to her had a predictable effect. His body didn't care about the hard bamboo flooring or the intermittent raindrops that seeped through the roof. It wanted to generate some heat and get back into action.

He was used to going without sex during overseas assignments, but that was different. The members of his SEAL team offered no temptations. Cuddling with a beautiful woman—one that he'd felt an instant connection to, along with an attraction beyond anything he'd ever experienced—was a special kind of torture.

"How did you get into cooking?" he asked, desperate for a distraction.

"My mom taught me. And my grandmother."

"The grandmother with the drill sergeant husband?"

"No. That's my dad's side of the family. My mom's mom lives in Texas. I didn't get to see her as often growing up. Just on holidays and stuff. Special times of the year. She was always in the kitchen."

"What kind of food?"

"Soul food. Creole. Some Southwest stuff, too. Gumbo, chili, seafood…"

His stomach growled with interest.

"Are you hungry again?" she asked, sounding amused.

"I could eat."

"My grandmamma would like you."

"Did you always want to be a chef?"

She rolled onto her back and rested her head against his arm. "I wanted to be a dancer, actually. I was in competitive dance for years."

"What happened?"

"I broke my ankle. I was practicing a leap near the edge of the stage and fell off. It healed, but I started dancing again too soon. Then I broke it a second time, and it was never the same after that."

"I'm sorry."

"It's okay," she said in a light tone. "Professional dancing is kind of a risky career choice, anyway."

"And you always play it safe."

"Yes."

He didn't find that odd, considering her background. She'd lost her grandfather in a tragic accident, and her father had been shot on duty. There was nothing wrong with being cautious, but it wasn't his style. Risks were inevitable in his line of work. They were part of who he was. No pain, no gain.

He wondered if she felt sad about giving up her childhood dream. She was a great chef. Cooking was another form of creative expression, and hardly a bad gig. She didn't seem bitter about her chosen path.

"It's funny," she said. "I always play it safe, but here I am. In the least safe situation imaginable."

"I can imagine worse," he said, flexing his left hand. It was falling asleep. "I've seen worse."

She lifted her head so he could move his arm. "In war zones, you mean?"

He nodded.

"What's the worst place you've been?"

"Syria."

She was quiet for a moment. "What if we don't get rescued?"

He didn't want to talk about Syria, but this subject wasn't any better. "Then we'll find a way to leave."

"How?"

"I'll repair the raft."

"It's shredded."

"There's a patch kit. I can fix it."

"You want to brave the open ocean in a patched-up raft?"

"If we don't get rescued, it might be our only option."

"I won't do it," she said, her voice shaky. "I'd rather stay here than get lost at sea again. I'd rather die."

"You don't mean that."

"Yes, I do."

He sat upright, incensed. He was trying to answer her questions honestly, and doing his damnedest to keep them both alive. Her words were an insult to everything he believed in. They were an insult to his dead comrades. "Don't ever say you'd rather die."

"You don't understand how I feel."

"Sure I do. You're miserable. You miss your family and the comforts of home. I get it. You think this is easy for me?"

She was quiet for a moment. "I think this is an exciting challenge for you."

He lay back down and took a deep breath, considering her point of view. He wasn't as rattled as she was. He thrived in dangerous situations. He had confidence in his skills, and the ability to adapt to extreme circumstances. This was an exciting challenge for him, but that didn't mean he was *enjoying* himself. "Let's focus on getting rescued. We've only been here three days. It's way too early to give up."

"You said they might not even be looking for us."

"We don't have to count on an organized rescue effort. Some random person could pass by in a boat or a plane." He told her about his idea for a signal fire. "Smoke from a high point can be seen for miles. We can build up the triangle. I also want to repair the raft, regardless. Having that kind of mobility is always an asset."

"You think someone will pass by?"

"Maybe."

"What about the kidnappers?"

"What about them?"

"Are they looking for us?"

"I hope so."

She frowned at him in the dark. "Why?"

"Because they have a better chance of finding us than a rescue team. If they spot our signal, they'll come ashore. And I'll be ready."

"You mean you'll kill them."

With relish, he thought. "If I have to," he said.

"Then we'll steal their boat?"

"Yes."

Although she didn't object to this plan, he could sense her unease. He could hear it in her rapid breathing. He knew she was afraid, and he didn't want her involved in any violence. If the kidnappers showed up, he'd hide her somewhere safe.

"Look, we're talking hypotheticals," he said. "The possibility of a second attack is low. It's more likely that a random plane or ship will pass by."

The conversation trailed off and the rain dissipated. She was stiff as a board beside him. He remembered how distraught she'd been the last time they'd tangled with the pirates. He regretted stirring up her fears, but she'd insisted on this discussion. She'd asked him to be honest with her about the dangers they faced.

He also wanted her to be prepared. He needed her to fight, even if she was scared. Because that was the key to survival.

## Chapter 10

Cady didn't sleep well in the new shelter.

Although they were protected from the worst of the rain, the bamboo pallet needed padding. She had to lie on her back on the hard surface, which was her least favorite position. Moisture seeped inside, dripping from the palm fronds and creating a damp chill she couldn't shake. She fretted half the night about Logan's gonzo plan to kill pirates. Then she drifted off in the wee hours of the morning.

The next thing she knew, it was sunrise. Logan was already up, of course.

She emerged from the shelter with a stiff body, but a calmer mind. She had to stop worrying about worst-case scenarios. That was a bad survival strategy, according to Logan, and it was mentally exhausting. She also couldn't prevent him from taking risks. She had to accept the situation, focus on simple tasks and live for today.

That was her plan, anyway. If she didn't succeed, she'd try again tomorrow.

She did some yoga stretches and drank water from a

coconut shell. She wondered if she'd be wearing them as a bra soon, complete with a hula skirt. Her dress was in shambles. The reattached strap kept slipping off. She tied back her hair, splashed her face with water and brushed her teeth with a twig.

They ate bananas for breakfast. She thought about other dishes she could make with the ingredients available. He started working on the shelter while she collected wood for the fire. Her feet felt better. The swelling was down and the cuts had scabbed over.

During her search for wood, she stumbled upon another treasure. A turtle shell had washed up on the shore overnight. It was oblong, about the size of a large serving bowl, and super tough. She picked it up and raced back to the shelter.

"Look what I found," she said.

He was sitting on the driftwood log by the fire, making an axe handle. His hand axe wouldn't chop down a tree big enough for the platform he was trying to build. He glanced up. "You can cook in that."

"Right on the fire?"

"I think so. Boil some seawater in it first."

She made a sound of excitement and set the prize by the fire pit. As she went back for the wood, she realized she'd squealed in delight over the prospect of cooking in a turtle shell. Who was she right now? She didn't even recognize this person.

They spent the morning working on separate projects. While she boiled the turtle shell and scrubbed it with a pumice stone, he made improvements to the shelter. They had coconuts for lunch. Then he asked for her help to raise the roof onto the platform. There was a lot of cursing and adjusting and heavy lifting.

By early afternoon, she was covered in sweat and dusted in a fine coat of sand. She felt satisfied with their accomplishments. She tried not to wish for a shower and clean clothes, but she was only human. She was a woman who enjoyed looking presentable. They shared the last of the water, eyeing each other.

"Need a break?" he asked.

"I need a bath."

"I need one more," he said in a gruff voice.

She smiled her agreement. Between the two of them, he was sweatier and dirtier. They went to the waterfall to refill the bucket. She wanted to strip off her dress and stand under the cool spray.

He had another idea: "Let's walk through the cave."

She didn't want to explore the dark interior, but she nodded, because she was curious about the other side. The cave was spacious, with water dripping from the cathedral-like ceiling. At high tide, the floor was completely submerged in water. As they moved away from the entrance, the light faded. She followed close behind Logan, taking careful steps. She couldn't see anything. She imagined sea kraits twining around her ankles. When her bare toe grazed a slippery object, she almost jumped out of her skin.

"What was that?"

"That was my foot. You stepped on it."

"Oh. Sorry."

"Do you want me to carry you?"

She shook her head and urged him forward, gripping the crook of his arm. The water level rose above her knees. Then it dipped again, and they were on dry sand.

Beyond the cave's exit, which was obscured in vines, there was another little cove with a secluded stretch of sand. It was similar to the beach they'd slept on the first night, surrounded by rock cliffs and largely inaccessible.

Logan studied the cliffs with interest. "We can get to that other waterfall from here. Maybe I can find some more eggs, or another breadfruit tree."

She followed his gaze, considering. She wasn't eager to hike again, but she wouldn't mind foraging for food. She was a chef, and he was hungry. They both were. His instincts were to protect her, and hers were to feed him.

He walked around a boulder in the middle of the beach to gain a better vantage point. "Whoa!"

"What is it?" she asked.

"Buried treasure."

It was a sand-colored plastic storage trunk, about four feet long, half-submerged in the sand next to the boulder. Logan dropped to his knees and tried to pry the lid open with his knife. It was locked, and wouldn't budge.

"Did someone leave it here?"

"It probably fell off a boat and floated here."

After about ten minutes, he managed to pick the lock. The lid sprang open, revealing a treasure trove of waterlogged supplies. There was a large canvas umbrella, two full-size deck cushions, two beach towels, two life vests, a kayak paddle, a diving snorkel with a mask and a yellow rain jacket.

"This is a huge score," he said, holding up the mask.

She helped him remove the deck cushions. They'd make perfect sleeping pads as soon as they dried in the sun. He swished his hand through the water in the bottom of the trunk and fished out a pink nylon bag. After a cursory glance, he handed it to her.

She gasped as she examined the contents. One pair of black bikini bottoms, size medium, with adjustable strings at the hips. One oversize T-shirt, white with a pink flamingo. One empty water container. One bottle of sunscreen, SPF 50.

Every item was like a precious diamond. She hugged the bikini bottoms to her chest, blinking away tears. There was no top, but she didn't care. She'd have paid a thousand dollars for a pair of fresh panties. Half a bikini was a godsend.

"I told you we'd have good days here," he said softly.

She nodded her agreement, sniffling. If someone had told her a week ago that she'd be weeping with joy over a bag of hand-me-downs, she wouldn't have believed them. A week ago, she couldn't have imagined feeling this way about anything.

Or anyone.

She wouldn't have survived without Logan. He'd been her rock from day one. He'd stayed positive during their days at sea, and he'd pushed her beyond her physical limits on land. She hadn't realized she was strong enough to keep pace with a Navy SEAL.

She hung up the wet towels and clothes to dry in the sun. "How far do you think that trunk drifted?"

"Not far," he said. "I'm surprised it didn't sink as soon as it went overboard. Maybe it came off a boat that was anchored nearby. Maybe it drifted a few miles. Either way, it hasn't been here long. There's hardly any deterioration."

The words were music to her ears. Human beings had been near this island before. Surely someone else would cruise by, and they'd get rescued. She hopped up and did a series of leaps on the beach, flying across the sand. Then she turned to face him. He was watching her with quiet awe. Her chest rose and fell with labored breaths.

It was too late to worry about getting attached to him. It had already happened. She'd turned over a new leaf today, and set aside her fears about the future. Maybe something else had shifted inside her, as well. When he looked at her like that, her heart skipped a beat, and she stopped thinking about getting rescued. She started thinking about making the most of their time together.

Was it really so bad, being stranded with a smoking-hot survival expert who made her pulse race with excitement? The real world was a difficult place, full of stress and strife. This island was a remote paradise, ripe with possibility. She'd never felt more alive than she did right now, right here, with him.

"I haven't done that in years," she said.

"You don't look rusty."

She laughed, tucking a stray curl behind her ear. She felt rusty and out of shape, but he didn't know any better. He stared at her for another few seconds, his face taut. Then he started walking toward the cliff. She grabbed the nylon bag and followed him. It was an easy climb, and a short hike into the jungle interior, but the heat under the canopy was sweltering. She'd forgotten how humid the air was here, compared to the pleasant breeze at the coast.

On the way there she found a taro plant, which had edible roots, like yams. They dug up several and tucked them into her bag. In the same area, there was a tree with lime-sized fruits. Logan plucked one and chopped it open. Several smooth brown nuts were nestled inside the fleshy white pulp.

"These are chestnuts," she said.

"Safe to eat?"

"Yes, but you have to roast them first."

They collected as many as they could carry, tucking

them into her new bag. They'd have roasted chestnuts and taro for dinner tonight. It wasn't coconut crab, but the meal would suffice. She was glad they'd explored this side of the island.

As they got closer to the waterfall, the jungle teemed with life. Logan had to draw his knife to slash through a thick section of foliage. Over the buzz of insects and birdsong, she heard the telltale sound of rushing water. He cut away a tangle of vines, his forearms flexing. Then they reached a clearing.

It was one of the most beautiful places she'd ever seen. A twenty-foot high waterfall tumbled into a sky-blue pool. Rocks lined the shore. Mossy cliffs framed the falls on both sides. She dropped her bag and stood at the water's edge, speechless.

Logan didn't hesitate. He peeled off his shirt, dropped his pants and waded in. Although he'd lost weight in the past week, he hadn't lost muscle. Every ridge and angle was sharply defined. His shoulders looked wider, his biceps harder. He dove under the water and came back up, sweeping a hand over his hair. Although she'd seen him shirtless on a daily basis, she still drew in a ragged breath at the sight of his wet torso.

"Are you coming in?" he asked, seeming puzzled.

"My dress," she stammered.

"Take it off. I won't look."

After he turned around, she pulled the dress over her head quickly. She kept her panties on and held one arm across her breasts, tiptoeing forward. He didn't look, not even when she submerged her entire body with a soft splash. He kept his back to her and swam toward the waterfall to drink from it.

She stayed near the middle of the pool, reveling in

sensation. The water was wonderfully cool and refreshing. It felt like heaven against her overheated, moisture-deprived skin. After days of harsh sun and saltwater residue, it was practically a spa treatment. She dipped her head under the surface to soak her tangled hair.

He glanced over his shoulder at her, his expression guarded. "Drink from the waterfall, not the pool."

She nodded, venturing into deeper water. She couldn't touch the bottom in some places. When he retreated from the falls, she swam forward to drink. The cascade made a sleek curtain of water to duck into. She stuck her head under the stream, rinsing her hair of sand and debris. He floated on his back, eyes closed.

He wasn't watching, so she removed her panties under the water. She wanted to burn them. Instead she scrubbed the lacy fabric and tossed the wet bundle on the shore. Those panties were well suited for a hot island night, but completely inappropriate for hot island days. They'd been giving her a nonstop wedgie.

With a sigh of relief, she washed from head to toe. She felt like a new woman, squeaky-clean and free of constrictive clothing. Too free, perhaps. She was acutely aware of her nudity, and of Logan's proximity. The fact that he wasn't steady-boyfriend material didn't matter anymore. They'd survived together, against all odds. Her body had decided that it wanted to celebrate life. She wanted to float on her back, like he was. She wanted to expose her breasts to the sunlight. And to him.

He turned toward her, as if he could sense her desire. She straightened in the water, lifting her wet hair off her neck. Her nipples flirted with the surface. His eyes darkened at the subtle invitation.

But the only move he made was to wade out of the

water, grab his shirt and start scrubbing it against a rock. She enjoyed the play of muscles in his shoulders and the cling of his boxer shorts against his taut backside. He washed his shirt with vigor, his jaw clenched. Then he rinsed the fabric and wrung it out, biceps bulging.

Lord have mercy.

"We should go," he said in a curt tone.

She blinked the stars from her eyes, with some difficulty. She didn't want to leave. She wanted to climb him like a tree.

He put on his pants, giving her an impatient look. "Are you ready? I'll turn around."

Her stomach clenched with disappointment. He wasn't interested. She didn't think he'd missed her signals. He wasn't that clueless. She also didn't think she'd misread him, an hour ago. He'd stared at her like he wanted to rip her clothes off and take her on the sand. Now that she was naked, he turned his back.

She waded toward the shore, stunned. She wasn't a vain woman, and she didn't consider herself irresistible, but she'd never been rejected before. When she offered a man her goodies, she expected him to jump on it.

To her chagrin, tears flooded her eyes. She felt vulnerable and exposed. She was trembling with embarrassment as she rose from the water. She chose her footing carefully on the slippery rocks along the bank. As she bent to pick up her panties, a centipede scuttled across the fabric. She hopped back and let out a little shriek of surprise.

He looked over his shoulder. "What..."

The question trailed off as he got a full frontal view. Before she could cover herself, he jerked his head the other direction. She donned the damp panties, flustered. Then she slipped into her stained, wilted dress.

"You did that on purpose," he said.

"Did what?"

He turned to face her, his neck flushed. "You know I want you," he said through clenched teeth. "You know you have a beautiful body, and I was already aching for a taste of it. Now I have to deal with that mental picture every time I close my eyes?"

She gaped at him in disbelief. "I don't know what you're talking about," she said, crossing her arms over her chest. "You think I planted a centipede to flash you? You've lost your damned mind."

"You didn't have to scream."

"Screw you," she said, still shaking.

He threw his hands out, frustrated. "I can't!"

She didn't ask him why not, though the question was on the tip of her tongue.

He tucked his knife into his belt and picked up the nylon bag. After a few deep breaths, he seemed to collect himself. "As far as I'm concerned, I'm on active duty. We aren't two survivors who just happened to get stranded together. I'm a SEAL, and you're a civilian. You were kidnapped because you were mistaken for my client. I have to treat you the same way I'd have treated Maya O'Brien."

"That's crazy."

"It's reality. I take my professional responsibilities very seriously."

"But you're not my bodyguard! I didn't hire you."

"I have ethical obligations, regardless. I took an oath to assist my country and its citizens in the event of an international emergency or terrorist attack. There's a strict code of conduct on the clock and off. I can't touch you."

"You already have," she said, remembering the kiss on the beach. He'd called a halt to that encounter, but he'd also started it.

He dragged a hand down his jaw, unable to dispute her.

"Look, it's cool. I get what you're saying. You don't want to take advantage of the situation, because we're not partners. We're not equals. You're a big-shot SEAL, and I'm a helpless baby bunny."

"That's not at all what I said."

She held her palm up to halt any further explanation. "I appreciate you being on the level. Now I know where we're at."

"You're twisting my words around."

"And you accused me of screaming for attention."

Instead of getting more defensive, he gave in, conceding her point. "That was out of line. I'm sorry."

She accepted his apology with a stiff nod. He tossed his wet shirt over his shoulder and picked up the nylon bag. Apparently the conversation was over. They walked away from the waterfall in silence. Now she understood why he'd been keeping his distance, but she didn't feel any better. She didn't want him any less. They were stuck here in this wild place, and they couldn't even do what felt natural.

When they got back to the beach with the storage chest, he handed her the bag of taro and chestnuts. The cushions were still a little damp, but the towels and clothing were dry. He carried most of their new gear through the cave and back to the shelter. Then he picked up his spear and headed to the tide pools.

While he was gone, she roasted the chestnuts and boiled the taro root. The turtle shell worked like a charm. He returned from the hunt empty-handed, which didn't surprise her. If he thought they were going to feast on crab and lobster every night, he was going to have to manage *his* expectations better.

After dinner, she ducked behind a tree to change her clothes. The T-shirt was soft and cozy. It covered her from neck to midthigh. The bikini bottoms weren't quite the right size, so she adjusted the string at each hip.

They sat in front of the fire for at least an hour. She watched the flames flicker. He worked on another spear, his head bent low. Then it was time to turn in. He placed the deck cushions on top of the bamboo pallet. The life jackets doubled as pillows. She crawled in next to him with a towel for a blanket.

The shelter was warmer and more comfortable, but sleep was as elusive as ever. She'd overreacted earlier. She'd asked him to be honest with her, and he had been. He'd said he was *aching for a taste* of her.

How was she supposed to ignore the heat between them, knowing that? They shared a sleeping pallet. She couldn't avoid his company, or turn off her desire. She also couldn't deny her feelings for him. They were depending on each other to survive. He'd been caring and supportive. She'd opened up to him about her grandfather. Their connection went deeper than physical attraction, and that made him even harder to resist.

He shifted beside her, equally restless. "I do think of you as a partner," he said. "You're not helpless. I value your contributions."

"I know. I was just mad."

They were both silent for another moment.

"I didn't scream on purpose," she said.

"I know. I was just...stupid."

She smiled at this apt descriptor.

"I meant what I said about treating you with respect and acting like a professional. But it's more than that. I feel like I let you down."

"How?"

"I let you get kidnapped."

"You're being too hard on yourself," she said, speaking from experience. She'd blamed herself for her grandfather's death for fifteen years. It was the nature of witnessing an accident you couldn't stop.

"It's my job to protect you."

She sighed, but didn't argue.

"Also, I don't have any condoms."

This practical concern gave her pause. She hadn't even thought about it at the waterfall, and she'd always insisted on safe sex.

"You're not...on anything?"

"No."

He let out a pent-up breath. "Sorry. I shouldn't have asked."

"You went to the bar without any condoms?"

"I wasn't planning to meet anyone. Then I saw you."

"What were you going to do when we got back to your cabin?"

"I was praying I had one in my luggage. I couldn't remember what I'd packed."

She laughed, shaking her head. "I thought you'd be prepared."

"In my defense, it was supposed to be a work trip."

They smiled at each other in the dark. Her heart twisted inside her chest. She reached out to hold his hand.

He took it, twining his fingers with hers. They couldn't act on their desires, but they didn't have to be at odds. They could still be friends, and partners.

"You didn't let me down," she said. "You're the reason we're alive right now."

"You're the reason we're not starving."

"Truce?"

"Truce."

## Chapter 11

He slept later than usual and woke up groggy.

For the first time in a week, or however long they'd been stuck together, he wasn't eager to rise and shine. The shelter was downright cozy with the new cushions. Cady was cuddled next to him, her hair a fluffy cloud of dark curls. He was warm, but he wasn't comfortable. His knee ached from overuse, and he had a raging hard-on.

A vivid mental picture of her naked body sprang into his mind. He'd seen everything. Every inch of her, sleek and supple and dripping wet. Her perfect tits, topped with ripe brown nipples. Her flat belly and gently curved hips. The sweet little triangle between her thighs. He hadn't lied when he said he was dying for a taste of her. Maybe he was just hungry, in general, but she looked delicious.

Smothering a groan, he got up and climbed out of the shelter. He studied his ravaged hands in the harsh daylight. Even if he had the privacy to take care of his own needs, there would be no physical release for him until his palms healed. These blistered, cut-up mitts would feel like sandpaper.

She emerged from the shelter, stretching her arms over her head. She was wearing that soft T-shirt, with the new bikini bottoms. Both garments flattered her curves. She joined him by the smoldering ashes, yawning. When she walked away, his eyes followed her ass. She bent over the water bucket to fill a coconut shell cup.

He returned his attention to the fire, poking it with a stick. He didn't think she was trying to tease him. It was just that they'd spent every moment together since the kidnapping. They'd become comfortable with each other. She wasn't self-conscious about her body, and she often seemed unaware of his gaze.

The chemistry was still there, of course. She'd proved that yesterday.

He hadn't expected her to issue such a blatant invitation. He'd thought sex was off the table for the duration of this adventure. When she'd given him that come-hither look, her breasts half-exposed, he'd almost swallowed his tongue.

It had been so hard to turn his back. *So hard.*

They had bananas for breakfast, as usual. He only ate two. He didn't want bananas. He wanted something else, and he wasn't going to get it.

"What's on the schedule for today?" she asked.

His mind swam with pornographic images. He blinked them away. "I want to finish the spear I started last night, and try out that snorkel. We should build up this triangle. I also need to scout a location for a signal fire."

"Where would you make it?"

He glanced around, considering. "A high point is ideal, but it also has to be accessible. If it takes too long to get there, I can't light it in time to signal anyone."

"Maybe we should conserve energy."

It wasn't a bad suggestion, considering how little protein they'd had. "We need to eat before we do anything else."

"How are your hands?"

He made a noncommittal sound. They were worse, not better, but the spear he was working on required dexterity. The bandages got in the way, and kept his hands moist. He preferred going without.

She wandered off to gather wood and look for washed-up treasures on the beach while he finished his spear point. She added some rocks to her SOS triangle. He kept his head down, determined not to stare at her.

"Can I borrow your knife?" she asked.

"For what?"

"I want to make a top out of this." She held up a narrow strip of torn canvas from the umbrella.

Instead of giving her his knife, he cut two holes in the material, where she wanted them. Then he sharpened two sticks and attached them to his spear point, forming a trident. This type of spear was a lighter, more agile tool. He stabbed it into the sand a few times to test its strength. When he was confident in its durability, he looked for Cady again. She was wearing her bikini briefs, with the canvas band across her breasts. She'd used her dress strap to secure it at the middle of her back. Her hair was neatly braided, tied with vine cordage.

He studied her with guarded eyes. She was adapting to their environment, even embracing it. She was a fighter, not a bystander. He admired that. He'd meant what he said about valuing her contributions. Having an equal partner took some of the pressure off, but it didn't reduce the sexual tension. He couldn't unsee her wet, naked body.

"I'm going to the tide pools," he said.

"Can I come with you?"

He shrugged, even though he'd rather be alone. Before they left, she grabbed the nylon bag and put a few things inside it. He brought the snorkel and both spears. If he didn't catch anything, he'd have to adjust his strategy. Maybe he'd make some basket traps. That meant putting off his other projects, because providing food was the top priority.

He was hungry. Always hungry. The gnawing emptiness had become his constant companion, along with unfulfilled desire.

As soon as they reached the tide pools, he stripped down to his boxers. They rode low on his hips. He'd probably dropped a full pants size. He was leaner than he'd been in years. Life on this island had robbed him of everything but muscle and bone.

Her hands met his shoulders, spreading cream on his skin. "You need sunscreen. You're already burnt."

Although her touch discomfited him, he allowed it. When she came around the front to put sunscreen on his face, he clenched his jaw in irritation. It was awkward as hell, being treated like a little boy while fighting a very adult male reaction. He jerked away before she was finished and picked up his trident.

He was being rude, but he needed space. He strode toward the water, taking ragged breaths. He couldn't stop fantasizing about those soft hands on his erection, stroking up and down. She was too familiar with him, too physical. Although he understood the basic desire for human contact, he felt like a pressure keg. If she wanted to touch someone, she was going to have to touch herself.

This idea gave him pause. He glanced over his shoulder, his blood thickening. She was sitting in the shade underneath a palm tree. Maybe she was going to slip her hand between her thighs right now, while he was busy.

Damn. He'd give his left nut to see that.

But he wasn't going to see it. He was going to drive himself crazy thinking about it. Frustration coursed through him in waves. Making a snarling sound, he turned around and walked toward her.

She scrambled to her feet. "Do you need me?"

He nodded, gesturing for her to join him. "Bring the other spear. I might want it, and I can't hold them both."

If he wasn't getting off, she wasn't either. End of story.

She grabbed the spear and hustled to catch up with him. She was so eager to help that he felt petty for making her tag along. He couldn't prevent her from pleasuring herself. He shouldn't even want to. If she took care of her own needs, she might stop looking at him with those sultry eyes.

They explored the tide pools together, side by side. She chose her footing over the sharp rocks carefully. The isolated puddles near the shore offered nothing of interest.

"Why are the pools empty?" she asked.

"Birds got here first."

"So we need to come at dawn?"

"I don't know. There might be other sea creatures at night. Rays, octopus. Anything that can move in shallow water."

"I like octopus."

"Yeah? I've never had it."

"It's good. Let's get one."

He grunted his agreement, but they didn't find an octopus lurking in the shallows. They waded into knee-deep water, where it was more difficult to use a spear with accuracy. There were plenty of tropical fish, bright-colored and elusive.

"Look," she said, pointing out an orange one. "It's Nemo."

"Can we eat it?"

"I don't know. I've never seen clown fish on a menu."

When he aimed his spear, the fish flitted away. He ventured farther out, donning the snorkel and mask. Cady swam alongside him, making ineffectual stabs at the reef. Her strategy stirred debris into the water, reducing visibility.

He didn't know if failing with her was better or worse than failing alone. He probably shouldn't have brought her along. She had no idea what she was doing, and he didn't have the patience to teach her.

She grabbed his arm, excited. "There's a giant clam."

"Where?" he said around his mouthpiece.

"That blue ruffled thing."

He adjusted his snorkel and peered down at the ocean floor. There was a clam about the size of a basketball. It looked like a pretty rock, with bright blue accents. He spat out the mouthpiece and shoved the mask up his forehead. "Should I get it?"

"How?"

"I'll carry it in."

"It's too big."

He scoffed at this and handed her his trident. "Watch the master."

The master dove underwater and attempted to lift the clam. It was about ten feet below the surface, nestled in the reef. He couldn't get a good grip on it. He ran out of breath and came up empty-handed.

"Give me the spear," he panted.

She passed him the one she'd been using, the original. He returned to pry the clam loose. It wasn't easy. After about a dozen turns from the sea floor to the surface, the stubborn shell broke free. He handed her the spear and dove under to claim his treasure.

Unfortunately, the clam was heavier than it looked. He tried rolling it along the ocean floor, but his progress was slow. The strain wore him down. He started getting light-headed, so he floated upward for more air.

Just before he surfaced, he spotted some dark shapes in the distance. He sucked in a breath and ducked under for a second look.

Sharks.

There were three or four of them, not more than twenty feet away. They were blacktip reef sharks, probably not aggressive, and too small to be deadly. Even so, he needed to get Cady out of the water now. If she started screaming and thrashing around, they might come over to investigate.

He ripped off the mask and snorkel. "You were right. It's too heavy."

"I'll help you."

"Nah. I'm tired."

She frowned at this uncharacteristic statement. "Really?"

"It's not going anywhere," he said, urging her along. "We'll get it later."

She swam with him toward the shallow water and waded to the shore. He kept her moving, his hand on her elbow. Maybe his grip was too tight, because she pulled her arm free as soon as they reached the sand.

"What's your problem?"

He glanced across the reef, reluctant to give a reason for rushing her.

"You saw a shark, didn't you?"

"It was a small one."

"A small one," she said in a shrill voice, scanning the water. "Are you kidding me?"

"No."

"You said you were tired."

"I was getting there."

"Why didn't you tell me the truth?"

"I thought you might…get loud."

"Get loud?"

"You scream a lot."

Her eyes narrowed at the charge. He thought she was going to argue, but she shoved his spear at him and stormed away. He watched her stomp across the beach, leaving footprints on the sand. Water dripped from her hair onto her bare shoulders. He admired the sway of her hips and her curvy backside.

He dragged a hand down his face, wishing she'd stayed to yell at him. Maybe if she slapped him across the face, he could retaliate by crushing his mouth over hers. Then they'd make out in the surf and roll around naked.

That was a nice fantasy. In reality, he was standing on the beach alone. He couldn't touch her. He couldn't even touch himself. This had to be an all-time low. He shook his head, laughing. It was either laugh or cry.

Instead of following her back to the shelter, he stayed at the tide pools. They both needed space. They were practically on top of each other every hour of the day, and not in a fun way. He was already wet, and he was hungry. He might as well keep trying. He left his snorkel behind and cruised the shoreline.

Hunting required patience and stillness. He couldn't expect to spear a fish every five minutes. Crouching behind a boulder in the shallows, he waited.

He needed some rope to get that big clam. That would be tomorrow's project. He'd retrieve the rope from the other side of the island. Harvesting the clam would give them meat for days, and some extra to use as bait. They'd have energy. He could make traps, build the signal fire, repair the raft...

While he was planning the next few days, he caught a glimpse of movement in the water. Something that looked like an algae-covered rock had flitted into his range. He jumped out of his crouched position and stabbed downward in one smooth thrust.

Got it.

He lifted the trident carefully. A creature flapped at the end, impaled by all three prongs. It was a mottled brown fish with ruffled fins and bug eyes, about the size of a softball. As he carried it toward the sand, its color changed to dark orange.

"Caught you, you ugly little bastard."

The fish stopped twitching. Logan let out a victory whoop, holding his spear high overhead. He hadn't felt this triumphant since he'd made fire.

Hell yeah.

He'd speared a fish, right out of the water. If he could do it once, he could do it again. This was a major turning point. He had a meal on a stick, and several more guaranteed by that giant crab. In the space of a single morning, they'd gone from struggling to surviving, maybe even thriving. Things were looking up.

He collected his other spear and strode away from the tide pools. When he reached the beach, Cady was sitting outside the shelter with a stack of palm fronds. She stood, letting the leaves fall off her lap.

"Check it out," he said, proud of his kill.

She didn't react the way he expected. Instead of celebrating, she clapped a hand over her mouth with a strangled scream.

"It's a fish," he said, because she didn't seem to recognize his accomplishment. He reached up to take it off the stick.

"Don't touch it!"

His hand froze.

"That's a stonefish," she said, flapping her hands. "It's deadly."

Her words raised a vague warning flag in his mind. He examined the unsightly orange lump, with its round belly and bumpy scales. Had he learned about stonefish in one of his survival classes? He couldn't remember.

She held a palm to her stomach, as if she felt sick. "They have barbs that release poison if you disturb them. Serious poison."

Logan arched a brow. "Can we eat it?"

"Yes, but you're missing the point. It could've killed you."

"Well, it didn't, so let's have it for lunch."

She frowned at his cavalier attitude. "Do you remember our conversation about the sea krait?"

"This isn't a sea krait."

"It's worse than a sea krait!"

"I didn't even know it was poisonous, Cady."

"Would you have left it alone if you had?"

He shrugged, feeling surly. "No."

Tears filled her eyes. "I told you about my grandfather for a reason. I don't want you to risk your life like he did."

His gut clenched at the sight of her distress. He hadn't meant to make her cry, but he also wasn't sorry he'd caught the fish. He didn't care how poisonous it was, as long as it was edible. His stomach rumbled with hunger.

"Give it to me," she said. "I'll cook it."

He held it out of her range. "I'd rather handle it myself, if it's deadly."

"Oh, you want to handle it yourself? Because it bothers you when I do something dangerous?"

He paused, trapped by this bit of logic. She was right about his risk-taking nature, and his discomfort with turning the tables. Although he didn't want to surrender control of the spear, he let her have it. She knew how to clean the fish safely. He had to trust her with the task. He watched her do it, his gut clenched.

Yeah, okay. Now he knew how she felt.

That didn't mean he was going to apologize for working hard to provide a meal for them. He wasn't going to be timid and cautious and wait for a rescue. He wanted to thrive here. It was what he did. It was who he was.

She wrapped the fish in banana leaves and placed it in the coals at the edge of the fire. "Heat kills the poison."

While the fish cooked, he went to refill the water bucket and retrieve his clothes at the tide pools. In his excitement, he'd forgotten them. When he returned, she served steamed fish with mashed taro in a coconut shell bowl. They used sticks for utensils. He cleaned his bowl three times.

"Thank you," he said. "That was delicious."

She nodded an acknowledgment and went to wash the dishes in the surf. He stayed near the shelter for the rest of the afternoon. He'd been pushing her too hard. They could both use a break, and it was hot as hell.

His first project was making a sheath for his knife out of yucca leaves. They were narrow enough to weave, but durable and waterproof. When it was finished, he attached the sheath to a piece of cordage and tied it around his waist. The next time he saw a shark, he'd have a backup weapon.

When that was done, he started working on a couple of basket traps. Trapping was a reliable method of catching fish. That giant clam would give them plenty of bait to use. He bent about a dozen long, flexible branches into a basket shape.

Cady was busy with her own projects nearby. She watched his technique for weaving yucca leaves, and she was a quick hand. By early evening, she'd made two rectangle-shaped sandals with vine cordage foot straps.

Then it was dark, and she roasted some chestnuts for a light dinner. Although they were both quiet, the silence wasn't uncomfortable. He didn't think she was angry with him anymore. She wasn't the type of woman who pretended everything was fine and hid her feelings behind a fake smile. When she was upset, she said it, straight out.

He wasn't used to that. The women he dated tended to be very accommodating. They gave him compliments, not criticisms. He didn't argue with them, either. Playing the field kept him from getting emotionally attached, so there was nothing to argue about. If a minor quarrel came up, he smoothed things over in bed. Or he just moved on to the next conquest. He didn't have time for relationship drama.

Unfortunately, he couldn't take Cady to bed. She was his partner in survival. They were stuck together, for better or worse. It was like a marriage, without the perks.

He had to listen to her concerns. He had to communicate and compromise.

This was unfamiliar territory for him.

Even so, he found himself kind of enjoying the challenge. He didn't mind being disagreed with. She was passionate and sexy. The "drama" wasn't killing his desire for her or driving them apart. If anything, it was bringing them closer together. He felt more connected to her every day, and less tied to the outside world.

A little voice in his head whispered that it didn't matter if they hooked up. They were already sleeping together. Sex was a natural progression. It was the ultimate morale-booster. It was practically a survival strategy. And it was personal.

No one had to know.

He squashed that idea before it could take hold. They'd only been here a week. It was too early for her to abandon hope, and for him to abandon his professional ethics. He wanted to thrive on this island, but he also wanted to get rescued.

Because when she was safe, he could make her his.

## Chapter 12

The days passed in an endless blur of heat and sunshine and hard work.

Cady stopped worrying about the kidnappers.

She also stopped worrying about the rescuers. If anyone was coming for them, they'd have been here by now.

She didn't know how they'd ever get off this island without help, but she tried to stay positive about their chances. She couldn't wallow in despair. She wasn't a risk taker, like Logan. She'd never laugh in the face of danger. Even so, her parents hadn't raised a quitter. Her drill-sergeant grandpa had fought in two wars. Her grandmamma in Texas had lived through Jim Crow and segregation before she joined the civil rights movement. Giving up wasn't part of Cadence Crenshaw's DNA.

So she crawled out of the shelter every morning at the crack of dawn, determined to contribute. She collected eggs and fruit and chestnuts. She gathered wood for the fire. She wove baskets like a native. In addition to the yucca-leaf sandals, she'd made two hats and an umbrella. She had wooden utensils and a twig toothbrush. She'd been thinking about making a grass skirt and a coconut shell bikini top, just for fun.

Logan had been keeping track of the days by marking notches at the base of a palm tree by their shelter. Three lines represented their time at sea. Beneath that was the island count. Today there were two groups of five, plus another one.

They'd been here eleven days.

They'd been lost fourteen.

In that time, she hadn't seen a single plane or ship. There was nothing in the sea, nothing in the sky. No bottle to put a message in. No convenient carrier pigeon.

Despite their overwhelming solitude, Logan had taken steps to attract the attention of a random passerby. He'd forged a path from the beach to the nearest peak and gathered all of the necessary materials for a signal fire. It was ready to light at the summit.

A few days ago she'd gone with him to retrieve the raft from the other side of the island. He'd managed to drag the inflatable portion to the cave, where he'd stashed it. They'd left the engine behind because it was too heavy to carry.

Today he was making a bamboo raft. He planned to paddle over to the cove, pick up the engine, and tow it back. He came out of the jungle with five pieces of bamboo that were about the length of his body.

"Are you making it big enough for both of us, plus the engine?" she asked.

He dropped the bamboo on the sand, giving her an impatient glance. His shirt was damp with sweat, his jaw scruffy. His clothes were getting ripped to shreds. So were hers. They looked like a couple of island bums.

They'd already argued about the trip to the cove. He

wanted to go alone, but she'd insisted on accompanying him. He'd agreed, with reluctance, and he still seemed irritated by the concession. He liked being in charge and getting his own way.

"If it doesn't hold us both, I'll swim," he said.

"What if a shark comes?"

"The only sharks I've seen around here are blacktips. They hang out by the reef, where the fish are."

That was true enough. She'd seen them hunting in the same area where he set traps and speared fish. That type of shark was small, only three or four feet long. As far as she knew, they didn't come close to him. He probably wouldn't tell her if they did. He didn't always communicate with her. They'd both been walking on eggshells around each other since that day at the waterfall.

The second week on the island had been easier than the first, however. He'd moved the storage box into the cave, where it was cool. Then he'd harvested that giant clam and stuck it inside. They'd had fresh meat for days. Now she had another boiling pot and a washbasin, made of clam shells. She'd been experimenting with cooking methods and spices. She'd collected salt deposits from the tide pools. Logan had found a passion fruit vine, which offered delicious fruit and plenty of leaves for tea.

Life on the island wasn't perfect, but they were surviving. Sometimes he flinched at her touch, as if it pained him. Maybe it did; he overexerted himself at every opportunity. The division of labor fell heavily along gender lines, with her hanging out at camp and cooking while he did the more physical jobs. His daily schedule looked like an Ironman workout. He was on the go from sunup to sundown, hunting and fishing and lifting and building. She couldn't convince him to take a break during the daylight hours unless there was a meal involved.

Instead of continuing the debate over the bamboo raft, she returned to her own project. She'd grated some coconut against a sharp volcanic rock and strained it into an empty shell. Then she boiled the liquid, let it cool and strained it again. By late afternoon, she had a half-filled shell of coconut oil.

Pleased, she crouched beside him to present the result. "Check it out."

"What is it?"

"Coconut oil."

He grunted his approval. "I'll catch you a fish to fry."

She dipped a finger in the fragrant oil and brought it to her lips. "It helps heal and moisturize, too. Want some?"

He shook his head, probably because his hands were busy. He'd been applying a coat of tree sap to the lashing on his raft. It was a sticky substance, like tar, that would prevent the vine cordage from coming apart in seawater.

Undeterred, she applied a drop of oil to his chapped lips. He didn't stop her, but his jaw clenched with unease. His skin was darkly tanned now, only a shade or two lighter than hers. His eyes met hers as she pulled her hand away. Although brief, the contact was intimate, and arousing. Her mind supplied more explicit uses for coconut oil. His expression told her he knew them all.

She imagined him rubbing oil over her sensitive parts with callused fingers. The fantasy was so sharp, she had to smother a moan. Flustered, she left his side abruptly. She almost dropped the coconut shell and wasted a half day's work.

He put his head down and finished the lashing, his face like a stone mask. When he was finished, he rose from the crouched position he'd been working in. She didn't miss his wince of pain as he straightened.

"Is your knee bothering you?" she asked.

"It's fine."

"Maybe you need to rest."

"That's the last thing I need," he said in a curt tone. He drank a cup of water and studied his hands, cursing. They were covered in tree sap. She'd used the substance to reinforce her sandals, so she knew it would wear off in a day or two. He seemed agitated about the inconvenience, as if it wrecked his plans somehow.

The coconut oil might have helped remove the sap, but she didn't offer.

He muttered something about checking the traps and left with his spear. He was having more success with the trident. He'd found a lobster in one of the traps yesterday. When he didn't bring back a fresh catch, she made do with chestnuts and side dishes. She had a stash of fruits and vegetables in the storage chest, along with a stack of wood. He'd brought the trunk over to their beach after the clam meat was gone. It kept the wood dry and the food protected from seabirds. Crabs were terrible scavengers, too.

She boiled some taro root while she waited for him to return. The water bucket was getting low, so she decided to refill it. She was restless, and he'd been acting strange. She hoped he wasn't out there hunting sharks.

That sounded like something he would do.

She didn't find him at the tide pools. She waded into the shallows, shielding the sun from her eyes with one hand. He wasn't in the deeper water beyond the reef, as far as she could tell. She continued down the beach, frowning.

When she reached the group of boulders just before the waterfall, she spotted him. He wasn't fishing at all. He was standing buck naked underneath the falls with his back to her. She stopped and stared.

Oh my.

He'd lost a few pounds in the past two weeks, but his body was still tight and right. He was bulky where it counted. His shoulders were wide, his hips narrow. Below the waist, his skin was several shades paler than his sun-bronzed back. Water streamed over his taut buttocks.

Lord have mercy.

She could have made her presence known at that moment. She could've quietly walked away without disturbing him. At the very least, she could've looked the other direction while he finished showering.

She didn't do any of those things. She sank to her knees behind the boulder and ogled him with thirsty eyes. Then he turned around, and her throat went dry. The front view was even better than the back. She'd seen his rock-hard chest before, and the dark tufts of hair beneath his arms. She'd seen him in wet boxer shorts. She hadn't seen him in his full naked glory, and it was a sight to behold. Even in a relaxed state, his size was impressive. He was naturally thick. Her breath hitched with excitement.

A gentle wave struck the boulder, wetting her knees.

It didn't cool her down. She'd been mildly turned on ever since she'd rubbed coconut oil on his lips. Now she was aching for release. She wanted him to touch her, but he wouldn't. So she slid her hand into her bikini bottoms to do it herself. In the next instant, her forgotten bucket got carried away in the surf.

She tried to reach for it, but she wasn't fast enough. Making a sound of panic, she scrambled after it on all fours. She grabbed the bucket and ducked behind the boulder, her heart pounding with trepidation.

Had he seen her?

Logan appeared beside the boulder a moment later, answering that question. He had his pants on, but no shirt. His expression was curious. She tried to think of a plausible lie, even though it was clear she'd been spying on him. He glanced toward the waterfall, where he'd been showering. Then his gaze moved to her bikini bottoms, which were slightly askew. His nostrils flared, as if he could smell her arousal.

She closed her eyes, mortified.

He didn't say anything. Not one word. After a short pause, he picked up the bucket and walked toward the falls. She rose to her feet, following him.

"I can do that."

He let her have the bucket. While she filled it, he retrieved his shirt and boxer shorts, which were wet. He wrung out the fabric and tossed it over his shoulder. Then he placed the full bucket on top.

He had a crab on his spear, ready to go. They walked back to the shelter in silence. She couldn't bring herself to apologize. She was too embarrassed to speak.

Back at camp, she boiled the crab with the taro root and some seaweed greens. He hung his wet clothes near the fire. They ate side by side, avoiding eye contact. It was the most awkward meal on record.

After she cleaned up, he reached out to grasp her wrist. "Sit."

She sank down on the driftwood log, her cheeks hot.

"I think I should build a separate shelter."

"Why?"

"Because of this," he said, gesturing between them.

She didn't want to sleep alone, no matter how excruciating the sexual tension was. "That's a lot of extra work."

He didn't disagree. "It's difficult for me to be close to you every night."

His confession surprised her. It wasn't like him to admit weakness.

"If I make my own space, you'll have privacy to do whatever. So will I."

She studied his face, embarrassed. She hadn't thought about how he spent his time alone. "You haven't…"

"Of course I have," he said, raking a hand through his hair. "I'd be going crazy if I hadn't. I'm going crazy anyway. It just doesn't hit the spot, you know? It's like eating vegetables when you really want dessert."

Her mouth dropped open. He was really laying it all out there. "For me it's the opposite."

"What do you mean?"

"Sex with someone else is the vegetable. Without dessert."

It took him a second to process what she was saying. "Touching yourself is the dessert? The only dessert?"

"Yes."

"Maybe you've been choosing the wrong vegetables."

She laughed at this, shaking her head. "Maybe I have."

He stared at her in that way of his. Half longing, half awe. She felt something shift inside her. It was like her heart had been balancing on this precarious edge. Now it was falling free, out of her hands and into his. He was the kind of man no woman could resist, and the intensity of his gaze just wrecked her. She felt more alive with him than she ever had before. More aware of herself, more in tune with her body.

She was capable of things she hadn't dreamed of. He made her want to live to the fullest. He made her want to take risks.

She was tempted to toss aside her misgivings and throw herself at him, but she couldn't do him dirty like that. It was wrong. He cared about his career and his professional ethics. She had to respect his boundaries.

"I'm sorry I spied on you," she said. "You don't have to build another shelter on my account."

"I'll think about it."

"Fine."

After a weighted silence, he said, "I'll sleep by the fire tonight. It's not raining."

"Suit yourself," she said, getting up to leave.

He reached out to stop her. "When we get back home—"

"What if we don't?"

His eyes met hers, contemplative. He didn't have an answer for that. Instead of making promises he couldn't keep, he released her. She crawled inside the shelter and curled up, alone. He took his cushion out to the fire.

She wondered how long they'd be stranded on this island. They could get rescued tomorrow, or next week. They could also die here, having never indulged their desires. The thought kept her awake for hours.

She wished for rain to bring him in, but it didn't come.

# Chapter 13

He slept off and on, plagued by vivid dreams.

In one, he was back at the waterfall with Cady. Instead of watching from a distance, she stripped naked and joined him. She wrapped her arms around his neck. Her lips touched his. He lifted her against the wet rock wall and took her like that, standing up, with the falls raining down on his shoulders.

Then the setting shifted, and he was on top of her in the surf. It was the same basic scenario. She was wet; he was hard. They were going at it while the waves crashed around them. But she slipped away from him somehow, leaving behind her red dress. He crushed the fabric in his fists and searched for her. She was in the raft, floating out to sea. One slender arm dangled over the side, fingertips touching the water. Sharks circled.

He jerked awake at dawn, chilled to the bone. A fine mist coated his face. He wiped the moisture away, blinking.

The fire was almost out, so he tossed some dry branches in the pit. Then he went to water a nearby palm tree. He was irritated that his sex dream had turned into a nightmare. He shook off and stretched his neck muscles, wincing.

What a day. What a night. What an unbearable situation. He was stranded with the hottest woman he'd ever met. She was so hot, she'd touched herself while watching him shower. He still couldn't believe it, and he'd seen the evidence with his own eyes.

The sight of her on her knees behind that boulder had undone him. He'd wanted to grasp her pretty hand and lick her fingers. He'd wanted to rip off her bikini and bury his face in her. He'd been so close to giving them what they both needed. So close.

Instead he'd dug deep for control, and found the strength to leave her untouched. He told himself that her actions didn't mean anything. She was responding to a naked male body with toned muscles or whatever, not to him as a person. It was flattering and sexy as hell, but rubbing one out wasn't a declaration of affection.

While he sat by the fire, imagining what she might have done if he hadn't interrupted her, she crawled out of the shelter. She was wearing her typical morning outfit, an oversize T-shirt and panties. She'd change into her bikini in an hour or two. Until then, he could see the shape of her breasts and her dark nipples poking at the fabric.

Building another shelter wouldn't help him ignore her sleek curves. It wouldn't stop his eyes from following her around camp. It wouldn't kill his desire. If he needed to be alone, he could walk into the woods. He'd stroked himself to a furtive climax a couple of times since his hands had healed.

He put on his shirt, which he'd hung up to dry by the fire, and decided to scrap the idea of separate spaces for now. He had more important projects to tackle. It was time to prepare for the long haul. They couldn't count on getting rescued. Waiting for help was a passive strategy. He wanted to take a more active role in his fate. He wanted to repair the raft.

With the raft, they'd have mobility. They could escape the kidnappers, if necessary. They could explore the shoreline, go out to meet a ship, or travel around the reef. The fishing possibilities were far greater. He could avoid sharks and rays, and cover more area. He could travel from one end of the island to the other.

The raft also offered the last and riskiest option: leaving the island. At some point, they'd have to talk about it. Months from now, though. Maybe even years. Because the chances of surviving a long journey across the ocean were slim.

Whatever they decided, he couldn't let the raft and engine components deteriorate. He had to get it in working order as soon as possible.

She made some kind of pudding for breakfast out of bananas and coconut milk. He'd rather have eggs and bacon, but he didn't complain. She was a wizard with the meager ingredients they had.

After they ate, he checked his bamboo raft. It was dry and ready to go. He gathered the rope and the kayak paddle. He also found a piece of palm bark she could use as a paddle. Then he stripped down to his boxer shorts and belt, with his knife secure in the sheath. His shorts were getting ragged because he used them for swimming so much. Pretty soon, he'd be wearing a damned loincloth.

Cady changed into her bikini and covered her hair before they left. She applied sunscreen, passing him the bottle. He wondered where she'd put the coconut oil. He had plans for a hot date with it later.

They walked along the tide pools and through the cave, to the beach where they'd found the storage trunk. They'd named it Treasure Cove. They were going to East Eden for the engine. Shelter Bay was their home base.

He launched the bamboo raft from the beach. She straddled the front section, and he straddled the back. Although the raft stayed afloat with both of them aboard, it didn't maneuver easily. Because of its narrow shape, it would be better suited to the calmer waters on the leeward side of the island. He could use it for fishing along the reef.

Navigating the choppy sea was difficult, but doable. They paddled past a set of sheer cliffs, into a section of no-man's land. The stark rock face made a striking contrast to the blue water. Although it was beautiful to look at, he felt a twinge of unease. There was no shoring area along these cliffs. If something happened to the raft, they'd have to swim.

Luckily, the raft held together fine. Cady seemed calm and focused. They had to paddle hard against the current to reach East Eden, but they made it without incident.

So far, so good.

The engine was heavier than he remembered. He tied a rope around it and dragged it across the beach the same way he'd dragged the clam shell. About halfway there, he had to stop and rest. His knee throbbed in protest when he started moving again. Cady helped him by pushing while he pulled. It took both of them to complete the task. He rolled the engine onto the raft in a final heave.

She dusted off her hands, smiling. "See? You needed me."

He hadn't wanted her to come along because it was mildly dangerous, but she was right. He'd needed her.

"You can just say it. The world won't end."

"I needed you."

"You couldn't have done it without me."

"I couldn't have done it without you. I'm so glad you're here. You're the queen of the island and I'm your humble servant."

She did a fancy bow, her toes pointed.

"What kind of move is that?"

"A curtsy."

"Were you a ballerina, too?"

"Not really. I did Acro. It's a blend of dance and acrobatics, with some ballet. You know Cirque du Soleil?"

He had a vague idea, so he nodded.

"It's like that. Very physical."

No wonder she was so fit, with her tight little body and sleek curves. She could probably do all sorts of twists and contortions.

He shoved that exciting thought out of his mind and focused on tying down the engine. He wrapped the rope around several times and secured it with a double fisherman's knot. He couldn't risk letting this prize fall overboard. If he lost the engine in deep water, they'd be screwed.

When he launched the raft from the beach, testing its buoyancy, it started to sink. He'd anticipated that, so he handed her the paddle and climbed off to swim. What he hadn't anticipated was the balance problem. Without his weight, the raft tipped forward. She bailed out before it flipped completely, treading water with him.

"I have to retie the engine in the back," he said.

"Why? We can both swim."

That was true. The raft looked stable with the engine in the middle. It would be easier to push and less likely to flip. "You don't have to swim with me. I'll drop off the engine and come back for you."

"Let's just go together. It's not that far."

He wasn't worried about the distance. It was less than a mile, and she was a strong swimmer, but they had to skirt along those sheer cliffs. If she got a cramp or panicked, they'd be in trouble.

"You don't think I can make it?"

"You can't go back once we start."

"I know."

He rested the paddle on top of the raft and pushed it through the water, kicking hard. Cady swam beside him. She didn't seem worried. She was better at swimming than paddling. They moved with the current, making steady progress.

"We're halfway there," he said. "You good?"

"I'm good."

He glanced behind them, just to confirm the distance traveled. His blood ran cold as he spotted the worst possible sight.

A dorsal fin.

Less than twenty feet away.

Judging from the height of the fin, this was not a small blacktip reef shark. It was an open water species, large and deadly. Although he knew that sharks tended to strike from below, rather than skimming the surface, his throat tightened with fear. This predator was tracking them. That wasn't necessarily a prelude to an attack— but it was really frickin' scary.

The next instant, the fin was gone.

That was even scarier.

"Come here," he said to Cady.

She followed his gaze, scanning the water. "What is it?"

"Just come here," he said, his teeth clenched.

When she swam closer, he pulled her into the space between the raft and his body, protecting her as much as possible. "Get on the raft, but be careful. I don't want you to tip it over or fall off."

The fin resurfaced in front of the raft. The shark was circling. He prayed it wouldn't take an exploratory bite.

She scrambled to get out of the water, eyes wide.

"Careful," he repeated.

The fin disappeared again.

She managed to climb on the raft, with his help. He grabbed her backside and hauled her aboard. She couldn't straddle either end of the raft without throwing off the balance, so she had to drape herself across the engine with her bottom in the air. It might have been comical if he wasn't afraid for their lives.

The shark circled around again, its dorsal fin cutting closer. He identified the size and species with growing unease. It was a tiger shark, about ten feet long. Tiger sharks could be aggressive, and they weren't picky eaters. He drew his knife from the sheath, treading water. She gaped at him over her shoulder.

"What are you going to do with that?" she asked in a hushed voice.

"Defend myself."

"Cut the engine loose and get up here right now."

He shook his head. "I can't lose the engine."

"Better it than you!"

The shark swept by his left leg, spooking the hell out of him. It was gone before he could make a stab in its general direction. He gripped the knife handle tight, worried about dropping it. He couldn't lose his knife. He couldn't lose the engine.

He couldn't lose *her*.

"You get up here, or I'm coming down," she said.

"Don't you dare move," he said quietly.

The shark bumped the raft.

She clapped a hand over her mouth to muffle a scream. He waited for the next pass, his knife ready. She was sobbing with terror. He couldn't hear her, but he could tell by the way her body shook. He felt oddly disconnected from his own fear. The thought of leaving her bothered him more than the thought of dying. She couldn't survive here without him.

He waited for the shark to attack, his heart in his throat.

After about thirty seconds, he returned the knife to its sheath. He was going to continue about his business. If the shark didn't like it, too bad.

He resumed swimming, pushing the raft forward. His stomach twisted in anticipation of teeth tearing into his flesh, but he tried to stay calm. Cady wept silently, her shoulders trembling. He concentrated on moving through the water with brisk efficiency. Soon they were in sight of Treasure Cove.

He didn't see any fins. Maybe the shark hadn't followed them.

When his feet touched the sand, he felt a surge of relief. They'd made it. They were on land, in one piece. They were both completely unharmed. The engine and raft were intact. She waded through the surf and collapsed in a heap on the beach. He shored the raft with relish. Then he flipped the shark two birds.

*Take that, you bastard. In your face.*

Cady didn't share his triumph. She glared at him with weepy eyes, as if she couldn't believe he would celebrate their narrow escape.

He rested his hands on his hips. "What?"

"You said the sharks hang out by the reef."

"The smaller ones do. That was an open water species."

"What if it had attacked you?"

He didn't have an answer for that.

"What if I'd panicked, or jumped in the water to help you?"

"I told you not to move," he said in a reasonable tone.

She gave him an incredulous look.

"Maybe you didn't hear me."

She made a strangled sound and closed the distance between them. "Hear this," she said, jabbing her finger at his chest. "You're a jackass."

He flinched at the insult, his muscles taut. He'd taken a risk by staying in the water, but it was a calculated risk. They'd needed the engine. The shark hadn't attacked. They were fine. Why not focus on the positive?

Instead of trading barbs with her, he untied the rope. He left the engine on top of the raft and secured the rope to the bamboo. It was easier to drag across the sand this way. He hauled the engine to the mouth of the cave and left it there, next to the deflated raft. Although the raft had a repair kit, he wasn't ready to start a big project. They hadn't eaten lunch yet. He hadn't explored the tide pools or checked his traps. It was his responsibility to provide for them. He was doing the best he could. She should respect that.

"Let's go," he said, walking through the cave.

She followed close behind him, but not by choice. She was afraid of the dark interior, especially at high tide. As soon as they reached the other side, she stormed off. He scowled at her slender back in frustration.

He found himself reacting just as passionately when they argued as when they kissed. That wasn't normal for him. He also didn't know how to resolve their conflicts. He couldn't take Cady to bed, so he had to find another way to please her.

While he headed toward the tide pools to check the traps, he considered different strategies. He'd had steady girlfriends before he'd become a SEAL. He tried to remember what he'd done to make them happy. They liked gifts, flowers, nice gestures. He could give Cady a fish, but that wasn't much of a peace offering.

What else? He'd never had any trouble communicating with women. They liked men who could carry on a conversation. They liked men who listened.

He hadn't listened to Cady's concerns just now. Instead of hearing her out, he'd asked if she'd heard *him* clearly. He hadn't stopped to think about her feelings. He'd told her to stay put, so he'd expected her to stay put. It occurred to him that her grandfather had barked the same order just before he'd died.

Logan massaged the nape of his neck, wincing.

Yeah. Maybe he'd been a little insensitive.

Although he didn't regret his decision to save the engine, he could've listened and communicated better. He also should have anticipated her reaction. He'd been in the water with an aggressive tiger shark for twenty minutes. Of course she'd been horrified.

Two weeks ago, she'd watched a group of the same

species tear apart a dead body. Most people were traumatized by stuff like that.

He didn't have much success at the tide pools. He returned to camp with one of those orange fish that looked like Nemo. It wasn't his finest moment. Her eyes were swollen from crying. She accepted the fish and cooked it in silence.

He cleaned up for dinner by washing his hands and face, and putting on his clothes. They had fried Nemo with mashed taro and seaweed. She could turn almost anything into a delicious meal, but not this. The fish was flabby and tasted strange.

He wouldn't be catching any more Nemos.

"I'm sorry I called you a jackass," she said, staring at the fire.

"I deserved it."

She seemed surprised by this admission. "I thought you were going to die out there."

"I know."

"How could you do that to me?"

He raked a hand through his hair, which was gritty with sand. "I didn't think the shark would attack."

"And sea kraits rarely bite?"

It was difficult to compare a shy, nearly harmless sea krait to an aggressive tiger shark. The second animal was far more dangerous. He'd made a risky decision, and he had to own it. "I'm sorry I scared you."

She rose from the driftwood bench, pacing in front of him. "I can't stand watching you be so careless with your own life. Or mine."

Two weeks ago she'd seemed a bit cavalier about death herself. She'd told him that she'd rather die than leave the island in the raft. It still bothered him, remembering that. "I didn't mean to put you in harm's way."

"Just yourself?"

"Yes."

"Why don't you get scared?"

"I do get scared, but I set the fear aside. I move past it."

She stopped pacing and crossed her arms over her chest. "You move past it."

He nodded.

She sat down again, facing the fire. "You know how I said my dad got shot in the line of duty? It took him a couple of months to recover from the injury. Then he went back to work on the same beat. He risked his life every day. I was afraid he'd die, like my grandpa. He moved past the fear, I guess. But I never did."

"That's why you play it safe?"

"That's why I play it safe. I'm not an adrenaline junkie, like you. And I don't enjoy worrying about people I love."

His heart did a flip inside his chest, even though she was talking about her dad, not him. "I don't know what to say."

"Say you won't scare me again."

He rubbed a hand over his mouth, reluctant to make promises he couldn't keep. "I'll try not to."

"You don't give an inch, do you?"

He'd like to give her every inch he had. Clearing his throat, he changed the subject. "I should teach you how to build a fire."

"No," she said, jumping to her feet.

"I want you to learn."

"Why don't you just keep yourself alive?"

"I could get sick. There could be a storm."

It smelled like rain right now, actually. Although it wasn't monsoon season, they'd grown accustomed to light showers in the afternoons and evenings. Heavier rains could strike. She started rinsing out the coconut shell cups and scrubbing her turtle shell, ending the conversation. They'd had more than enough conflict for one day, so he stayed quiet.

Clouds gathered low in the night sky, shrouding the beach in mist. He wouldn't be sleeping outside tonight. He covered the fire as well as possible and climbed inside the shelter. They lay side by side, silent. A light drizzle began, pelting the roof. The drizzle turned into rain, and the rain became a downpour.

The storm had arrived.

# Chapter 14

It rained for the next five days—and they both got sick.

Cady wasn't sure if it was the clown fish or something else, but she woke up that night with severe stomach cramps. Logan suffered alongside her. They took turns leaving the shelter to throw up in the rain. The nausea persisted throughout the next day. He slept it off while she stared at the ceiling, shivering. She was miserably ill. She couldn't decide which was worse, succumbing to food poisoning or dying of thirst.

He recovered from the bout before she did, probably because she got hit with a double-whammy: her period. She noticed the blood in her bikini bottoms on the second day of rain. She wasn't prepared for this inconvenience, of course. She returned to the shelter with a palm pressed to her belly.

"What's wrong?" he asked. "Still sick?"

She curled up on her side, grimacing. "I got my period."

Logan didn't seem phased by this declaration. He tore the end of his towel into strips and gave them to her.

"That's your blanket," she protested.

"You need it more than I do."

She folded one of the strips of terrycloth into a rectangle shape and tucked it into her bikini bottoms. She'd have to wash the rags and reuse them, but she didn't mind. "Thank you," she mumbled.

Although the rain interrupted Logan's big plans to repair the raft, he didn't sit idle. He transferred some hot coals from the fire into one of the giant clam shells, covered it and brought it inside. This strategy gave them a backup fire source and kept them warm. She was glad they had plenty of dry wood and food in the storage bin. Despite these reserves, he ventured out in the rain every few hours to hunt and forage. He wandered around with his spear, checking the tide pools for fish, impervious to cold and discomfort. She stayed indoors and wove a mat out of palm fronds.

For the bulk of the time, they were sandwiched together in a tiny hut, unable to escape. His long legs ate up all the space. His lungs sucked up most of the oxygen. She was suffering from stomach cramps and cabin fever.

"There's no air in here," she said. "And no room."

"I'd make a skylight, but then the rain would pour in."

She nudged his ankle with her bare foot. "Are you familiar with the term 'manspreading'?"

"Is it like manscaping?"

"It's when men on the subway spread their legs to take up as much space as possible, regardless of other passengers."

"People do that?"

"You probably do it."

"I never ride the subway."

She rolled onto her side, feeling irritable. Her back

ached, and her emotions were on edge. When she started rubbing the sore muscles with her fingertips, he took over. Tears sprang into her eyes at his strong, soothing touch.

"Here?" he asked gruffly. His thumbs made circles on either side of her spine.

She murmured a series of contradictory-sounding instructions. "Lower. Higher. In. Out."

He did his best to find the right spot. "If this is how you direct men in the bedroom, no wonder they have trouble."

She laughed weakly. "Lower."

He spent another few minutes on her lower back and moved on, massaging the nape of her neck. She almost purred in response. It occurred to her that Andrew had never done this. He'd treated her period like an infectious disease. He also hadn't taken direction well, in or out of the bedroom. She couldn't remember why she'd fallen in love with him. His confidence had appealed to her. He was a brilliant chef, handsome and financially stable. He'd seemed controlled, reserved…safe.

"Thank you," she said, when Logan's hands stilled.

"Better?"

"Yes."

"I'll try not to take up so much space."

Her lips twitched into a smile. "Why don't you have a girlfriend?"

"I don't know. It's so hard to meet women on this island."

"Before this, I mean." She turned to face him, curious. "You said you pick up women at bars."

"Yeah. Sometimes."

"You don't date any nice girls?"

He arched a brow. "They're all nice."

"You're avoiding the question."

He stretched out on his back, tucking his hands behind his head. "I had a steady girlfriend during BUD/S training. Liliana."

Cady tried not to bristle at the name. *Liliana.* She pictured a sultry, straight-haired beauty. "What happened to her?"

"We drifted apart, I guess. She wanted me to take her out every weekend and give her lots of attention. I was more focused on making the cut. Then I got deployed, and that was it. I think she liked the idea of being a SEAL's girlfriend more than the reality."

"That's too bad."

He shrugged, as if he'd dodged a bullet.

"Don't some of your teammates have wives or girlfriends?"

"Sure, most of them do. Hud had a wife, at one point."

"What happened to her?"

"He came home from his second tour in Iraq and found out she was three months pregnant. He'd been gone six."

"Ouch."

"Yeah. The job is hard on relationships, and on families. It takes a certain kind of person to sign up for that."

"What kind of person?"

He studied the palm frond ceiling. "Someone independent and self-sufficient, who can handle long separations with little or no contact. It's not easy to wait for a call from overseas, and stay in the dark about every detail."

"You haven't met anyone who would wait?"

His gaze connected with hers. "I haven't met anyone I wanted to ask to wait."

She tried to imagine what would have happened between them if she hadn't been kidnapped. Would they have shared anything beyond a hot vacation fling? She doubted it. They had great chemistry, but she wasn't the type of woman he'd described. She couldn't stand the thought of waiting up at night, worrying about him. Because she already knew what kind of man he was. Logan Starke was a risk taker who considered himself indestructible and killed without blinking an eye. He'd die for his country, its citizens and his comrades. Waiting for his call would be like watching him swim with sharks every day.

"It's a big ask," she said.

"Yes."

The conversation reminded her that they were fundamentally incompatible—in the real world, at least. Here, none of that seemed to matter. She couldn't deny that she felt safer in his arms than she ever had with Andrew.

For the duration of the storm, she wavered between being grateful for Logan's company and desperate to escape the close confines of the shelter. She felt like a prisoner of war. At least she wasn't dying of sexual tension.

On the fifth day, she woke up alone. The sun was shining. Birds were chirping. It was a beautiful morning.

She climbed out of the shelter to greet the day. Logan was already up. He tossed some wood on the fire and went to gather more. She stretched her arms overhead, smiling. Shelter Bay made a pretty picture after the rain. Soft pink clouds edged the horizon. The sand was strewn with palm fronds, fresh coconuts and who knew what else. She couldn't wait to go exploring.

Chuckling at her eagerness, she took stock of the storage bin. They were out of chestnuts, taro and breadfruit, but they still had bananas. Her stomach rumbled with hunger as she put some water to boil for tea.

Logan returned with two eggs, to her delight. They shared a hot breakfast, basking in the sunlight.

"How are you feeling?" he asked.

"Good."

"No more cramps?"

She shook her head, wondering if he'd go back to sleeping outdoors. Her period had been an effective buffer between them, but now that was over, and she felt more connected to him than ever. She anticipated some serious moments of weakness in the future. Keeping her distance would be difficult.

The storm had destroyed one of Logan's fish traps and damaged the roof of the shelter, so they had work to do. On the plus side, plenty of loose building material had blown down from the palm trees, and some new treasures had washed ashore. There was a multicolored parasail floating in the surf. She helped Logan untangle it from the reef.

"This could be our ticket home," he said.

"Really?"

"If I can repair the raft, and add a modified sail…it could travel a far greater distance. Well beyond the limits of the gas tank."

Her chest tightened with unease. "On the open ocean, you mean?"

"Yes."

She dropped the sail in the water. "You're still thinking about leaving the island?"

"Of course. Why do you think I was so desperate to save the engine?"

"You said the raft would help us get rescued."

"I'm still counting on it to do that, and to help us with daily life. Leaving is a last resort. But it's something to consider if we run out of other options. With a sail, we can control our direction of travel, and not just float on the current."

"I won't go with you."

Scowling, he dragged the sail to shore on his own. "It's just an idea. A backup plan."

"It's a crazy idea."

He rested his hands on his hips in an impatient gesture she'd grown familiar with. "Look, I'll do whatever it takes to survive. I'll risk the open ocean if I have to. What's crazy is spending the rest of our lives here."

"You'd have to go alone."

He strode forward and grasped her upper arms, startling her. His eyes were dark and his tone vehement. "If I go, you're coming with me. I'll drag you along, kicking and screaming. I won't leave you behind to die. I can't do that again."

She stared up at him in surprise. "What do you mean, again?"

He let her go. "Never mind."

"Did you leave Hud?"

He sucked in a sharp breath, telling her she'd hit a sore spot. "You don't know what you're talking about."

"I know what you yell in your sleep."

A muscle in his jaw flexed. "What's that?"

"His name, mostly."

"You cry out random stuff in your sleep, too. It's a lot of moaning and begging and 'Logan, please.'"

Her cheeks warmed at his mocking tone. Had she really done that? "You're changing the subject because it's painful."

"I didn't leave him," he said curtly. "Not the way you're suggesting. I got injured en route, so he went ahead without me."

"Then what?"

"Then the building he was in blew up." He spread the parasail out on the sand and knelt to inspect the fabric for tears. "Another unit searched the rubble in the aftermath, but there was nothing to recover, due to the force of the blast. There were no bodies in the impact zone, just dust. So yes, we left him."

She sank to her knees beside him. "I'm sorry."

He seemed lost in the memory. His eyes were far away, his brow furrowed. When she slipped her arms around him, he allowed it. She stroked his broad shoulders, trying to give him a small amount of comfort, the same way he'd comforted her in the shelter the other day. She didn't know if her touch soothed him, but it felt right. His muscles bunched beneath her fingertips, and his heartbeat thudded in his chest.

She was afraid he'd misinterpret her gesture if she lingered too long, so she patted his back and let him go. His face revealed nothing of the emotions within. She focused on rearranging the multicolored nylon. It made a pretty kaleidoscope on the sand.

They left the sail to dry and continued to the tide pools. Logan caught a small octopus, battered by strong waves. He ended its misery with the tip of his spear and brought her the prize. She'd make tentacle soup for dinner.

He spent the rest of the day working on repairs while she collected driftwood and other necessities. Instead of building a separate shelter, he improved the existing structure. He extended the roof and added a sitting area next to the sleeping pallet. When he was finished, they had more space to move around inside. Room to breathe.

She returned from her final beach expedition with a collection of shells to cook with and two exciting new finds. The first was a vintage glass bottle that she'd dug out of the sand. She planned to store coconut oil inside. The second object she couldn't identify. It was a tool of some kind, pale and marble-smooth, with a grooved handle. It reminded her of the stone mortar and pestle she used to grind herbs.

She showed it to Logan, who stopped what he was doing immediately. "Wow."

"What is it?"

"It's a whalebone club."

"For hunting?"

"I don't know if it would take an animal down from a distance, but it could certainly finish one off. It's probably more of a close-quarters combat weapon. It looks old, too. It might be worth a lot of money."

She wasn't as excited about a killing weapon as he was. He did some martial arts moves, testing his new toy. She removed the shells from her nylon bag and put her towel inside. She'd rinsed off in the waves this morning, but she longed for the clean feel of freshwater. Some fresh clothes would help, too. Her red dress had faded into a rose-pink after hanging out in the rain. She tucked it into her bag before she set off.

"Where are you going?"

"To the waterfall."

He nodded and went back to his tai chi or whatever. She took her time at the falls, scrubbing the grit from her hair and body. After she was finished, she washed her bikini and T-shirt. Then she put on her dress and panties, feeling like a new woman. She picked up the parasail on the return trip, dropping it at Logan's feet.

He gave her a dark look and walked away to clean up while she made dinner. The octopus soup reminded her of San Francisco. She felt a pang of homesickness, even though she didn't live there anymore. She didn't have a home to speak of. She hadn't decided where to go. The job on the cruise ship had been temporary, but she didn't want to drift around forever. Before the breakup, she'd been ready to settle down and have kids. She'd already done her share of traveling. She'd been to Europe and India and South Africa.

She knew where she *didn't* want to go: out on the open ocean with Logan. She wouldn't take that risk, with or without a sail. If he tried to drag her away, she'd jump overboard and swim back to shore.

They ate in the early evening, hours before sunset. He devoured several bowls in a row. Judging by his appetite, the soup was a hit. She cleaned up and he started one of his projects. He needed cordage for his new bludgeon. It had a small hole bored through the handle, as if the original owner had kept it tied to his belt or wrist. She imagined that it had belonged to a powerful Polynesian warrior.

Cady wasn't content to sit down by the fire and weave another basket. Maybe his frenetic pace was rubbing off on her, or she'd been cooped up in the shelter too long. She wanted to do something physical, but relaxing. She wanted to relieve her tension, and release all of the emotions she'd been keeping bottled up inside.

She wanted to dance again.

She walked toward the shore, where the sand was smooth and flat. She started with some basic stretches.

She wasn't as flexible as she used to be, but she could still do a standing front split, with her left foot planted and her right pointed at the sky. She held that position for as long as she could, hugging her right leg. Then she let go and sank to the sand for a center split. From there she leaned forward into a pancake, her chest flat.

Not bad.

Not effortlessly graceful, but not bad. She tried an elbow stand and fell over repeatedly. The Valdez she'd nailed at fourteen was out of reach. She didn't even attempt an aerial. Her back walkover felt rusty, but she managed a back bridge without trouble. She could still do an excellent one-handed cartwheel, toes pointed.

Before she knew it, night had fallen. She dusted off the sand and returned to the fire pit. She gulped water. A light perspiration coated her skin, and she was breathing hard. Even so, she felt good. She felt strong.

Although she hadn't been weak or inactive before she came here, she'd felt sort of lost and adrift, without an anchor. The hard work had whittled her into shape. She hadn't been this toned since her competitive dancing days. But the real change was on the inside. She was a stronger person. If she could survive here, she could survive anywhere.

When she returned to the fire, Logan glanced up at her. He was building a new fish basket. His shoulder muscles were tense, his neck corded. "You dance like a pro," he said in a low voice.

She nodded her thanks, flushed with pleasure. She hadn't known how he'd react to her practice session. They were both on edge, humming with desire. If he'd been practicing martial arts shirtless, she'd have watched with hungry eyes. But she hadn't forced him to watch. She hadn't been trying to tease him.

She hadn't even been dancing for him. She'd been dancing for herself.

Maybe it had been a small act of defiance, because he'd threatened to physically overpower her. She wasn't sure if he meant that, or if he was just working through his feelings about his fallen comrade. Either way, the prospect of him dragging her away like a caveman excited her. She was thrilled by his display of passion, his raw masculinity, his strong-willed determination.

She wouldn't bend to his will. She might enjoy the tussle, but she wouldn't bend. She wouldn't leave on that raft.

Anything else he wanted? She'd do.

# Chapter 15

For the next few days, Logan buried himself in the raft project.

Like everything else on the island, it posed a greater challenge than he'd anticipated. First he dragged the deflated raft out of Sea Krait Cave to inspect it for tears. After washing the material, he discovered the damage wasn't limited to small punctures. There were several jagged tears along the hull where the raft had crashed against the reef. The patch kit was intact, but it was useless. The patches wouldn't cover the tears.

He'd paced up and down the beach, swearing. He couldn't order another kit, or slap some leaves over the gaping holes. He needed waterproof glue and larger patches. The canvas umbrella might work. The only adhesive he knew of was the sticky sap he'd used to reinforce the lashing on the bamboo raft. He'd have to heat the sap and mix it with something to make tar. With tar and canvas, he could make patches.

Collecting sap from several different trees took him all day. Transforming the sticky substance into tar proved even more time-consuming. He boiled the sap in one of Cady's cooking shells and mixed in some ashes from the fire. That made a lumpy paste. He added coconut oil and ended up with something that looked like wax. He had to dump out the mess and start over. For the next batch he used sand, which hardened immediately and ruined the shell. He chucked it into the ocean with an angry roar.

On the third day he ran out of sap. He tried to harvest more, but the trees were tapped, so he peeled away sections of bark to use instead. He piled the bark pieces into another clam shell and burned them at high heat. It was similar to the process Cady had used to make coconut oil. The result was a dark, pungent liquid.

"What's that?" she asked.

He wasn't sure, so he just shrugged. "It smells like kerosene."

She gave him a dubious look. She'd been helping him by gathering wood, but she didn't know the proper ingredients for tar. Apparently he didn't know, either. He should've studied more long-term survival strategies.

"Try not to blow yourself up," she said.

He set the liquid aside, gritting his teeth. The sand by the fire was getting cluttered with his failed science projects. The wax he'd made yesterday had formed a hard lump. He tossed it over his shoulder, irritated. She snatched up the wax and studied it with interest. Then she dipped it in the water bucket and rubbed it against her skin.

"This is genius," she said. "You made soap!"

He wasn't impressed by this accidental achievement. Soap wouldn't repair the raft. Neither would kerosene.

"I'm going to use this right now," she said, squealing

with delight. She grabbed her towel and rushed down the beach to take advantage of the novelty.

He watched her go, his eyes narrow. He had enough trouble keeping his thoughts pure when they were both filthy. Imagining her naked in a soapy lather didn't help. Between his struggle to make tar and his struggle with desire, he was in a constant state of frustration. He'd been restless, cranky and quick-tempered.

He blamed his dark mood on her evening dance sessions. She was so goddamned beautiful with her sleek silhouette against the sunset backdrop. Every move she made took his breath away. Of course he looked at her body and imagined them entwined in a series of inventive, acrobatic sexual positions. But he also admired her physical strength. He appreciated the form of art. The exquisite grace of her motions.

Something had strengthened inside her, too. She was getting used to basic survival. She was getting *good* at it. She collected wood and foraged for food like an expert. When he didn't catch any fish, she provided a plethora of tasty vegetarian dishes. She didn't jump at every shadow or scream when a bug crawled on her. Dancing had given her a new sense of calm. Her morale was way up.

So was his dick, unfortunately. He couldn't tell her not to dance, and he couldn't seem to look away. He spent his nights by the fire, alone and aching. Taking care of his own needs hadn't put a dent in his desire. Denying himself might be a better strategy. He needed his body to go into sexual hibernation. Maybe at some point, he'd stop wanting her.

He wasn't going to hold his breath.

While she was gone, he sharpened his knife and polished it against his pants. Then he held up the blade and studied his blurry reflection. He almost didn't recognize himself. He'd been taking care of his teeth and washing regularly, but he looked rough. More like a scraggly pirate than a clean-cut soldier. His beard itched with sweat.

She'd left half a cake of soap behind, so he warmed up some water on the fire and attempted to shave. Although the soap didn't really make bubbles, it smelled nice, like smoky coconut, and made a slick surface for his blade. He ended up with a smooth jaw and a few patches of stubble.

He checked his reflection again. Better.

She returned from the waterfall with a smile on her face and a pink flower in her hair. She was wearing an outfit she'd made from extra scraps of parasail. It consisted of a sarong skirt and a triangle-shaped top. The fabric clung to her breasts like tissue.

Yeah. Not holding his breath.

"Oh my God," she said, dropping her bag. "You shaved."

He touched his cheek, self-conscious. "Does it look okay?"

She stared at him for a couple of seconds. Her throat worked as she swallowed. "Yeah," she said in a husky voice. "It looks okay."

He got the impression that she thought he looked better than okay. Warmth suffused his chest, because it felt good to be admired. It felt good to be admired by her, the object of his obsession. He'd forgotten how important routine comforts were to survival. Something so basic as shaving had become a luxury—and it made him want more luxuries. He longed for the comfort of physical contact.

The center of his desire wasn't always below the belt.

Right now it was in his hands, which itched to touch her skin. It was in his mouth, which watered to taste hers. He didn't need to throw her down and rip off her clothes. He just needed to kiss her. He needed to remember how it felt to hold a woman.

He could tell she was on the same page. It wasn't hard to read her. She was standing there with a flower in her hair, fragrant and doe-eyed, lips parted in invitation.

When he pulled his gaze away, it felt like he was ripping the bandage off a wound. He glanced around for a distraction, his face hot. He couldn't stay here with her another minute without crossing the line. His fishing gear was in the shade nearby.

He had to cool off. It was either that or spontaneously combust. "I'll be at the reef," he muttered, grabbing his snorkel and spear.

Fishing had been more miss than hit lately. He hadn't been getting lucky near the shore. Both of the fish baskets were empty, which had been the case since the storm. He wondered if some fish were seasonal, traveling with warm currents, or if they learned to avoid traps. Could fish learn? On impulse, he dragged the bamboo raft out of the sea cave and launched it. He'd seen some lobsters on the other side of the reef.

He ventured into the turquoise water, his trident resting on the raft beside him. His shoulders relaxed and some of his tension uncoiled as he took in the spectacular view. There were lush green kelp beds and bright coral blooms.

This is exactly what he'd needed. Some alone time on the ocean to commune with nature and clear his head.

He selected a promising-looking spot before donning his mask and snorkel. Then he dove under the surface, trident in hand. The sediment had settled since the storm, leaving the water crystal clear. The sea floor was painted with brilliant colors, teeming with vegetation. He didn't even hunt on his first few dives. He just enjoyed the sights.

His patience was rewarded with a flash of red shell. He struck fast, pinning the lobster against a rock with his trident.

Victory.

Grinning around the mouthpiece, he kicked toward the surface. Then a dark shape appeared in the water, like a cloud blocking the sun.

Shark.

Before he could even identify the species, the shark struck. Logan's spear snapped in half and a heavy tail smacked him in the face. His snorkel flew out of his mouth as if he'd been backhanded. Stunned and out of breath, in a flurry of swirling water, he realized what had happened.

The shark had robbed him.

He broke through the surface, gasping for air. He shoved his mask onto his forehead and stared at his broken spear, dumbstruck. His raft was about twenty feet away. Although the shaft of the spear could be used as a weapon, it would also slow him down. The shark circled, as if considering a second bite.

It was his old friend, Mr. Tiger.

Logan dropped the spear shaft and swam for his life. His heart thundered in his chest with every stroke. The raft seemed like it was a mile away. As soon as he reached it, he heaved his body out of the water with lightning-quickness. The raft rocked back and forth, threatening to dump him. His paddle toppled overboard with a splash.

Shit.

He rested on his stomach, quaking with fear.

Yeah, he felt fear. He felt it hard. That shark was ten feet long, with razor-sharp teeth and powerful jaws. It had snatched the lobster right out of his hands. It could have easily taken off his arm.

He had his knife strapped to his waist, but he didn't draw it. He hadn't brought the whalebone club with him. He gripped the wet bamboo and stared at the paddle floating beside him. It was a better weapon to fend off the shark. It was still within reach.

Should he go for it?

He lifted his head to search the area. His breath came in short pants and his vision was blurred, especially on the right. Maybe he had a black eye. The shark's tail had slapped the hell out of him. Colors were strange and shapes were fuzzy. He felt like he was looking at an X-ray. He didn't see the shark.

He had to make a decision. Paddle or knife. Paddle or knife.

If he chose the paddle, he'd have to stretch his arm out. That was risky. So was sitting upright and strad-dling the raft to defend himself, with his legs dangling like bait. His other option was to draw his knife and stay in this prone position. He wasn't a fan of that, either. He couldn't even see out of his right eye. He didn't want his face near the water.

He took a deep breath, praying the shark wouldn't bump the raft and knock it over. Or just come up and take a bite out of it. If he didn't act fast, the paddle was going to float away. Gut clenched, he extended his left arm. His fingertips glanced off the handle and pushed it out of range. Cursing, he used his hand to dog-paddle closer. He reached out and gripped the handle, yanking it toward him.

And the shark struck again, jaws open.

His entire body jerked from the impact. The paddle flew out of his grasp. Teeth met flesh. Bamboo splintered. Blood splattered.

Then the shark rocketed away, fin flashing.

Logan tucked his injured arm against his body and tried not to panic. He didn't fall off the raft, by some miracle. His left hand was wrapped in a tight fist. The rest of his arm was intact as far as he could tell. Warm blood trickled from his elbow into the water.

Logan didn't know if the shark had aimed for his arm or the paddle. Maybe the predator had learned that humans meant easy fish. Meat on a stick.

He moved into a straddle position. The raft was damaged, but still buoyant. The view was still spectacular. It was surreal. The wounds above his elbow appeared superficial, to his relief. He was damned lucky. If he hadn't been holding the paddle, he might have lost his arm. The aluminum handle had taken the brunt of the blow. There were several seeping punctures, but no hanging skin flaps or missing chunks.

He was going to live—as long as the shark didn't come back for more.

Now he drew his knife, because he had nothing else to defend himself with. He gritted his teeth, ready to stab the bastard in the eye. But the shark didn't return.

He sheathed his knife and paddled to shore with his good arm. When he reached the sand, he dragged the raft to a safe spot and stumbled down the beach. He wasn't looking forward to Cady's reaction. She was going to say he was reckless, that he took too many risks and that she didn't want him to die.

He grimaced, holding his arm close to his body. He was okay. He was in shock, because getting bitten by a shark was a major ordeal, but his wounds weren't serious. He probably didn't even need stitches. He wouldn't get any, regardless.

When he reached Shelter Bay, she was heating up water in her turtle shell pot. She took one look at him and rushed forward.

"Oh my God. What happened?"

He couldn't play off a shark bite as something else. The punctures formed a telltale half crescent on the underside of his arm. "I had a little accident."

"Little? Are you for real?"

He sat down on the driftwood bench. Now that the adrenaline had worn off, he felt weak. "I hope you're not squeamish. I need you to clean it."

She collected a bunch of rags and brought hot water. Blood trickled from the punctures, dripping down his forearm. Her mouth pursed with anger. It was pretty adorable. He liked how she tilted her head to one side when she was mad, and didn't hold back her opinions. And he knew, in that moment, that he would never feel this way about another woman.

She sponged his arm with hot water. He sucked in a sharp breath. "What kind of shark did this?"

"A tiger shark."

"You said those don't come near the reef."

"Apparently this one does."

"How did you escape?"

"I climbed on the raft and it went away."

She continued working on him. She wasn't squeamish. She cleaned the wounds with a thoroughness that was borderline sadistic. Then she mashed up some cooked taro leaves. She claimed it was a natural pain reliever that promoted healing. After applying the paste carefully, she bandaged his arm with a dry strip of towel.

He curled his hand into a fist and bent his elbow to test the bandage. It felt good. Not too loose, not too tight. "Thank you."

"What if it gets infected?"

"You can cut it off."

"I'm serious."

He could see that, but he was reluctant to argue about hypotheticals. "I don't know what you want me to say."

She stood abruptly. "I don't want you to say anything! I want you to be more careful."

"I understand that," he said in a clipped voice. "But I wasn't being reckless. The shark came out of nowhere."

"The same shark that almost attacked us three days ago?"

"I think so."

"So you took the raft out—the same raft that shark already followed—and you didn't even worry about it. That's your story?"

"It sounds stupid, the way you tell it."

"This isn't funny, Logan."

"I wanted a lobster. That's what I was worried about."

"You could've died."

He rubbed a hand over his mouth, sighing. He wasn't taking unnecessary risks. He was busting his ass to provide for them. She wouldn't have complained if he'd brought back a lobster. No, she'd have made a delicious meal and danced on the beach while he fantasized about her doing the splits on his lap.

"What do you expect me to do?" he asked. "Not fish?"

"You won't be able to until that wound heals."

He couldn't argue there. With a muttered curse, he lumbered to his feet. "I left my pants at the reef."

"I'll get them."

"I can walk."

She followed him anyway. He lengthened his stride just to annoy her. When they reached his pile of clothes, she stood there like a hall monitor, waiting for him to get dressed. He didn't like putting his pants on over damp shorts, especially this late in the day.

"Do you mind?" he asked.

"Do I mind what?"

"I'm going to take off my shorts first."

Her eyes dropped to his crotch. His boxer shorts were riding low on his hips. The wet fabric was torn in places and faded in others. The button that held the flap together had fallen off. He figured they'd be useless within a week.

She turned around to give him privacy. Not that she hadn't already seen everything, of course. His gut clenched at the memory of the day he'd caught her behind the rock on the beach, flushed and breathless.

*Don't think about it.*

He dropped his shorts and stepped into his pants, wincing as he extended his left arm. He wouldn't be doing any heavy lifting in the near future, which meant his raft project was on hold. Damn it all to hell.

"Do you need help?" she asked over her shoulder.

Yeah, right. He needed her hands on his fly like he needed a hole in the head. "I'm good."

While he fumbled with the buttons, she gathered his shirt and snorkel from the sand. The bamboo raft was lying nearby, a chunk missing from its side. She clapped a hand over her mouth when she saw the damage. He had to admit, it looked sinister. His arm had been sandwiched between the bamboo and the paddle, and he'd still sustained a nasty bite.

"You could've died," she repeated.

Here we go again.

"That shark is going to come back and kill you."

"He'll have to get in line behind the sea kraits and stonefish."

Her mouth twisted with displeasure. "Now you're mocking me. You're mocking my fear."

He started walking back to camp, hoping she'd drop the subject.

No such luck. She hurried to follow him. "What is your problem? You've been acting like a jerk all week."

"You're my problem."

"Me?"

"Yeah. You." He gestured from her head to toes, indicating the entirety of her person. "Everything you wear, everything you say and everything you do."

"Oh? Am I bothering you?"

"Yes," he ground out. "When you rub coconut oil and sunscreen on me, I'm bothered. When you wear a see-through top, I'm bothered. When you do the upside-down splits in a skirt, I'm bothered."

"You think I'm trying to tease you?"

"I know you are."

"I could say the same about you."

"What?"

"Your boxer shorts leave nothing to the imagination.

You don't even hide your morning erections anymore. Your pants ride so low I can see your pubic hair. And speaking of hair, who are you shaving for? It's like an invitation to climb aboard."

He stopped in his tracks, stunned. He knew she felt desire, of course. But he'd been under the impression that women weren't as visual, and had classier sexual fantasies than men. "You want to climb aboard...my face?"

"Forget it," she said, seeming flustered.

He'd never forget it. Never.

"I'll try not to touch you," she said. "But I can't help you with the rest. If looking at me bothers you, look away."

He didn't think he could. He was Logan Nathaniel Starke. He didn't quit. He didn't lose. He'd handled every challenge the world had thrown at him. He'd taken on the deadliest overseas assignments. He'd just survived a shark attack. But he could not look away from Cadence Crenshaw to save his life.

Denying himself the pleasure of having her now, after everything they'd been through, would be like putting a storm back in a bottle. This thing between them had already been unleashed. It was a juggernaut, hurtling toward completion.

Survival wasn't just about following a routine and working hard and staying alert. Sometimes it was about letting go.

"I can't," he said, cupping her chin. "I can't fight this anymore."

"Then don't," she said simply, and lifted her lips to his.

## Chapter 16

She couldn't believe she'd told him that she wanted to climb on his face.

It was true, of course.

It had been true before he'd shaved. But still, she shouldn't have said that. He hadn't shaved to dazzle her, any more than she'd danced to mesmerize him. The chemistry between them was just there. They were both caught up in an electric current of desire and emotion. She understood why he couldn't look away, because she couldn't look away, either. The instant she'd caught a glimpse of his smooth jaw, she'd been lost. She wanted to feel his mouth, his skin and his hands on her body.

Her lips parted in invitation, but he didn't kiss her. Not yet. He swept his thumb over her mouth, marking the territory he was about to claim. She sucked the tip of his thumb and watched his eyes go dark. She liked the effect she had on him. She liked his pained expression.

He removed his thumb from her mouth and replaced it with his tongue, devouring her. She kissed him back with an eager moan. She couldn't get enough of him. Their mouths were hot and hungry, hands roving. She clung to his neck and pressed her body against his. He was already aroused. So was she. Not surprising, as the past three weeks had been a long, tortuous session of foreplay. She made a whimpering sound, low in her throat.

He didn't stop kissing her, despite the urgency between them. She'd have let him take her right here on the sand, but he didn't tear off her clothes. He didn't rush into second base. He just held her face and feasted on her mouth.

She wanted more. Her nipples hardened into taut peaks against the hard wall of his chest. His erection prodded her stomach. She thrust her fingers in his hair. She could feel the soft sand beneath her bare feet and the ocean breeze on her flushed skin.

His hand left her face, finally, and landed at his favorite place: her ass. Every time she turned around, his eyes were on it. Now his hands were on it. Both of them, lifting her against his throbbing erection. He let her slide down in a delicious drag.

Sparks of sensation rocketed through her. She ached for another dose of that good friction, up and down. She'd never been this turned on before. The encounter in the hallway paled in comparison, and it had been her sexual high point. Now that they were about to take it to the next level, she was…well, she was melting. That was the best way to describe it. She was melting from the inside out.

He squeezed her bottom and grinded against her, still kissing. Her panties got damp and her nipples hurt. She dug her fingernails into his shoulders. When he finally broke the kiss, she blinked drowsily, drunk on lust.

"Lie down," he said.

The only thing to lie on was the shark-bitten raft,

which should have been a turnoff. But she was so far gone that a bucket of ice water wouldn't have been a turnoff. If he'd dumped one on her, she'd have shivered and said yes please.

She sat down on the bamboo and reached behind her neck to untie her top. It fell to her waist, exposing her breasts. Her nipples were dusky points. His gaze caressed them as he stretched out beside her on the sand.

"You're beautiful," he said in a husky voice.

She wasn't self-conscious about her body. She appreciated the advantage of a streamlined physique for dancing. She valued strength and athleticism. But she also knew what men typically liked, and small breasts weren't it. Even so, Logan didn't seem to find her lacking. He stared at her chest the same way he stared at her ass, with bold appreciation. He cupped one breast, then the other. She bit her lower lip as he trapped her nipples between his thumb and forefinger. Her sex pulsed, and her skin tingled with awareness.

"Do you like that?"

"Yes."

"What else?"

She didn't want to say it. She just wanted to do it.

He untied her sarong, his knuckles brushing her flat belly. Her black lace panties barely covered her. The fabric was damp, clinging to her swollen flesh. His nostrils flared, and his eyes blazed with hunger.

He looked, but he didn't touch. His mouth lowered to her breasts. She cried out as he suckled her hard nipples, one after the other. He went back and forth at least a dozen times, making her spine arch and her skin burn. She gripped his broad shoulders, unsure if she wanted his mouth to move up or down.

He lifted his head. "Are you tapping me out?"

She half laughed, half choked. "Please."

"Please what?"

"I feel like I'm going to come before you even…get there."

"That would be hot."

She groaned, clenching her hands into fists. He took pity on her and pulled her panties down her legs.

"Damn," he said, his breath catching.

She was too aroused to feel embarrassed about his perusal, even though it had been a month since she'd waxed. He didn't seem to care. He stared at her slick center and moistened his lips, as if she looked delicious. His erection jutted at the front of his pants, drawing her attention. She wasn't content to lie back and let him do all the work, so she reached out, molding her palm over him. He felt rock-hard and nicely thick.

"Hello," she said, fluttering her lashes. "What do we have here?"

"He's friendly. You can pet him."

She undid the buttons on his fly with a breathy laugh. Then she stopped laughing. Because wow. His erection bobbed up against his belly, blunt-tipped and impressive. She encircled his hot flesh in her fist and stroked. "Good boy."

He grunted his pleasure, shuddering a little. Then, after a minute, he stilled her hand. "Sorry, he gets too excited. He's going to make a mess."

She squeezed his shaft. "I don't mind."

He peeled her eager fingers away, nonetheless. Then he moved lower, settling between her legs. Glancing up, he kissed her inner thigh. "Now pet the kitty."

Her eyes widened at the order. For a clean-cut mama's

boy, he was a dirty talker. After a short pause, she slid her hand down her belly. He'd already caught her in the act, so why play coy? She knew how to pet the kitty. She wasn't sure why he wanted her to do it, but she was willing to indulge him. He watched intently as she touched herself. She dipped one finger inside, where she was hot and wet. Then she circled the tight bead above her opening.

"Nice kitty," he said, kissing her inner thigh again.

Her stomach quivered with anticipation. She was acutely aware of her body, of his mouth and that handsome face, so close to her pulsing heart. She'd never done this in front of anyone before. She'd never been this excited before, either. Most of the time she felt too self-conscious to enjoy oral sex.

He kissed her slippery fingers. She paused, panting with arousal. He sucked her fingers, tasting her. Then he settled his mouth over her already-stimulated flesh and blew her mind. She couldn't believe how good it was. Her breath came in short pants as he licked and stroked her. Maybe he'd cheated a little by letting her do the warm-up, but she wasn't complaining. She was writhing in ecstasy. He flicked his tongue over her, and she went off like fireworks, screaming his name to the tops of the palm trees.

When it was over, she collapsed on the bamboo raft, her legs splayed out like a rag doll. He straightened to a kneeling position again. His erection jutted from his open fly, in desperate need of attention.

"I'm close, just from looking at you," he said in a guttural voice.

She moistened her lips, ready to return the favor. "Let me."

He grasped her hand and wrapped it around his shaft. He wasn't shy about showing her the right grip and rhythm. While she stroked him, his gaze moved from her mouth to her jiggling breasts to the still-tender flesh between her thighs.

Then he came with a strangled groan, splashing her breasts and belly.

She didn't rush to rinse off. He didn't rush to button up. He just studied her with that awed look, as if they'd done something special and lovely, and he was committing every detail to memory. And she felt beautiful, even with her legs spread and his fluid on her skin. She felt cherished, not sullied. She sat forward, touching his face.

He covered her hand with his. "I want to watch you dance tonight."

"Why?"

"Because now I can actually enjoy it."

She smiled, happy to oblige. He helped her to her feet and waited while she knelt in the surf to wash her belly. His eyes traveled down her wet, naked body, alight with pleasure. At sunset, the water seemed to sparkle on her dark skin. When she rose, he took her by the hand and kissed her knuckles.

"Don't get dressed," he said. "Stay like this."

She indulged him easily, gathering her small bundle of clothes. They walked down the beach together, hand in hand. It felt strange and wonderful to be completely nude on their own private beach. He was still wearing his pants, but no shirt. There was something erotic about the picture they made. She was an island nymph with her castaway lover.

As soon as they reached the shelter, he brought out the grass mat she'd made and placed it on the flat sand near the edge of the surf, where she liked to practice. He sat down to watch her from the closer vantage point.

"You want me to dance…naked."

He nodded, his throat working in anticipation.

Although she wasn't that kind of dancer, she couldn't deny him. He was so handsome, with his newly shaved face and bandaged arm. He didn't seem to be in pain, but he was good at hiding that. The way he looked at her, as if she was the sexiest woman alive, made his request irresistible.

She started with a basic stretch, bending at the waist and flattening her palms on the sand. She was aware that he could see everything, but that was kind of the point. There was no way to stretch naked in a modest fashion. She straightened, lifting her leg high in a standing split. It was easier to do now, after several days of practice. Her muscles felt warm and strong. She tried a few tumbles and a side split leap.

His sharp intake of breath told her he was impressed. Or aroused. Probably both.

She was aroused by the performance, as well. She sank into another side split with her back to him, her thighs splayed wide and her hips tilted forward. The damp sand tickled her private parts. She would rinse off again when she was finished. Her goal now was to drive him crazy with desire. A glance over her shoulder indicated that she was getting there. His eyes were dark, fly distended.

She transitioned into a pancake, her belly flat on the sand. It abraded her nipples nicely. She moved out of the splits and rolled over into an elbow stand. She held it for as long as she could, her heart pounding. Then she rose to her feet and lost herself in a short series of free-form moves, whirling and leaping.

He caught her and pulled her into his arms. She'd done some partner dancing, so she knew instinctively that he could learn how. Not tonight, but someday. He had the upper body strength to hold her in a number of different poses.

Even with his injured arm, he lifted her with ease. He crushed his mouth against hers and kissed the hell out of her. She could feel all of the pent-up frustration he'd experienced over the past few weeks. He smelled like soap and salt and something darker, like blood. She hoped his wound didn't hurt too much. His arousal pressed into her, hard and hot. He stumbled toward the mat and fell to his knees, still kissing her. She threaded her hands through his hair and kissed him back hungrily. A thrill raced through her at his grunting sounds. He gave her bare bottom a rough squeeze and let go, breaking the kiss.

His hands moved to his fly. She watched him release the buttons with excitement, thinking he might throw caution to the wind and thrust inside her. But he didn't. He rolled onto his back, breathing heavily. "We can't do that."

"I know."

She helped him take his pants off with a coy smile. Then she pulled him to his feet and waded into the surf. She sank to her knees and rinsed the sand from her body, looking up at him. His erection strained forward.

She wrapped her wet hand around him, stroking up and down. Then she rained kisses along the side of his shaft, where the veins stood out in harsh relief. He was so hard, it looked painful. She soothed the skin with her soft mouth. Then she brushed her lips over the blunt tip, stroking upward.

"You're killing me," he groaned.

She curled her tongue around him, tasting salt. After a few teasing licks, she opened her mouth and went to work. He seemed surprised by how deep she took him, but she wasn't inexperienced at this. She'd always been eager to please her partners.

With him, the pleasure was all hers. She found herself enjoying his taste, his thickness, the smooth velvet of his skin. He had a very nice piece of equipment, and she liked filling her mouth with it. She liked his hands in her hair and his thrusting hips. She alternated between stroking and sucking, her eyes half-lidded.

He didn't tell her to stop before he climaxed. He warned her by gripping the base of his shaft, ready to direct his aim elsewhere. She made a soothing sound, low in her throat, letting him know he didn't have to. He exploded with a hoarse cry, his legs locked and his shaft pulsing in her tight mouth. Spurts of hot fluid filled her throat. She swallowed every drop. When he was finished, she released him and rocked back on her heels.

"Jesus," he said, sounding dazed.

She laughed and rose to her feet. The sun had dipped low on the horizon, and the air was starting to cool. She gathered the mat and went toward the fire, which was burning low. He followed her, pants in hand. He tossed them on the driftwood log and stretched out on the mat. She drank a cup of water, smiling.

"Come here."

She sank down on the mat beside him. He held her face in his hands and kissed her thoroughly, worshipping her mouth. His shaft hardened against her belly, raring to go. She couldn't believe he was aroused again.

"Do you want to ride my hand or my face?"

She flushed at the question. She didn't know if she was brave enough to climb on his face, despite what she'd said earlier. He extended his right arm on the mat and lifted two fingers in offering. After a short pause, she straddled his hand and sank down on his fingers. He had big hands, with long, blunt-tipped fingers. Even though she was soaking wet, it had been months since she'd been penetrated, and she felt the stretch.

He felt it, too. He inhaled a ragged breath. "Does it hurt?"

"No."

"Ride me, then."

She moved up carefully and slid back down, making them both groan. It felt good, so she did it again. It felt even better to rock her hips back and forth, rather than up and down. There was no pressure to satisfy him with an in and out motion, so she focused on her own pleasure. His fingers went deeper, and she shivered. He rested his thumb on her slippery bead, rubbing back and forth with every little thrust of her hips.

"Touch your nipples," he panted.

She pinched them into hard points, biting on her lower lip. She was aware of him watching her with hot eyes. She was melting again. Melting all over his hand, her moisture slicking his fingers. His erection bobbed against his belly, neglected. She knew they couldn't have intercourse, but there were other things to do. Things she'd never done.

She came with a sharp cry, her sex clenching and her hips bucking. Something about the dual stimulation of his thumb and fingers gave her a deeper, more full-bodied orgasm. It went on and on, rippling through her like an earthquake.

When it was over, he removed his fingers and she collapsed beside him. She'd never felt more relaxed in her life. Her skin was dotted with light perspiration, her head buzzing but her thoughts quiet.

"How was it?" he asked.

"Like I died and went to heaven."

He kissed her lips softly. "I've never had better."

She nodded her agreement. This was the best sex she'd ever had, and it was just foreplay. "Do you want…more?"

"I'm good. Just rest for a minute."

She propped her head on one hand, smiling. "I mean, do you want real sex?"

"This is real sex."

"Penetration. Penis in vagina."

He gave her a sidelong glance. "Yeah, I want that. But it's a bad idea."

She knew it was. Letting him come inside her was too risky. If she ended up pregnant, they'd be screwed—whether they got rescued or not. Even so, she wasn't sure they could resist. She also wasn't sure it mattered, in the long run.

This island was as deadly as it was gorgeous. Today had proven that more than any other. There was a ten-foot tiger shark prowling the reef. She hadn't seen a plane or ship since they arrived. Repairing the raft seemed impossible. They were stuck here. They could die tomorrow. Why worry about the future when your days were numbered?

He put his arm around her, as if he could sense her

uncertainty. "No matter what happens, I'll take care of you."

Her eyes filled with tears, unbidden. She pressed her face to his chest. Maybe it was the sexual release, or all the tension she'd felt about the shark attack. Maybe it was just an outpouring of emotion. She *was* depending on him to take care of her.

She was also falling in love with him.

The realization rocked her to the core. She was falling in love with a man who seemed to have no fear, and she was helpless to stop the events in motion. The flimsy walls between them had come down. She couldn't give her body without surrendering a piece of her heart. Now that she'd let him touch her, there was no turning back.

And that was the greatest risk of all.

## Chapter 17

Logan spent the next few days recuperating from his injury and bringing Cady to dizzying heights of pleasure.

It was a glorious time to be alive.

He almost wanted to kiss that tiger shark for setting off this chain of events. He didn't know why he'd held out so long. Making love wasn't a crime. He'd seen too much war and death on his overseas assignments. What they were doing felt like a beautiful expression of life and passion. They both needed it, badly. If his commander begrudged him the affair, so be it. He'd never regret touching her.

The wound on his arm healed quickly. He stayed out of the ocean. Cady kept the area clean and bandaged. Even after it scabbed over, he didn't venture beyond the reef. He searched the tide pools, content to look for easy meals.

He hadn't given up on hunting in deeper water, but he'd been forced to acknowledge the recklessness of it. There was a predatory shark trolling the reef. Swimming alone was too dangerous, and the bamboo raft had offered little protection. If he finished the repairs on the inflatable raft, and took Cady with him as lookout, he could try again.

He found himself eager to please her, and more willing to compromise on safety issues. When she was happy, he was happy.

There was one thing they couldn't do, but it wasn't the most important thing. He could bring her to climax without penetrating her. He was well satisfied by her efforts, in return. They'd shared hours of creative, erotically charged encounters. Not being able to fall back on the old standby had sparked something new and surprisingly dirty inside him. He'd explored every inch of her. He couldn't get enough. She was so sexy and responsive. They'd both been insatiable.

But he still wanted to drill her.

He couldn't help it. He was a man. It was in his nature to dominate and plunder. Whenever they were together, he imagined rolling on top of her and thrusting into her tight body. Although he loved using his hands and mouth on her, he longed for a deeper connection. He wanted to fill her to the hilt.

He knew they shouldn't. He was already crossing the line by touching her. Even so, the temptation to take the final plunge, with no barriers between them, was overwhelming.

She had something special planned tonight, on their one-week anniversary. He'd caught two good-sized crabs in his basket this morning. He'd also managed to make tar, after many failed experiments. He'd patched all of the tears in the raft and rigged a primitive bellows to blow air into it. Tomorrow they'd take turns pumping the bellows. It would probably be a lengthy, exhausting process. He couldn't wait.

While she made dinner, he cleaned up at the waterfall. He thought about shaving again, but decided against it. He'd washed his pants earlier and hung them over the boulder he called Cady's Rock, just to tease her. His boxer shorts had given up the ghost two days ago, and he didn't bother with a shirt unless it was cold. He'd acclimated to the intense sun, little by little. Now he had a tougher hide.

After donning his pants, he plucked a flower from the overhanging vines by the waterfall. Then he strolled down the beach, whistling. Cady wasn't by the fire. He saw a covered basket near the coals that was giving off steam and a delicious aroma. He approached the shelter, his stomach rumbling with hunger.

"Don't come in," Cady cried.

"Why not?"

"Because I'm not ready."

He'd seen her in every state of undress, but he shrugged and went to sit down on the driftwood log.

"Cover your eyes," she said a moment later.

Lips quirking, he held one hand over his eyes.

"Keep them covered."

"What are you doing?"

"Just wait."

He could hear her fidgeting with the basket. The scent of steamed crab drifted into his nostrils, mixing with the hibiscus flower in his opposite hand. He also smelled coconut oil and female skin.

"Okay," she said. "I'm ready."

He uncovered his eyes…and almost swallowed his tongue. She was standing in front of him with a platter she'd woven out of palm leaves. It was loaded with fresh crab, mashed taro and steamed greens. Everything looked amazing, but he hardly glanced at the plate. Because the real treat was her.

She was wearing a skirt she must have been working on in secret. It was made out of banana leaves, strung together and tied low on her hips with cordage. The short leaves tickled the tops of her thighs. On her head, she had a lush green wreath, Polynesian-style. Her dark curls were more relaxed than usual, as if she'd applied a magic potion to her hair.

Oh, and she was topless.

He stared at her, slack-jawed. The flower fell out of his hand. There was a dewy sheen on her lips, and on her dark nipples. Had she oiled her breasts? He pictured her massaging her smooth skin until it shone, toying with the stiff peaks.

He was instantly, powerfully aroused by that mental image, and by the erotic presentation before him. He was also aware of the effort she'd put into her appearance. The headdress alone had probably taken hours. She'd done this for him. To please him. His chest tightened with emotion, because he didn't feel worthy. He'd shown up, shirtless and barefoot, with a flower he'd plucked on impulse. He had nothing else to give her.

"I was going to make a coconut shell top," she said, seeming flustered. "I wanted it to be a whole outfit."

"This is better," he said, with complete honesty.

"Do you like it?"

"I love it."

Her eyes lit up with pleasure. "You do?"

He nodded, giving her another slow perusal. "Put down that plate."

She laughed and shook her head. "Not yet. I have to feed you first."

He reached out to take the platter, but she didn't release it. Instead, she sank to her knees at his feet and literally fed him out of her hand. He ate the crab from her fingers, his heart pounding with excitement. She held his gaze while she took a bite herself.

He was so turned on, he almost couldn't stand it. She was topless, kneeling at his feet, serving him. He felt mildly ashamed of himself for enjoying it so much—and that shame added to his arousal, stoking it higher.

"What's for dessert?" he asked in a low voice.

"Coconut cakes."

Not what he wanted. She fed him and herself bite after succulent bite, finishing the plate. Then she rose to get a drink. He watched the sway of her skirt, mesmerized. He made a choking sound as he realized she was completely bare beneath it.

He stood up, his erection straining his fly. She smiled and handed him the cup. He took a drink, because he was thirsty. Then he tossed the cup aside and lunged forward. She let out a breathy laugh, evading him easily. Before he knew it, she was running down the beach, her bare bottom jiggling beneath her skirt, and he was chasing after her.

He couldn't quite believe they were doing this, but what the hell? They were alone. The island was their prison and their playground. She was his queen and his prey. He was a predator. He was going to catch her—and eat her.

In the back of his mind, he knew they were playing a dangerous game. Because they weren't playing. This chase was real, and it didn't end with him holding her down and ravaging her with soft kisses. It ended with him buried deep inside her.

He wanted it. She wanted it. He could see it in her hot gaze as she glanced over her shoulder. He could smell it. He'd feel it in the slick heat between her legs. They were racing toward ruin, perhaps, but damn. It felt good to run.

She was fast and nimble, giving him a merry chase. He relished every second of it. His knee hadn't been bothering him at all lately. He kept a steady pace, aware that her endurance was no match for his. He could jog like this for hours. She slowed after a few minutes. He caught her around the waist and lifted her over his shoulder in one fluid motion. She let out a high-pitched shriek as he carried her toward the shore.

He dumped her on a flat rock near the tide pools, triumphant.

She braced her weight on her elbows and looked up at him, biting her lower lip. "Careful, you'll make me scream again."

He fell to his knees before her. "I like it when you scream."

"You didn't used to."

"I was a fool," he said, and kissed her. She tasted like cool water, intoxicating and invigorating. She tasted like the elixir of life. He smoothed his hands down her sides and buried his tongue in her sultry mouth. She arched beneath him, twisting her fingers in his hair. He loved it when she did that.

He loved her. Every inch of her.

His plan to unbutton his pants and take her, quick and rough, transformed into something gentler. There was no need to rush. As he lifted his head, warm surf cascaded over her body. Her lips were parted, thighs spread. His chest twisted with emotion.

She was so goddamned beautiful.

He slid his palm over her slippery breasts, thumbing her sweet nipples. Then he lowered his mouth to taste, flicking his tongue over the oiled tips.

She gripped his hair, groaning.

He moved between her thighs. The leaves of the grass skirt had separated, revealing her pretty sex. His mouth watered to taste her. She looked pouty and ripe, like an erotic delicacy. He couldn't resist having her for dessert. When he touched his tongue to her sensitive flesh, she let out a soft cry. She started to writhe her hips, riding his face. He grunted with pleasure, licking and sucking her until she screamed his name.

After her shudders subsided, he wiped his mouth, studying her. She'd lost her wreath in the surf. The last rays of sunlight shimmered on the surface of the water, lovely and transient. Although she looked well satisfied, and eager to be taken, he had to make sure. They needed to discuss the consequences.

"If we don't get rescued—"

"I don't care anymore," she said.

"It's a health risk."

"This entire island is a health risk."

He frowned at her response, suddenly uncertain. But when she unbuttoned his fly, he surged into her hand. Her mouth made a soft moue. And then the moment of restraint was over. He fit himself against her opening. She clung to his neck.

He held her gaze as he thrust into her. Her lips parted with a quick intake of breath. Not pain; her eyes were half-lidded, smoldering with heat. So was her body. She was lusciously wet, enveloping him like a slick fist.

He groaned at the snug sensation, his arms trembling.

She twined her arms around his neck and put her mouth near his ear. "Don't hold back," she said, panting softly. "Make me scream."

Jesus.

How could he deny that request?

Jaw clenched, he started to move. He withdrew halfway and slid back in, testing the waters. She shuddered and tightened her thighs around his hips. He did it again, in and out, thrusting harder.

"Yes," she cried.

After a minute or two of intense pleasure, he knew he was in trouble. To his chagrin, he was already close to finishing. His erection throbbed inside her and his arm muscles flexed. He wanted to drive them both toward an earth-shattering climax, but it would probably be a solo ride at this point. He slid his hand between their bodies to help her along. The quick rhythm of his fingertips offered no finesse, but she didn't seem to mind. She made little gasping noises, encouraging him.

Damn. She was so hot.

As soon as he felt her inner muscles flutter around him, he was lost. He crushed his mouth over hers to swallow her scream. Then he thrust twice more and came hard, his body quaking from the power of the release.

It occurred to him, while he was collapsed on top of her, that he hadn't pulled out. He'd meant to, but he'd been so caught up in getting her off that he'd forgotten to take the most basic step toward prevention.

He couldn't believe it. He removed himself clumsily, stunned by the mental lapse. "I came inside you."

"I know."

He did a quick countdown in his head. She'd had her period two weeks ago. "Is this a bad time?"

"We're probably okay. I have irregular cycles."

He wasn't an expert in the rhythm method, having never failed to use protection before. He had the vague idea that it was unreliable. Kind of like pulling out. He rolled off her and watched as she went to rinse away his semen in the gentle surf. The idea of her belly growing round with his child might have appealed to him under any other circumstances. But the thought of it happening here, away from the safeguards of modern medicine, terrified him. He'd seen women die in labor before.

He buttoned up his pants. "We can't do that again."

She glanced over her shoulder at him, her expression wary.

He swallowed hard, rising to his feet. "We can't... I can't touch you anymore. Not the way I have been."

"Why not?"

He gestured to the rock they'd just christened. "Because this is going to keep happening. Obviously I can't resist you."

"Resist me? I didn't twist your arm, Logan."

"No, you didn't." She'd twisted something a little lower. He cleared his throat, flushing. "I take full responsibility for the mistake."

She rolled her eyes heavenward. "Please. I was an equal partner and then some."

He threw his hands in the air. "Well, I'm sorry."

"You're sorry, all right," she said under her breath.

"What does that mean?"

"It means that you waited until after we had sex to

decide it was a bad idea. When your dick was hard, it was all good."

"I tried—"

"You tried what? To stop? To talk me out of it? You chased me, threw me down like a caveman and gave me a screaming orgasm."

"You wanted it like that."

"We both did."

He couldn't argue there. He didn't know why they were arguing at all. They'd been getting along great before that sex bomb had gone off. Now they were back to square one. He still wanted to be with her. They just couldn't be together physically.

She brushed by him, her arms crossed over her bare breasts.

He felt a surge of helpless frustration. Didn't she understand that he was trying to protect her by keeping his hands off? Didn't she know that he couldn't resist making love to her because he'd fallen *in* love with her?

Maybe she didn't know. Maybe he should tell her.

He reached out to grasp her wrist. "Cady, wait—"

She skirted around him and stepped into one of the shallow tide pools near the shore. With a sharp cry of pain, she stumbled sideways and sat down, her face frozen. She clutched her right foot. In the shallow pool, a stone moved.

Not a stone. A stonefish.

His heart wrenched at the sight. "Oh my God," he said, lifting her into his arms. "What can I do?"

"Hot water," she said through stiff lips. "Soak it."

He carried her to the shelter as fast as he could, his blood pumping with adrenaline. When he set her down by the fire pit, her foot had swollen twice its size, and her breathing had slowed to a dangerous rate. He filled the turtle shell with water and added wood to the fire. By the time he returned to her side, she was unconscious.

## Chapter 18

Cady woke up screaming.

Intense pain radiated from the sole of her foot to the top of her thigh. It struck in sickening waves, creating an endless loop of agony. She felt like her skin was melting off the bone. Her foot was grossly swollen, wrapped in rags. Something was wrong with her brain, too. It was as if she'd taken psychedelic drugs. Reality was warped beyond recognition. Her thoughts were sluggish, her vision blurred. Logan held her arms in a tight grip, restricting her movement. She screamed until she passed out.

When she came to again, he was tying a hot rag around her foot. She tried to kick free, but he held strong. The scalding heat penetrated her skin, stealing her breath away. She couldn't seem to get enough air. Her entire body ached, and her throat was raw.

"What happened?" she croaked.

"You got stung by a stonefish."

Oh my God. She collapsed on her side, sobbing. Flames licked the night sky and palm trees bent forward, rubber-like, before snapping back again. Her stomach twisted, as if an electric eel had taken residence inside her. She vomited on the sand several times. No eels, just bile. He wiped her face with a wet cloth and moved the grass mat away from the bile. Then he lay down and drew her into his arms.

"Help me," she said.

"I will."

"I need to go to the hospital."

"I know."

"When are we leaving?"

"Soon."

Although she suspected that was a lie, she didn't argue. She alternated between thrashing around and moaning weakly. Hallucinations plagued her. Sometimes everything went black, and she could rest. Sometimes it was a carnival of pain and nausea, swirling like an untied parasail. She closed her eyes and prayed for oblivion.

Her dreams were no solace, because they were littered with monsters. Tree monsters that pelted her with breadfruit and captured her in their branches. Fire monsters that exploded out of a volcano and ate souls. She fled across the burning lava, only to end up on a pirate ship. Pirates made her walk the plank with blistered feet. Then she was forced to dance across hot coals. She was burned at a stake while Logan watched, his hands tied behind his back.

They finally escaped the pirates somehow and ended up lost at sea again. She was sitting in the inflatable raft, soaked in sweat, her belly round and legs splayed. Labor pains ripped through her abdomen. Logan knelt between her thighs and told her to push. With a strangled cry, she delivered the baby in a wet gush.

He cradled the squirming lump to his chest, but it

wasn't a baby. It was a stonefish. His body jerked as the powerful sting went straight to his heart. He dropped the fish and careened overboard, dead in the water.

She woke with a start. She was alone in the shelter. Sunlight filtered between the cracks in the weaving. Her T-shirt stuck damply to her skin.

She studied her injured foot, which was wrapped in a strip of towel. The swelling had gone away. She pressed against the tender spot with her fingertips. It felt sore, like a bruise. She had a mild headache and a scratchy throat. Otherwise, she was okay.

She crawled off the pallet and peered out the entrance. Logan set a bucket of water down in the shade nearby. She emerged from the shelter, wincing at the bright sky.

"You're awake," he said, examining her.

"I'm thirsty."

He brought her a cup of water and a fresh banana. They sat in the shade together. She drank sips of water and ate half the banana, studying his face. He looked tired, even haggard. His jaw was shadowed with stubble, his hair was disheveled and he had a dark bruise on his cheekbone. Her heart did a little flip inside her chest anyway, because he was still handsome, and she was hopelessly in love with him.

"I guess you're feeling better," he said.

"Much."

"Do you remember what happened?"

She nodded. She remembered the outfit she'd made, the dinner they'd shared, the dizzying eroticism of the chase and capture, and the amazing sex they'd had on a rock by the tide pools. Then he'd ruined it by voicing his regrets, and she'd stepped on a stonefish in a fit of pique. "How long was I out?"

"Two days. You were unconscious about half the time, delirious the other."

"Did I give you that shiner?"

"You did."

"I'm sorry."

"It's nothing," he said, clearing his throat. He met her gaze and held it. "I thought you were going to die."

She knew how that felt. Her chest tightened, and her eyes watered with emotion. She took a deep breath, blinking away the tears. "Never a dull moment around here."

"I shouldn't have touched you."

"Not that again."

He glanced at the waves, frowning. He seemed to be searching for the right words to apologize for rocking her world.

"It was a freak accident," she said.

"You got stung because of me."

"It wasn't because of you. Even if it happened while you were on top of me, it wouldn't have been your fault."

Color suffused his neck, as if he'd already pictured that scenario. She knew he felt responsible for her safety. He felt responsible for her kidnapping, and everything else. There was a new strain in his features, as if the past two days had aged him. Her illness must have really thrown him for a loop. The timing of the sting was disturbing, she had to admit. She'd been writhing in ecstasy one minute, doubled over in pain the next.

"I got stung because I wasn't watching where I was going, and stonefish look like stones. You didn't cause the injury."

"You were angry with me."

"Do you really want to rehash that?"

"I think we should talk about it, when you're well enough."

"I feel fine," she said, finishing the banana. She didn't want to have this conversation. It stirred up her anxiety, and she was still rattled by the nightmares. Now that she was lucid, she had to consider the consequences of their actions. Cadence Crenshaw, who always played it safe, had engaged in some incredibly risky behavior. She was going to spend the next few weeks with her fingers and her legs crossed. "I know we made a mistake. I won't try to jump on you again, if that's what you're worried about."

"You didn't jump on me. I jumped on you."

"I started it."

"And I ended it. Badly."

"We were both wrong."

"I'm the one who came inside you."

Her cheeks heated at the memory, but she pushed it aside. "I was upset about what you said, not what you did. It reminded me of something that happened with Andrew."

His brows drew together. "You had unprotected sex with Andrew?"

"No. We slept together once after he cheated."

"Why?"

She sifted sand through her fingertips, contemplative. "I don't know. I went to his apartment to get the last of my stuff. He was there, and… I wasn't going to take him back, but I still had feelings for him. I guess I wanted him to choose me over her."

"Did he?"

She shook her head. "As soon as it was over, he said he'd made a mistake and rushed me out the door."

Logan made a grunting sound, low in his throat. "Is he still with her?"

"No. She found out about his slipup with me and dumped him on the reality show. They competed against each other in the finale. She won. Then he started texting me again, saying he was sorry."

"What an asshole."

"Yeah," she said, but the memory caused no pain. A few months ago, it was the worst thing that had ever happened to her. Now it seemed like a lucky break. Maybe she'd never really been in love with Andrew. Her feelings for Logan were so much stronger. "Have you ever cheated on a girlfriend?"

"No."

"I guess it's easier when you don't have steady girlfriends."

He reached out to hold her hand. Then he brought her knuckles to his lips. "When we get back to the US, I want you to be my girlfriend."

She pulled away from him. "I don't think we should make plans."

"Why not?"

"You got bit by a shark this week. I got stung by a stonefish. This island makes its own plans."

His eyes darkened at her claim. "This island isn't in charge. We are. We've come this far, and we're going to find a way home."

She wanted to believe him. It was herself she doubted, more than him. When they'd arrived here, she'd been at a low point. She'd been uprooted from her job and her home. She'd faced an uncertain future. The trauma of the kidnapping and being lost at sea had diminished her further. She'd felt weak and helpless.

She was a different person now. Her heart had healed well enough to love again. Her body was toned, her feet tough. She was stronger than she'd ever been, but she'd never be as brave or as optimistic as he was. She couldn't shake her feelings of dread.

"I had a dream that you died," she said.

"Me? I'm indestructible."

"We were in the raft, and I was…in labor."

His expression changed, revealing an emotion she hadn't seen before. It took her a few seconds to recognize it as fear. Apparently the thought of her having his baby was the one thing that truly scared him.

"I gave birth to a stonefish, and it stung you in the chest."

He schooled his features into a blank mask. "Was it a boy stonefish or a girl stonefish?"

This was the way he dealt with fear. He brushed it aside and made jokes. "Is that all you have to say?"

His jaw clenched with determination. "I'm not going to die here, and neither are you."

"What if we don't leave?"

"We will."

"You mean *you* will."

He studied her for a long moment. She remembered the threat he'd made about dragging her along. It didn't strike her as sexy anymore. There was a new edge to him, as if he'd been to hell and back over the past two days. "I won't leave you."

"Then we'll stay."

"No."

She rose to her feet, stomach roiling. "The raft isn't even seaworthy."

He stood with her. "It will be when I'm finished. I'll

make a sail, and we'll take plenty of food and water. I want it to be ready before monsoon season."

"You said it was a last resort!"

"That was before."

"Before we slept together?"

"Before you almost died in my arms," he said.

She stared at him in disbelief. "What happened to waiting it out? What happened to hoping for a passing ship?"

"I'll wait a few weeks. To find out if you're pregnant."

The blood drained from her face. "And if I am?"

"Then we'll go."

"I already said no. What are you going to do, knock me unconscious?"

"Of course not. I'll tie you up."

She crossed her arms over her chest, fighting tears. He could overpower her easily. He outweighed her by at least sixty pounds. The thought of him using brute force to take her choices away devastated her. His eyes told her that it devastated him, too. He wasn't the kind of man who put his hands on a woman unless she wanted him to.

"I won't stay here and watch you die in childbirth," he said.

"I'm probably not even pregnant."

"Maybe not now, but you will be. I can't keep my hands off you forever. I can't live here with you and not touch you."

"You're crazy."

He gripped her upper arms and held her close. "I'm not crazy. I'm in love with you."

She shoved at his chest. "No, you're not! You wouldn't even think about risking both our lives if you were!"

"I'm trying to save us!" he shouted back.

She studied his tense face. A muscle in his jaw flexed, and his eyes blazed with emotion. She thought he might shake her senseless or yell at her until she agreed, but he didn't do either. He released her and retreated a step.

"There was a woman, in Al-Hasakah," he said, after a pause.

"Where's that?"

"Syria. We'd been working with her husband. He was our interpreter. We promised them visas for helping us, but he got killed by insurgents after a few weeks. She was pregnant."

Cady leaned against the palm tree, feeling weak.

"She went into hiding, and we lost contact with her. One day a boy came to our camp saying she needed a doctor right away. We brought the medic, but it was too late."

"The baby?"

He shook his head, and her chest tightened with anguish.

"It wasn't your fault, Logan."

"Hud took it harder than I did. He'd recruited the interpreter, and he was still kind of messed up about his own wife having some other guy's kid. I think that's why he didn't retreat with us in Telskuf. We were targeting the same terrorists who killed the interpreter. Hud was out for blood."

"I'm sorry," she whispered.

His gaze met hers. "You asked me once if I've ever failed at anything. I have, and people died because of it. Those failures led me to this moment. I have to go get help before it's too late. Do you understand?"

Her eyes filled with tears and her throat closed up. He wasn't going to change his mind. He'd get that damned raft repaired. He'd work on it day and night. There was nothing she could do to stop him.

When she didn't answer, he picked up his spear and walked away. As if the discussion was over.

She watched him go, tears spilling down her cheeks. Then she curled up on the sand and cried for a long time. She cried for her parents and her dog and her best friend. She cried for her favorite foods, her favorite clothes, her favorite TV shows. She cried for toiletries and hair products. She cried for everything she missed and everything she'd lost.

After the tears dried up, anger settled in. She should have expected this. He'd been a bullheaded overachiever from day one. He was too damned antsy to stay here and wait for rescue. Of course he couldn't wait to try his luck at sea. He was a hotshot daredevil. He lived for opportunities like this.

Damn him.

And damn her, for falling in love with him.

She stared at the shoreline, feeling hopeless. She didn't know which was worse, staying here alone or going with him. She couldn't face the open ocean again, with its endless days and shark-plagued nights. But if she stayed behind, the torture of worrying about him would be equally unbearable.

Not that he was giving her a choice. He wouldn't leave her. End of story. He said he'd wait a few weeks, to find out if she was pregnant.

She slid her hand down her belly, eyes closed. They'd been so careless. She hadn't even thought about telling him to withdraw. She'd been too focused on her own pleasure. For the first time ever, intercourse had felt better than foreplay, and she'd reveled in his touch. She wouldn't have stopped him for the world.

He'd said he loved her. He'd said he couldn't keep his hands off her because he was in love with her. The confession weakened her knees, but it didn't improve their situation. It didn't assuage her fears about sailing away in a patched-up raft.

She took a deep breath and tried to look on the bright side. Maybe all of this arguing and angst was premature. Her cycles had always been irregular. The possibility of pregnancy from one encounter was low, especially under these circumstances. She'd lost weight. She hadn't been getting enough rest, or a balanced diet with the proper nutrients. The past month had been a roller coaster of stress and trauma. Plus, she'd just been stung by a stonefish!

There was no way she was pregnant. Her body was focused on purging the poison from her system, not fertilizing an egg.

She rose to her feet, frowning. They were fighting over a remote, hypothetical situation. That was against survival protocol. He always told her not to get hung up on worst-case scenarios or let fear take over.

He wasn't following his own advice, was he?

She headed in the direction he'd gone, hobbling on her sore foot. She found him sitting on a rock by the tide pools. He was repairing one of the fish baskets. He'd promised not to venture into deep water unless she was with him, acting as lookout. Apparently he'd broken that promise. He arched an arrogant brow, daring her to complain.

"I'm not done talking about this," she said.

He dusted off his hands and stood, ready to hear her

out. His lips curved into a humorless smile. She wasn't fooled by his hard face and obstinate attitude. He'd told her he loved her, and she hadn't responded in kind. He might not admit it, but he was feeling vulnerable. He was afraid of what the future held.

So was she.

"It's highly unlikely that I'm pregnant," she said. "My cycles have always been irregular. After what my body just went through, it's almost impossible."

"Okay," he said, shrugging. "But what if you are?"

"I don't want to go, either way."

"I get that."

She moistened her lips, nervous. "I think you're using this as an excuse to leave. You can't stand staying in one place. You're bored. You're ready to move on to the next challenge. Or the next conquest."

His stunned expression told her she'd hit a nerve. "Jesus," he said, raking a hand through his hair. "This is why I don't have girlfriends. Even on a deserted island, you can still manage to sound jealous."

"Am I wrong?"

"Yes," he said through clenched teeth. "You're wrong. I'm not bored with you. I don't want a new challenge. I just want you to be safe. I want to take action before it's too late. Why is that so hard to understand?"

She studied him for a moment, wavering. "It's a huge risk."

"It's a calculated risk," he said, setting aside the fish basket. "I've thought about every detail. All of the elements have to be perfect. If the patches don't keep a tight seal, or the sail doesn't work right, we won't go."

"And if I'm not pregnant, we'll stay?"

He rubbed a hand over his mouth. "Yeah. We'll stay."

"And we can go back to plan A? Waiting for a ship?"

"I can't wait forever."

"How long?"

"I don't know. Six months, maybe a year."

Although she didn't like his vague answer, she figured it was the best she'd get. She couldn't make him put off the journey indefinitely. He might not be looking for a new conquest, but he wouldn't let the island win. He wouldn't accept defeat.

"Do we have a deal?" he asked.

"There's one more thing."

"What?"

She took a deep breath and met his gaze. "You don't have to worry about this problem coming up again. I won't let you touch me."

His eyes darkened. "Fine."

She held out her hand. He shook it, agreeing to a deal they both disliked. They were going to avoid physical contact for the rest of their days here. Funny how she'd once thought that getting stuck on this island was a fate worse than death. Now she was clinging to it like a lifeline, terrified to leave.

It had been paradise, hadn't it? For an unfairly short time.

She believed he was sincere in his affections, despite her claim otherwise. They shared the same pain. His voice had been raw when he'd confessed his feelings for her. He'd told her the truth, and it was tearing him up inside.

In the real world, they wouldn't have been together long enough to fall in love. Here, they couldn't escape it.

That didn't mean she was going to tell him how she felt in return. She'd conceded to his plan. She'd already given him her body. She had nothing left. If she surrendered her heart, she'd crumble into a pile of sand and blow away.

So she offered him something else instead. "What do you need help with?"

He seemed surprised by the question, but they both knew he couldn't move the engine on his own. Maybe the raft would help them get rescued in the next few weeks. "I need help with the air pump, if you feel strong enough."

"Let's go."

# Chapter 19

It wasn't his best week.

Logan worked on the raft for several hours a day, in between fishing and other tasks. He needed Cady's help, and he was trying not to overtax her. She seemed to be recovering well, but she'd been quiet. He'd been downright silent.

What was there to say? He'd poured his heart out to her, and she'd accused him of wanting to leave because he was *bored.*

He wasn't bored. He was afraid.

She had no idea what he'd gone through after she'd gotten stung. He'd held her limp body in his arms and cried. He'd soaked her foot and bathed her clammy skin and prayed for her to wake up. He'd considered cutting into the wound and sucking out the poison, even though he knew it was an ineffective strategy. He'd been desperate.

After a long night and an endless day, her condition had improved. She'd gone from unconscious to merely sleeping. Then guilt had settled in. He'd started agonizing about life, rather than death. He'd thought about all of the reasons he shouldn't have touched her. He'd recognized that his mistake might have grave consequences. Nine months from now, she could die in childbirth. He imagined thirty-six hours of labor, with him as midwife. It was his worst nightmare.

Even if she managed to deliver a healthy baby…then what? He couldn't leave her here with a newborn. Babies were fragile. They needed stuff. The chances of survival, with no supplies or medicine, were not good.

But Cady refused to focus on that reality. She didn't want to risk the open ocean. She didn't believe she was pregnant. She thought he was overreacting, and making a rash decision based on a remote possibility. Maybe he was. Maybe she'd get her period next week, and he'd collapse in relief. Maybe she really wouldn't let him touch her for a year. Maybe they'd get rescued tomorrow.

He wasn't counting on any of that.

He was willing to relax his time line, however. She'd told him she might not get a period, even if she wasn't pregnant, because of her irregular cycle, plus the harsh conditions on the island. She'd also said that women often had miscarriages in the early stages. He'd promised to wait a few months.

He went to the tide pools at dawn, his mood dark. He was still angry with himself for failing to protect her. He'd been incredibly stupid and reckless. Now they faced the worst possible circumstances. What the hell was wrong with him? He wanted to beat his head against a rock, every single day.

It had taken an entire week to air up the raft. He'd found several leaks, which he'd repaired with tar patches. Then the engine didn't start, and he'd had to take it apart to study the components. After some tinkering, he got it going. He'd circumnavigated the island, alone at first. Cady had gone with him the second time around. The patches held. She'd studied the vast expanse of ocean, her curls flying in the wind. They didn't speak.

He'd stashed the raft in the cave, anchored so it wouldn't drift out to sea. His next step was building the sail, which might prove to be the most difficult phase of the project. He didn't know what kind of sail to make. He wasn't sure what the weather conditions would be. He had no idea where they were. His best guess was between Hawaii and Tahiti. They'd traveled on a west-flowing current to get here. That same current would take them away from the island.

They seemed to be entering a dry season, which meant he wouldn't be able to collect rain for drinking water during the trip. That was bad. But he also might not have to worry about storm swells and monsoons. That was good.

He swam out to deeper water to check his fish basket. They were in luck; a hefty mahimahi was trapped inside. He brought the fresh catch back to camp with pride.

"Nice," she said, as he dumped the fish on the sand.

"Let's have this for breakfast and take it easy today."

"Take it easy? You?"

"We can hike to the pool, collect some chestnuts."

She gave him a suspicious look. Hiking uphill wasn't exactly taking it easy, but spending a day at the big waterfall was a rare treat. It was her favorite place on the island, a paradise within a paradise. He liked it, too, even though visiting meant swimming naked with her and ignoring his base desires.

It wasn't as hard as it used to be. Well, it was still hard, but his physical needs paled in comparison to the emotional turmoil he'd experienced since her illness. He'd told her he loved her, and she'd pushed him away. Sexual frustration was insignificant.

She cleaned the fish with a deft hand, and they returned to the fire pit for a hot meal. Sometimes they ate bananas for dinner and fish at dawn. They both looked like beggars, with bare feet and frayed clothes. He worried about her slender form. She wasn't too thin yet, but she was compact and small-breasted, with a tiny waist. She'd never be lush and round here, no matter how much fish he caught.

After breakfast, they made their way uphill. He'd blazed a new trail a few weeks ago. Now they could access the waterfall from Shelter Bay without having to go through the cave and around the backside of the island. It was a short but challenging hike. Her foot had healed well enough. So had his arm. The shark bite scar was an ugly pink crescent above his elbow. His knee didn't hurt at all anymore.

When they arrived at the pool, he pretended to take a nap in the shade while she splashed around in the water. She hadn't danced since the stonefish incident. She hadn't screamed, either.

He missed both.

He heard her wade out of the pool, but he didn't look. She sat down on a mossy rock to braid her hair. He kept his eyes closed, listening to the sounds of tree frogs and rustling birds. When she wandered off to collect chestnuts, he took a turn in the water. He ducked his head under the rushing falls, scrubbing away the stink of a long week. He hadn't bothered with showering or washing his clothes lately. It felt good to immerse himself in clean, cool water. It felt good to massage his sore muscles.

When he was finished, he helped her gather bread-fruit and chestnuts. He'd brought the whalebone club with him. It acted sort of like a boomerang, knocking down fruit from high branches. They filled two bags before they headed downhill.

They took the scenic route on the way back because he wanted to check on the raft. He paused inside the cave, where the raft was anchored. The rope appeared to have loosened during the night.

"I have to retie this," he said. "Do you want to go on ahead?"

She nodded, eager to leave the dark recesses of the cavern. He secured the raft in a better spot and continued after her. On impulse, he plucked a red hibiscus flower from the vines overhanging the waterfall. He couldn't touch her, but his feelings hadn't changed. He was hopelessly in love with her. Maybe someday, when they were safe, they could be together again. As he strode down the beach, an ear-splitting scream rang out.

It was Cady, and this was no ordinary scream. He appreciated the sound now, and understood its nuances. He recognized the difference between her little shrieks of surprise, her throaty cries of pleasure and her real screams of terror.

This was the third kind, ratcheted up to ten.

He dropped the flower and started running. He passed Cady's Rock, his heart pounding with panic. Then he saw her. She was racing toward him on the narrow strip of sand between the tide pools and the cliffs. There was a man in hot pursuit.

A man.

One of the kidnappers, if Logan wasn't mistaken.

It was the same Polynesian man he'd choked out on

the mother ship. Logan hadn't seen another man in so long that he almost couldn't process the sight. He felt like he was dreaming. He was dreaming and running at the same time. He blinked to clear his vision, but it didn't help. The man was still there, chasing Cady.

Was this really happening? Had he stepped on a stonefish? Was he hallucinating?

Cady screamed again as the man tackled her around the waist. The sound cleared Logan's mind of everything but counterattack. His hand closed around the whalebone club at his belt. His feet barely touched the sand as he sprinted toward them. The man took Cady down, but he didn't have time to subdue her. He jumped up and whirled around to confront the bigger threat.

Logan closed in on him, holding the club high. The man's eyes glinted with recognition. He remembered Logan. He didn't appear intimidated, but why would he? Logan probably weighed one-seventy-five now, dripping wet. This guy was a hard-muscled two-fifty—and he had a knife.

He drew a wickedly curved blade and smiled.

Cady lay on the sand behind him, stunned. Logan hoped she wouldn't interfere. He didn't want her getting in the middle of this.

"Surrender," he said in French. It was the only French word he remembered.

The man replied with something guttural and profane-sounding. It wasn't an agreement; Logan knew that much. He stepped forward and feigned a right swing, which was the usual starting point. For amateurs. The man shifted his stance to avoid the hit, leaving his left side vulnerable. Logan transferred the weapon into his opposite hand behind his back and struck for real, aiming a brutal blow across the man's temple.

But his opponent was no amateur, either. He ducked.

Logan had been counting on the larger man to be clumsy and slow. He wasn't. He jabbed forward with the blade, narrowly missing Logan's torso. Cady screamed and kicked the sand, trying to trip him. The man jumped over her legs easily, but the split-second distraction worked in Logan's favor. He transferred the weapon to his right hand again and swung across his body, bringing the club down on his opponent's forearm.

It was a devastating hit, flaying skin and shattering bone. A strangled sound emerged from the man's throat. The knife dropped from his now-useless hand. Unfortunately, he didn't make the fatal mistake of retreating. Most wounded men took an instinctive step back, inadvertently giving their opponent the chance to strike again. This experienced warrior lowered his shoulder and drove forward, slamming into Logan's midsection.

In the next instant, they were rolling across the sand. Logan ended up on his back, unable to dislodge the heavier man. He was at an extreme disadvantage now. The man locked his left hand around Logan's right wrist and applied crushing force. Logan didn't let go—until he got head-butted in the temple.

His skull vibrated and black spots danced across his vision. The club slipped out of his slack hand. He couldn't free his arms to defend himself. The only way to avoid getting knocked by the next blow was to rock forward to meet it. He gritted his teeth in anticipation.

But the blow didn't come. Not to him, at least. Cady attacked from behind, cracking the man over the head with the club. His body went limp. Logan shoved him away and broke free, scrambling to his feet. The Polynesian man was facedown on the sand, unconscious.

Logan picked up the discarded knife and looked around, still reeling. He couldn't see Shelter Bay from here. They were in a secluded spot, close to the cliffs. He'd have to walk past the tide pools, to the flat rock he'd named Logan's Folly, for a better view. "Where are the others?"

"I don't know," she said, her lips trembling.

"What did you see?"

"I saw a ship in the bay, and a raft at the shore. I didn't stop to stare. I just turned around and started running."

"You did good," he said, kissing her forehead. She'd saved his life. She'd probably saved her own life with that scream, but she also might have alerted the other men. There had to be others. The Polynesian hadn't arrived here on his own. "Let's go."

He ran as fast as he could on unsteady legs. They reentered the cave, wading through the knee-high water. His hands shook as he untied the anchor rope he'd just secured.

"Where are we going?" she asked as they climbed inside the raft.

"Around the island. I have to sabotage their raft first. Then we can take the ship."

"Forget the raft," she said. "Let's just take the ship."

"Too risky," he said, starting the engine. It sputtered twice and turned over. "If they have guns, they'll follow and shoot at us."

He drove out of the cave as fast as possible. There were no kidnappers on their tail as he rounded the southernmost tip of the island. He hooked a left, cruising by

Treasure Cove. Before they reached East Eden, he slowed down. "You have to get out."

Her lips parted in shock. "What?"

"Stay here and hide. I'll come back for you when it's safe."

"I'm not getting out!"

"Get out, or I'll throw you out," he said in a hard voice. He meant it.

She stared at him in dismay. Tears filled her eyes, but she didn't argue. "Promise me you'll come back."

"I'll come back," he said, crushing his lips to hers. "Nothing could keep me from you."

With an anguished sob, she climbed over the side of the raft and swam the short distance to the shore. He waited until she ducked behind a cluster of rocks. Then he continued on his journey, hoping he hadn't lied to her.

Praying he wouldn't fail—again.

If he couldn't execute this plan, they were both doomed.

Cady couldn't believe he'd left her.

She sank to a sitting position behind the rock, filled with dread. She shouldn't have been surprised he'd left her behind. She knew he'd do anything to protect her. He was more than willing to risk his own life. She remembered how hard he'd fought during the kidnapping, and how aggressive he'd been with her captors. The sight of him using lethal force had terrified her. It still did. She was trembling uncontrollably, her heart racing.

She squeezed her eyes shut and took deep breaths.

Damn it.

If only she wasn't crazy in love with him. If only he wasn't crazy.

After a slow count to ten, her tremors subsided. She hated being here alone, but maybe it was better than watching him in action. She didn't want to see him taking on men twice his size, or gutting his opponents like fish. She didn't want to fight alongside him. She'd tucked the whalebone club into her waistband, though the thought of using it again made her queasy.

She heard the whine of an approaching engine, which was strange. Logan couldn't have circled the island already. He'd only been gone two or three minutes. The motor sounded funny to her ears, buzzing too high. She froze as she realized it wasn't him.

It was the kidnappers, looking for him.

They were going to find him at Shelter Bay. Or they'd follow him back here. She bit the edge of her fist, horrified.

She had to do something to help him. She had to take the risk. If she caused a distraction, Logan might have time to get away.

Decision made, she jumped to her feet and ran for the cliffs. There wasn't really a path, so she couldn't climb fast. The last time she'd done this with Logan, she'd almost plummeted to her death. But she was stronger now, and more confident about her abilities. She grabbed a handhold and pulled herself up. The whining motor grew louder. She glanced over her shoulder, swallowing hard.

Then two men in a raft flew by.

She didn't recognize either of them. The man Logan had fought near the tide pools wasn't in the raft. For several breathless seconds, she thought they weren't going to see her. Then her foot slipped, sending a spray of peb-

bles down the cliff. She clung to the rock face and locked
eyes with the passenger. He pointed at her.

The driver slowed, turning the raft around.

She reached the top of the cliff and searched for a hiding place. There was no convenient boulder to crouch
behind, so she got down on the ground among a thick
tangle of vines. She covered her head with her arms, an-
ticipating gunfire. Her pulse pounded with adrenaline,
and her life flashed before her eyes.

The men didn't shoot at her or even dock their raft.
They had a short conversation she couldn't hear. Judging by their gestures and expressions, it was contentious.
As she watched them through the foliage, the passenger jumped overboard and started swimming. The raft
sped away.

Cady didn't know what to do next. She hoped she'd
given Logan an extra minute, and a fighting chance.
Maybe she'd put herself in danger and done nothing helpful whatsoever.

That was the problem with taking risks. You never
knew when they'd pay off.

She waited for the passenger to reach the cliffs, staying low. As soon as his attention was focused on the
climb, she leaped to her feet and kept going. It would be
easy to hide in the jungle interior. She had the advantage here. She was familiar with the terrain. She knew
the rocks, the plants, the water, the soil. She'd become
one with it.

She ran into the jungle and immersed herself in the
foliage. He'd never find her. She was a sea krait in shallow water, a centipede scuttling across a rock, a stonefish camouflaged by the ocean floor.

She wasn't six feet tall and fearless, like Logan. She

didn't have his muscle mass or his nerves of steel, but she was a force of nature in her own right. This island had taught her that the smallest things could be the most deadly.

And she would attack, if she had to.

## *Chapter 20*

Logan surveyed the scene as he arrived at Shelter Bay.

The mother ship was docked about a half-mile from the reef. It was the same cabin cruiser he remembered. In the harsh afternoon sunlight, it looked shoddy and worn down. Even so, it was a beautiful sight. A sea-worthy ship beat his patched-up raft by a long shot. His spirits soared at the thought of stealing it from the pirates and sailing away with Cady. That kind of poetic justice was what dreams were made of.

But his dream evaporated as soon as he got closer, because there was no other raft to sabotage.

What the hell?

The man Cady had knocked out cold was sitting on the driftwood log by Logan's fire pit, eating a banana that Logan had picked. Logan's gaze narrowed in irritation. He should've cut the guy's throat when he had the chance. Killing a defenseless man was unpleasant, but sometimes it was good strategy. He hadn't been thinking clearly. Spending a month here with Cady had turned him into a goddamned hippie.

The Polynesian had roused, dragged himself down the beach and alerted his friends. They'd probably taken their raft on a trip around the island. There was a chance that they'd spotted Cady. His gut clenched with unease. When he'd left her, she'd been hidden. She wouldn't have done anything to attract attention.

Would she?

Swallowing hard, he made a beeline for the mother ship. Stealing it wasn't an option at this point, because he wouldn't go anywhere without Cady, but he could use the radio and look for a gun.

He hadn't gone far when the pirate raft appeared, racing toward him at full speed. There was only one man inside. Another European. Logan got a glimpse of a long face and graying beard.

Logan cursed under his breath and changed course again. Now he didn't have time to climb aboard the mother ship. Graybeard would catch up to him before he got there. Even if the guy was unarmed, which Logan doubted, his instincts told him to evade and outmaneuver.

He sped along the reef, pushing the limits of his patchwork raft. Judging by the sound of the motor, the man wasn't hot on his tail. A glance over his shoulder revealed the reason. Graybeard had stopped at Shelter Bay to pick up reinforcements. The Polynesian climbed into the raft before they continued after him.

Logan returned his attention to the shoreline, his jaw tight. He really shouldn't have let that guy live. They'd tussled twice, and he'd needed Cady's help to win both times. He didn't feel good about a third matchup.

He drove into the dark recesses of Sea Krait Cave, grateful for high tide. His pursuers were less than a minute behind him. They hadn't seen him come in, but they'd figure it out soon enough. He cut the engine, jumped into the shallow water and waded toward the opposite exit. He waited there, his heartbeat thundering in his chest. He strained to listen for the pirates. Then he spotted the raft.

The driver cruised by and doubled back to look for him, just as Logan had expected. The instant they were out of sight, Logan emerged from the cave and started climbing the outside wall. It was technically difficult. He'd never done it before. He wasn't sure it could be done. That didn't stop him.

He had to kill both of these bastards. He could not fail. His plan was risky, but it was his best chance of survival. It was also his best chance to save Cady. If he succeeded, he could salvage their relationship and win her heart.

First, he had to survive this climb.

He managed to get to the top somehow. It was half adrenaline, half insanity. He reached the summit and lay flat on his belly, looking down over the falls. He was perched on a perilous, moss-slick slope. There was a basketball-sized boulder within reach. He'd seen it from Cady's Rock, ironically. The day she'd been spying on him, he'd glanced toward the falls from her vantage point and spotted that boulder. He'd made a note to check its stability because it looked like a hazard. Then he'd noticed her flushed face and twisted bikini bottoms, and his brain had short-circuited.

The forgotten boulder was easy to dislodge. He held it there, ready to roll.

The pirates didn't enter the mouth of the cave at first. Graybeard returned to the opposite side of the island to drop off the Polynesian. Logan watched as the Polynesian jumped into the water, swam ashore at Treasure Beach, and went inside the back of the cave to flush Logan out.

Graybeard drove back to the main entrance and parked there. He left his raft at the edge of the sand. He was tall and lean, with the confidence of a man who trusted his muscle to take care of business. Even so, he released the snap on his gun holster, wiggling his fingers in anticipation.

Logan waited for him to approach.

He had no idea who these men were, why they'd targeted Maya O'Brien, or if they even knew Cady wasn't her. He wasn't sure why they'd landed here, but he was going to make them regret it.

*Come and get me, you bastards.*

When the Polynesian man appeared at the entrance, empty-handed, Graybeard swore in French and stepped closer to take a look. Logan pushed the boulder down the slope—and almost went tumbling after it. He slid several feet, struggling to regain his handhold, as the boulder picked up momentum. It dislodged rocks and rained pebbles down the falls. It also rolled off target, and might have missed both men completely if Graybeard hadn't panicked. He shoved the other man's shoulder in an attempt to get clear. The Polynesian stumbled and caught the boulder like a cannon.

He fell flat on his back, his chest crushed.

Logan had been aiming for Graybeard, but at least he'd hit something. He expected Graybeard to flee into the recesses of the cave. He didn't. He glanced up, spotted Logan and lifted his arm to shoot.

Logan was stuck. Retreating wasn't an option, because he couldn't scramble back up the slippery slope. He was fully committed to this course of action. There was no escape route or eject button. He could either get shot or attack. So he attacked.

He let himself slide down the falls and tumble over the edge, making a human boulder. He kicked Graybeard in the face. The gun fired, sending a bullet ricocheting through the cave. They both went down hard in the shallow water.

Graybeard's body absorbed most of the impact, which saved Logan from broken bones. He still got slammed, though. The air rushed from his lungs, leaving him lightheaded. His temple throbbed from the earlier blow.

Logan shook it off and grabbed Graybeard by the front of the shirt. Instead of fumbling for a weapon on his belt, he used his fists. It wasn't a graceful or particularly efficient form of combat, but he made every strike count. Graybeard seemed stunned by the assault. He didn't even fight back.

"You killed my brother," the man said in stilted English.

"He deserved it," Logan replied.

The man looked around for his gun. Logan spotted the weapon on the wet sand nearby. When Graybeard reached for it, Logan shoved a forearm across his throat, holding him underwater. It was a struggle to finish the job. He needed to rest, to catch his breath. Finally Graybeard's body went limp, and Logan heard a telltale splash behind him.

Someone else was coming.

Cady climbed a breadfruit tree and watched the passenger ascend the cliff.

She knew better than to try to ambush him. He was a short man, but not slight. He had broad shoulders and a cap of curly reddish hair. In a physical altercation, he'd win easily. She had to stay safe and put as much distance between them as possible.

He paused at the edge of the jungle, squinting. The most direct route to Shelter Bay was straight ahead. He headed that way, as expected. As soon as he was out of sight, she climbed down the tree and hurried south, toward Treasure Beach. She could cut through the sea cave and take the longer route to Shelter Bay. She might get there first. It was difficult terrain to navigate. The pirate might wander around in circles for hours.

Or he might double back and surprise her.

She ran as fast as she could.

The sharp crack of gunfire echoed in the distance, cutting through the muggy air. Her heart lodged in her throat. She stumbled and almost fell, sobbing with panic. As soon as she reached the cliff overlooking Treasure Beach, she dropped to her belly to study the scene below. She didn't see anyone on the beach or near the back of the cave. She didn't hear the buzz of engines as two rafts drag-raced around the island. She had no idea where Logan was. He could be waiting for her at East Eden.

Or he could be dying of a gunshot wound in Shelter Bay.

She leaped to her feet, pulse pounding. She could either stay here and play it safe, or keep moving and fight for her man.

She kept moving.

She scrambled down the side of the cliff and raced across the beach. Before she entered the cave, she took out the whalebone club. Inside, the cave was darker and spookier than ever. She proceeded with caution, creeping forward. She could smell gasoline and something acrid, maybe gunshot residue. When the wet sand at her feet turned into black water, she shivered. But she didn't stop.

Two figures were locked in battle at the mouth of the cave. One man appeared to be choking the other, who was half-submerged in the shallow water. She could see the silhouette of broad shoulders, framed by a sunset backdrop.

It might be Logan. It might not.

She gripped the club tighter, ready to brain someone. Disturbing images flashed through her mind. She remembered Logan on the night of the kidnapping, grappling on the floor with veins popping out of his neck.

She blinked away the memories and kept going. Water swirled around her calves, snakelike. When she was close enough to strike, the victor let go of the man beneath him. He glanced back at her.

It was Logan.

She dropped the club and fell to her knees beside him. He turned to embrace her, burying his face in her neck. Her chest swelled with emotion, and she sobbed with relief. They were okay. He'd risked his life for her, and she'd done the same for him. They'd survived.

He thrust his hands in her hair and kissed her forehead. Then he just looked at her, as if he wasn't sure she was real. She glanced around, shivering. They were alone, other than the two dead bodies near the mouth of the cave.

"Is there one more?" Logan asked.

"Yes."

He picked up a gun from the wet sand and tucked it into the waistband of his pants. Then he approached the pirate raft and stabbed his knife into the side. It began to deflate immediately. Hand in hand, they waded back into the cave to retrieve their raft. She climbed inside with him, eager to escape.

She didn't know what to expect as they sped away from the shore. The redheaded man stood on the beach at Shelter Bay. Now he was stranded. She thought he might try to follow them, but he didn't. She thought there might be another man on the ship, waiting to kill them, but there wasn't.

She used the ladder to board the ship after Logan declared it safe. She helped him load the raft on the deck. It felt strange to be on the pirate ship. It felt strange to be anywhere but on the island. He used the navigation system to chart a course to the nearest hub of civilization, a place called Nuku Hiva. It was more than a hundred miles away.

As she watched Shelter Bay grow smaller and smaller, she considered all the things she'd left behind. Her cooking shells. Her coconut cups. The baskets she'd woven. The shelter they'd built together. Tears pricked her eyes, because she'd miss it. She'd miss dancing on the shore and bathing in the waterfall. She'd miss the sunsets. She'd miss the person she'd become and the man she'd fallen in love with.

Nothing would ever compare to this. Nothing would ever be the same.

# Chapter 21

It took them twelve hours to reach Nuku Hiva.

The trip was arduous, but uneventful. Logan kept his hands on the wheel and his eyes on the dark sea, which seemed to go on forever. They'd truly been out in the middle of nowhere. According to the ship's navigation system, they'd been stranded on an island called Eiao. From Eiao, you could travel thousands of miles in almost every direction without hitting land. Or you could head southeast to Nuku Hiva.

"Would we have made it in the raft?" she asked.

"No."

"Not a chance?"

"The odds aren't good. The current would've taken us the wrong way."

She stayed by his side, leaning her head against his shoulder. She'd found an old blanket to keep them warm. He'd told her to go belowdecks to lie down, but she couldn't. She couldn't sleep on this ship, in the same space the pirates had inhabited. In the same space she'd been terrorized. She didn't feel safe.

She worried about underwater obstacles, lost shipping containers and rogue waves. She worried about a second pirate ship, although he assured her there wasn't one. She worried about the GPS and the sonar and the fuel gauge, all of which he claimed were in working order. She wouldn't relax until they were on dry land.

Maybe not even then.

The night stretched on, endless as the ocean. They didn't talk about what had happened, or celebrate their escape. It didn't seem real. She felt like she was dreaming. She might wake up any moment, still stranded.

At dawn, they finally reached Nuku Hiva, and she could hardly keep her eyes open. She was exhausted, physically and emotionally. She wondered if fatigue was a symptom of trauma. She remembered shutting down after the kidnapping. Shutting him out.

Less than two months later, she wasn't as affected by death or danger. She hadn't become inured to it, but she wasn't frozen in fear. The second attack hadn't rattled her as much. She'd been hardened by the harsh conditions on the island and the daily struggle for survival. She was a warrior now, battle scarred.

He docked the ship in a port among a handful of other vessels. There were shiny yachts next to beat-up fishing boats. A local policeman was patrolling the dock. He didn't speak English, so Cady asked him in French where they could go for help. He escorted them a short distance to the Gendarmerie Nationale.

From there, Logan called the Naval Air Station in Coronado and asked to speak to his commander. The man didn't seem to believe it was him. Logan had to recite a security code. Then he laughed into the receiver, and everything was okay. His boss wired them money and faxed a copy of Logan's credentials.

Cady wanted to call her mother, but Logan said they had to wait for an okay. They also had to stay put for a few days. His boss was sending someone to assist them, but Nuku Hiva was a remote location, thousands of miles from the nearest US Embassy.

Cady didn't mind waiting. She was too exhausted to travel, anyway.

There was a hotel across the street from the gendarmerie, and a pharmacy, and a little tourist shop with casual clothing. Cady was wearing Logan's shirt with her bikini bottoms. Logan was wearing his pants, and nothing else. They were both barefoot. He'd left his weapons on the boat, but he still looked like a savage.

They bought a few necessities at the pharmacy first. She lingered in the makeup section, delighted by the sparse selection. His eyes lit up at the sight of a disposable razor. These were precious commodities now, to be cherished. After paying for the items, they went next door to pick out new clothes. Dockers for him, with loafers and a basic T-shirt. She found a pair of sandals and a cute flower-print dress in pink and white.

He booked two rooms. She didn't know why, because he stayed with her and ordered room service. They ate a huge breakfast of eggs, bacon and pancakes. He cleaned his plate and finished hers. She thought her stomach might burst.

Her heart, too.

They curled up on the too-soft bed, marveling at the modern amenities. Running water. Air-conditioning. Carpet.

They didn't even shower. They just slept.

* * *

When Cady woke again, it was early evening and Logan was gone.

The note on the pillow read "dinner downstairs, 7:00 p.m."

It was 6:15.

She rolled over and stretched her arms, groaning. Sleeping in a real bed was disorienting. It was too comfortable. She felt like she'd been drugged in luxury. Getting up, she went to the bathroom and turned on the light.

She winced at her reflection. Mirrors were another luxury she could do without. Her hair was a frazzled mess. Her eyes were puffy, her cheekbones prominent. She filled the bathtub with water and stripped down, studying her naked body.

She'd lost weight, no doubt about it. She covered her teacup-sized breasts with her hands and turned around. She hadn't been this slim since her competitive dancing days. She still had some curves. She looked pretty healthy, considering. Dropping a few pounds wasn't the worst thing that could've happened. It was a miracle they were alive.

When she settled into the hot bath, she felt instantly transported. Submerging herself in warmth was glorious. She closed her eyes and lingered in the tub, smiling. Then she washed her hair and shaved her legs languidly. After she got out, she slathered her skin with moisturizer, pinned up her damp curls and tried on her new dress. It looked nice. The bright pink color set off her dark skin tone. She didn't have any underwear, but the dress was knee-length and demure. No one would know.

She applied makeup, because the natural look only went so far. Then she walked downstairs to meet Logan.

He was sitting at the restaurant bar. The beer bottle in his hand was the same brand he'd been drinking the night they met.

He rose to his feet and did a double take. "Wow."

She smiled at the compliment, doing her own double take. He'd shaved, which served to highlight his best features. He had an angular jaw, a strong chin and a very sensual mouth. The soft cotton T-shirt clung to his hard torso and broad shoulders. He smelled as good as he looked. "Wow, yourself."

"We clean up nice, don't we?"

"We do," she said, studying his face. He was leaner than he had been on the cruise, and more darkly tanned. There was another difference, in his eyes. His gaze carried more weight than it had before. He was still a heartbreaker, unfairly handsome, but he didn't seem as restless. He looked rock-steady, like a man who knew what he wanted.

"Are you hungry?" he asked.

"Starving," she said, though it wasn't quite true. She couldn't use the exaggeration without remembering how hunger pangs felt.

They were led to a quiet table with an ocean view. She sat down across from him. The lighting was low and romantic, adding to the ambience. A waiter appeared with menus. She asked for a glass of white wine. Logan lifted his empty beer bottle. After the waiter left, Logan glanced at his menu.

"I'm not ordering fish," he said in a low voice.

"Are you sure?" she teased. "They have a nice *poisson cru.*"

"What's that?"

"It's like ceviche."

"No way," he said, closing his menu. "I want a steak."

She laughed in agreement. When the waiter returned, she ordered for both of them. Someday she'd try *poisson cru*. Right now, she couldn't stomach it. As much as she loved seafood, she might not eat it again for weeks.

He stared at her from across the table, his expression inscrutable. She could sense his tension, and it wasn't just sexual. There was unfinished business between them. Unanswered questions about their relationship.

On the island, she'd been afraid to make plans for the future. Now they were here. The future had arrived, earlier than expected. They were safe, but were they officially together? He'd said he couldn't touch her because of professional ethics. Was she supposed to pretend nothing happened?

"I'm going back to Eiao," he said.

She tilted her head to one side. "What?"

"Tomorrow, or the next day. I'm going back with my team."

"Why?"

"We have to apprehend the last guy, and recover the bodies."

"Why do you have to go with them?"

"I know the layout of the island. I know all the hiding places. I want to go, and there's no reason for me to stay behind."

"Oh."

He picked up his beer bottle, and set it down again. "That's not what I meant."

"You didn't mean that I'm not a good reason to stay?"

"It's a short assignment. Six men against one. There's nothing to worry about."

She drank a sip from her wineglass. It was nice, but

she needed something stronger. It hadn't occurred to her that he wouldn't take time off to recover. They'd been on that island for more than a month. They'd barely survived the second attack. She was still reeling from that narrow escape, and trying to sort out her feelings for him.

"We just got here," she said.

"I know."

"We haven't even been safe twenty-four hours, and you can't wait to go back?"

"I didn't say that."

"No, you said there was no good reason to stay."

He picked up his bottle again. This time, he drank.

"You killed two men yesterday."

"I remember."

"Why are you so eager to risk your life again?"

"I'm not. I don't want to leave you."

"But you're jumping at the chance."

He leaned forward and held her gaze. "I want to assist the investigation. I want to know why those men targeted Maya O'Brien, and who they're connected to, and if there are any other attacks planned. This is my job."

"Are you required to be there?"

"No. I volunteered."

"Of course you did."

"What do you expect me to do?"

She couldn't ask him to choose her over his career. She wouldn't even ask him to sit out this particular assignment. Although it wasn't an unfair request, she knew he wouldn't grant it. This was who he was. She could take it or leave it.

"I won't be gone long," he said. "Maybe a couple of days. When I get back, we can spend more time together. I'll come to visit you."

"Let's not make plans."

He flinched at her words. "Why not?"

She gestured to the space between them, indicating their relationship. "This might not even work in real life. We got attached to each other because of the circumstances, but we're not stranded anymore. Feelings change."

"My feelings won't change," he said.

The waiter arrived with two plates, interrupting the conversation. It was just a basic salad with vinaigrette, but her mouth watered at the sight of fresh vegetables. They both devoured every bite.

"Can we start over?" he asked. "I don't want to argue. We should be enjoying ourselves. We're in a room with four walls, sitting at a table with real utensils. We're eating food that I didn't have to catch with a spear, and you didn't have to cook it on a campfire. My beer is cold. This is amazing."

She finished her glass of wine. It was pretty amazing. She didn't want to argue, either. She didn't want to think about him leaving. "If we're starting over, I'd rather go back to the night we met."

He arched a brow. "You want to finish our date?"

"It wasn't really a date."

"Whatever it was, it got rudely interrupted."

She smiled in agreement. "Yes, it did."

"We can pretend it didn't."

Her stomach fluttered with awareness. A do-over would be perfect. They could pretend they were still on the cruise ship. "Okay."

He took another swig of beer, giving her a measured look. "I want you to know something first."

"What?"

"I meant what I said on the island. Every word."

Her eyes filled with tears, and her throat closed up. She nodded an acknowledgment. He'd told her that he loved her. She loved him, too, even if she couldn't say it yet. She wasn't ready to take that risk. They'd only known each other a month, and they'd been isolated the entire time. She couldn't give him her heart, but she could surrender her body. She could enjoy his. They could make the most of this night together.

"Do you want another glass of wine, or is one your limit?"

"Are you trying to get me drunk?"

"Just tipsy," he said, his mouth quirking.

She let the waiter refill her glass, already halfway there. She was willing to take some risks tonight. When their meals arrived, she tried to eat slowly and savor every bite. She was acutely aware of his gaze, and of her nudity beneath the dress. He watched her like a wolf waiting for his prey to start running. She shifted her bare legs together, remembering the excitement of the chase. She remembered how he'd looked at her on the dance floor, as if he'd wanted to devour her on the spot. He still looked at her like that. If he knew she wasn't wearing any panties, he'd probably leap across the table.

Her cheeks warmed at the thought.

The waiter appeared to take their plates away.

*"En dessert?"* the waiter said, describing the options.

"What do they have?" Logan asked her.

"Coconut cake and bananas flambé."

He laughed at the choices, shaking his head. They could pretend she'd never been kidnapped, but they couldn't pretend to want coconut or bananas.

*"Chocolat, s'il vous plaît,"* she said to the waiter.

The man gave a polite nod and disappeared again.

"Where did you learn French?" he asked.

"I spent a semester in Paris. Study abroad program."

They spoke about the different places they'd visited, keeping the conversation light. Then they shared the chocolate mousse that came five minutes later. It was deliciously rich and decadent, with a froth of whipped cream on top. She moaned in delight. She'd missed chocolate, and spoons, and ice-cold refrigeration.

He fed her the last dollop. She licked the spoon and leaned back in her chair, satisfied. She was full, but not as full as she'd been after breakfast. She'd paced herself.

He paid the check and sat quietly while she sipped her white wine. The jukebox started playing some French reggae music. It reminded her of the Bob Marley song they'd danced to on the cruise ship. His eyes connected with hers, and they traveled back in time.

"Want to dance?" he asked, just like before.

"There's no dance floor."

He stood and offered her his hand. "We don't need one."

She walked outside with him. Her bare legs brushed together with every step. The restaurant's back patio was deserted. Moonlight sparkled over the bay. He skipped the dancing-apart step and pulled her into his arms. She clung to his neck, already breathless. They swayed together as one, their bodies close together. Within moments, he was aroused.

So was she. She'd been aroused since she got here. The ocean breeze caressed her skin. She rubbed against him.

He paused, stilling her motions.

"It's the dress, isn't it?"

"It's not the dress. It's what's underneath the dress."

"Nothing," she whispered in his ear.

His hands flexed at her hips, as if he wanted to draw the fabric up to expose her to the night air. Then he went off script and crushed his mouth over hers. His kiss was deep and desperate, his tongue searching. She threaded her fingers through his short hair and kissed him back with an eager moan.

He broke the contact before they got too carried away. "We should take this somewhere private."

"Okay."

"My room or yours?"

"Let's try mine."

"Good idea."

They rushed through the restaurant and headed upstairs, hand in hand. He kissed her on the landing, and again outside her room. It was just like old times. It was better. She laughed into his mouth as he fumbled with the key. Then they were inside the room.

He pressed her back against the door and devoured her. She wrapped her arms around his neck and her legs around his waist. His hands found her bare bottom beneath her dress. He froze, panting against her neck.

"I thought you were winding me up."

"No."

He tugged the bodice down and lowered his mouth to her breasts. She gasped at the sensation of his tongue on her tight nipples. It was so good, she couldn't stand it. She threaded her fingers through his hair, dying of pleasure.

He went down on his knees and took it to the next level. Shoving her dress to her waist, he studied her exposed flesh. Then he looked up at her, his face taut. "I can't believe you went to dinner like this."

"I've done it before," she reminded him. "Just not in public."

His nostrils flared at the memory of her feeding him with her bare hands, wearing nothing but a grass skirt. He'd clearly enjoyed that, and she'd gotten a thrill out of serving him.

"Spread your legs," he said.

She almost swooned at the order. Letting her head rock back against the door, she widened her stance. Then she kicked off her sandal and lifted one foot to his shoulder, giving him even better access. He kept her dress bunched in his fist and kissed her swollen sex, his tongue hot.

She panted with arousal, already close. His teasing licks weren't enough. She wanted one of those screaming orgasms, followed by a hard pounding against a rock. He appeared to share her urgency. Instead of finishing her off with his mouth, like she'd expected, he rose to his feet and removed his shirt.

"Yes," she said, to his bare chest.

"Yes what?"

She moistened her lips, unsure what he was asking.

"How do you want it?"

She pushed her dress to the floor. "However you want to give it to me."

He must have bought condoms at the pharmacy this afternoon. He took one out of his pocket, studying her naked body. It took him about ten seconds to drop his pants and suit up. She wrapped her hand around his latex-covered shaft, biting her lower lip. He was deliciously hard and thick.

He pushed her hand away and lifted her against the wall. She let out a strangled cry as he thrust inside her.

Then he paused, as if gauging her reaction. He didn't have any trouble holding up her weight. She felt pinned by his gaze, impaled on his length. Watching her face, he withdrew halfway and drove deep again.

"Ohh," she said, her eyes rolling back in her head. "God."

He gripped her bottom with big hands, rocking her body with every thrust. He did it again, and again, driving her wild. She dug her fingernails into his shoulders, sobbing. Her cries were getting really loud.

"What do you need?" he asked.

He knew what she needed. His erection throbbed inside her, huge and hot, but it didn't pinpoint her pleasure. It brought her to a fever pitch, teetering on the edge.

"Please," she said.

He took pity on her and carried her away from the wall. When he reached the bed, he fell down on his back. His shaft went deep and high, hitting a place no one had ever been before. She was stretched tight around him, filled to the hilt. He groaned at the sight. His hands roved her body, skimming her waist and hips. He pinched her hard nipples while she rode his slick shaft. She felt a surge of wetness between her legs and moaned, moving up and down.

He licked his thumb and placed it right where she wanted it. She bucked her hips as he stroked her slippery sex. "I love this," he said, burying one hand in her hair. The other stayed between them, strumming gently. "Tell me you do, too."

"I love it."

"Tell me you love me."

"I love you," she said, her inhibitions gone. She tipped over the edge, her body shuddering with the most powerful orgasm she'd ever experienced. It rocketed through her like a freight train, going on and on. He petted her expertly, drawing out the pleasure. Then he covered her mouth with his, swallowing her cries with a sensual kiss.

She was still feeling the aftershocks when he rolled on top of her.

"I love you," he said in a guttural voice. "I love your body and your mouth and your hot, wet—"

He broke off, his shoulders quaking from the power of his release. He buried his face in her neck and thrust hard, driving deep one last time. Then he collapsed over her, sweaty and spent. She hugged him close, listening to his thundering heart. She relished his loss of control, his intense lovemaking. He was raw and wild.

Here, in this middle place between reality and fantasy, they were wild together. They were meant for each other.

He was hers, she was his, and nothing else mattered.

# Chapter 22

Logan woke the next morning with a massive sex hangover.

It felt pretty great.

He'd spent the entire night in bed with Cady. Well, mostly in bed. He'd also taken her in the shower, against the sink, and on the floor. They'd gone out for ice cream once. They'd napped between encounters. But they'd made the most of their time together and then some. He'd worshipped her body. She'd worshipped his. He'd told her he loved her again. She'd said it back to him—on her knees.

It didn't get any better than that, did it?

He curled up next to her, kissing her bare shoulder. She was fast asleep, facing away from him. The sheets were tangled around her hips. He studied her soft hair on the pillow and her smooth, dark skin. His blood thickened with arousal, and his chest swelled with emotion. He'd never get his fill of her.

She made a sleepy sound and snuggled into the covers. Most of her back was exposed, almost to the cleft of her buttocks. He pressed his lips there, at the base of her spine. Then he worked his way up to the nape of her neck. By the time he arrived, she was awake, reaching back to twine her fingers in his hair.

He growled against her ear, pushing the blankets aside. His erection pulsed against her bare bottom. He wanted to enter her from behind, maybe bite her neck a little. He was an animal with her, insatiable. There was nothing he wouldn't do to her.

She shifted her hips, encouraging him. He toyed with her taut brown nipples, which were so damned succulent, he couldn't stand it. Then he smoothed his hand down her flat belly. She spread her sleek thighs. He kissed the side of her neck and slid one finger into her snug heat, groaning.

He was always hard for her. She was always wet.

He gripped his shaft and imagined thrusting inside her, just like that. He'd been using condoms every time, and he had a box by the nightstand. The urge to proceed without one was tempting. It would feel good, going bare. He wouldn't do it, but he wanted to. She glanced over her shoulder at him, her eyes half-lidded.

Then someone started knocking on the door.

Not her door, but his, which was adjacent.

His stomach dropped. He scrambled out of the bed, searching for his pants. His erection could pound nails.

The knocking continued, along with the murmur of male voices.

"Who is that?" Cady asked.

Logan wasn't sure which team members his commander had sent. He yanked his pants up his hips and went to the door. When he opened it, he saw three SEALs standing in the hall outside his room. Gonzales, Pepperdine and Samir.

"I told you we had the wrong room," Samir said.

"What's up," Logan said. He was glad to see them, even under these circumstances. "Give me a second to get dressed."

"Don't bother," Pepperdine said, lifting a rucksack. "I brought you some utilities."

All three men strode toward his door. Logan accepted the rucksack with a grunt of thanks. It held a combat utility uniform, which meant they were leaving Nuku Hiva right now. "I'll be ready in ten."

Gonzales seemed amused by Logan's cagey attitude. "We took a twenty-four hour flight to get here, and you're going to make us wait outside?"

Logan had opened the door partway to set down the rucksack. He couldn't slam the door in their faces without arousing suspicion. He also couldn't prevent them from crowding around and glancing in. They all got a glimpse of Cady, wild-haired and obviously naked, with a sheet clutched to her chest.

"Oh," Pepperdine said.

Gonzales licked his lips. "Who's that?"

Logan dragged a hand down his jaw. They knew who she was. They wouldn't be here if they hadn't been briefed. Gonzales was angling for an introduction. Logan stepped back, letting the door fall open. "This is Cadence Crenshaw," he said. "Cady, this is Petty Officer John Pepperdine, Petty Officer Omar Samir and Petty Officer Richard Gonzales."

"Ma'am," Pepperdine said.

Samir said hello.

"You can call me Ricky," Gonzales said, flashing his movie-star smile.

Logan gave him a warning look.

"We'll be downstairs," Pepperdine said. "See you in ten."

After they walked away, Logan shut the door. "Sorry," he said to Cady. "I didn't expect them this early."

"You're leaving right now?"

He opened the rucksack and pulled out his pants. "I'd stay if I could."

"No, you wouldn't. You already got what you wanted."

"That's not true."

"Isn't it?"

"I want more than one night with you, and you know it."

She rose from the bed, wrapping the sheet around her body. "You already took more than one night."

He didn't know what she meant, and he didn't have time to argue. "Can we talk about this when I get back?"

"You wrung a confession out of me. That wasn't fair."

He put his pants on and tucked himself in. "I didn't make you do anything but come a lot. If that's a crime, I'm guilty."

"Tell me you love me," she said, mimicking his masculine voice.

His face suffused with heat. He had said that. He'd said it with his finger on her trigger, after he'd reduced her to begging. "Okay, you win. I made you say it. I made you admit that you feel the same way I do."

"Maybe I didn't mean it."

He tossed his shirt aside and stepped forward, gripping her upper arms. "I don't believe you."

She jerked away from his hold, as if he was hurting

her. Then her brow furrowed, and she turned her back on him. He studied the bare shoulders he'd kissed this morning, wishing they hadn't been interrupted. He didn't want to say goodbye like this. He knew she cared about him, or she wouldn't be so upset about him leaving. But did she love him? Or had she told him what he wanted to hear in bed?

"You did mean it," he said. "You're just afraid to feel. You're afraid to take a risk."

"I'm afraid of losing you, you idiot!"

He grasped her upper arms, gentler this time. "I'll come back to you," he said, kissing the top of her head. "I promise."

"Just go," she said, her voice choked with tears. "Go be a hero."

He grabbed the rucksack and left without another word.

## Chapter 23

Cady didn't have much time to cry over Logan.

She paced around the room for a few minutes and threw some pillows at the door. That wasn't satisfying, so she crumpled to the floor and pounded her fists against the carpet. She hated this feeling. She cursed him for leaving her, for making her fall in love with him and for being too damned good in bed.

Then the phone rang, interrupting her pity party. She wiped the tears from her eyes and picked up the receiver. "Hello?"

"It's Logan." He sounded as miserable as she felt.

"What do you want?"

"We're leaving now, and I might be hard to reach for the next few days. I thought I'd let you know what to expect while I'm gone."

She shifted the phone to her other ear. "I'm listening."

"Two intelligence officers are on the way from Tahiti. They'll interview you about the kidnapping, and all of the events between then and now. Tell them whatever you want. Whatever you remember."

She interpreted that as an invitation to be honest about their sexual relationship. "Okay."

"After the interview, someone will escort you to Papeete. It's a more centralized location. You'll be safe there."

Ironic, that he was concerned about *her* safety.

"I left some money for you at the front desk, but you won't need to pay for anything. You'll be well taken care of."

"What about you?"

"I'll be fine. This is a level-two mission, very low risk." There was some noise in the background, a combination of voices. "I have to go now."

She hung up before he could turn her into mush with another declaration of love. She was still mad about him leaving. He'd almost died on that island more times than she could count. He knew how she'd feel about him going back. Even so, he'd jumped at the first chance to return, completely disregarding her concerns. She wasn't ready to let him off the hook yet.

She put on her flower-print dress and walked across the street. She used his cash to buy some underwear, a canvas bag and a second outfit. After she ate breakfast, a man in a suit arrived with two US Marshals, one male and one female. They escorted her to the Gendarmerie Nationale. The marshals waited in the front office while she sat down in a private room with the intelligence officer.

She told him the truth, but she didn't say anything about having sex with Logan, on the island or anywhere else.

Officer Sloan listened carefully, making notes here and there. "We don't have footage of the kidnapping.

Several witnesses saw you leave the bar with Petty Officer Starke. There were signs of activity in the cabin, but no proof of foul play. Investigators called it an accident. They thought you'd fallen over the balcony, and he went in after you."

Cady inhaled a sharp breath. "Was I considered missing, or…?"

"You were presumed dead. Both of you."

She clapped a hand over her mouth, making a sound of distress. Her parents had been notified that she was dead? Tears filled her eyes at the awful thought.

Sloan wanted to know about the kidnappers, but she could only give vague descriptions. He opened a laptop and showed her some photographs. The main suspects were two brothers. They had a cousin with red hair. All three were from an island called New Caine, on the edge of French Polynesia.

Cady couldn't identify them. The only man she'd seen up close had been Polynesian. "Why would they want to kidnap me? Or Maya O'Brien?"

He closed his laptop. "They belong to a faction called the FNF, or French National Front, in New Caine. France bought the land to use as a penal colony in the 1800s. It recently achieved independence, with help from the UN. There's been a history of unrest between the descendants of French prisoners and the natives."

"The natives are Polynesian?"

"No, they're Melanesian. Like indigenous Australians. The Polynesians in New Caine aren't friendly with these natives. Neither are the French nationals, who don't want to cede any territory to them, as directed by the UN Security Council."

"President O'Brien is involved in that."

"Yes. The FNF threatened retaliation against him specifically."

She found the news unsettling. She'd always liked President O'Brien. She'd been eighteen when he took office, and so proud to be an American at that moment. She'd watched his daughters grow up. They didn't deserve to be targeted by terrorists. "I'm glad they failed," she said, her voice quavering.

"So am I," Sloan said.

"Should I be worried about someone coming after me?"

"I don't think so. Three of the four perpetrators are dead. The other will be captured in short order. His associates have no reason to harm you, and they're all on a watch list, unable to enter the US."

"When can I go back?"

"Now," he said, his brows raised. "If you feel well enough to travel."

She did, so the female marshal drove her to a tiny little airport. They took a plane called an "island-hopper," which made her stomach lurch with every dip in elevation. She closed her eyes, wishing Logan was there. She really needed to hold his hand.

They reached Tahiti in the early afternoon. A bone-deep fatigue settled over her, making her brain fuzzy and her eyelids heavy. She'd hardly slept last night, but she couldn't wait to go home. She couldn't wait to see her parents, and feel safe again. The marshal booked them on the first flight to LAX.

The next day, she was back in Long Beach, sobbing on the couch with her mother. Her parents were over the moon. Even her dad cried. They'd been planning a wake!

She told them about the kidnapping, and being lost at sea. Then she crawled into bed and slept for hours.

When she woke up, she had a note on her door about a doctor's appointment. She was supposed to see a doctor as soon as possible because she'd been exposed to so many health hazards during her extended stay on Eiao.

Her mom took her to the appointment, after making a giant breakfast to "fatten her up." Cady ate every bite dutifully. There was nothing like home cooking.

The physician at the Army-Navy hospital seemed alarmed by the fact that she'd been stung by a stonefish and received no medical attention afterward. Cady got a full workup, complete with blood and urine tests. She waited for the results in an exam room, hoping she didn't have scurvy, island fever or brain damage.

When the doctor returned, she had a serious look on her face.

"Oh, God," she said, holding a palm to her heart. "I have malaria, don't I?"

The doctor smiled. "No, no. Nothing like that."

"What is it?"

She reached out to squeeze her shoulder. "You're pregnant."

Cady heard a series of warning bells go off inside her brain. This couldn't be true. There had to be some mistake. "Are you sure? Because I have irregular periods, and I was unconscious for two days, and I lost ten pounds in a month, and I was under so much stress..."

"The test results are positive."

"Oh, God," she said. She moved her hand from her chest to her flat stomach. "Oh, God."

Logan had been right.

How was this even possible? The only time she'd ever

had unprotected sex—the only time she'd ever taken that kind of risk—she'd ended up pregnant.

Unbelievable.

"I understand that you were the victim of an international crime," the doctor said.

"Yes."

"If there was a sexual assault…"

"No," she said, swallowing hard. "It was consensual. The man who rescued me is the father."

"Okay," the doctor said in a calm voice. "You're only a few weeks along, so you have plenty of time to think about your options. If you don't wish to terminate the pregnancy, you can start taking prenatal vitamins and make an appointment with an OB. There shouldn't be any ill effects from the poison, because implantation occurred after the sting."

Cady remembered her nightmare about the stonefish baby. Feeling queasy, she accepted a free sample of prenatal vitamins and walked into the lobby. Her mother knew something was wrong at first glance.

"What is it?" she asked.

"Let's sit down," Cady said. They found a quiet corner in the back. Then she took a deep breath and told the whole story. She started with their arrival at Eiao and ended with the test results, blinking away tears.

Her mother gave her a tissue. She didn't seem horrified by the news. "This man loves you?"

"He says he does."

"And you love him?"

She nodded, her face crumpling.

"But you don't want to have a baby with him?"

"Of course not. We've only known each other for five weeks."

"You've spent every single day with him for five weeks."

She hadn't thought of it that way. The hours probably added up to six months or more with a regular boyfriend.

"Is something wrong with him?"

"Yes. He's a Navy SEAL."

"And?"

"You know how careful I am. He's a risk taker." She crumpled the tissue in her fist. "He's not a safe choice."

"He got you back here in one piece, didn't he?"

Cady couldn't argue there.

"You think he's going to run around on you, like that other fool?"

"No," she said, because it wasn't her main concern. Logan might have been a player before they met, but she believed he would be faithful. He was loyal to his team. When he did something, he didn't do it halfway. "I think he's got a dangerous job, and he's going to drive me crazy with worry. He's doing it right now."

"Oh."

"Don't you worry about Dad?"

"Of course I do. But I deal with it."

"How?"

"I keep busy. When you were little, I had my hands full taking care of you. Now I have a career, and hobbies and friends."

Tears filled Cady's eyes again. She made it sound so simple.

"Are you afraid he'll get hurt, or that you will?"

"Both," she said. If her relationship with Logan didn't work out, she'd be devastated. She couldn't stand the thought of losing him. Loving him was the ultimate risk.

"I've never felt this way before, like I might die if he breaks my heart."

"You won't die. He might break your heart and drive you crazy, but you won't die. You're a survivor."

She took a deep breath. She was, wasn't she?

"He also might be perfect for you. He fell for you for a reason. It takes a strong woman to love a man like that."

"You think I'm strong?"

"I know you are."

Cady's chest tightened with emotion. She hadn't felt strong before she met Logan, but she hadn't been weak. She'd just been lost. In a way, the island had revived her. She'd found love, and she'd found herself.

Tears spilled down her cheeks. She didn't know if it was the pregnancy or the epiphany that was making her so weepy. Either way, she needed to let it out. Her mother put her arms around her and held her while she cried.

## *Chapter 24*

Logan found a bloodbath on Eiao.

He hadn't expected any serious danger there. It was one man against six. The worst he'd imagined was a long, drawn-out search process, in which the target attempted to evade capture by disappearing into the jungle.

What they encountered wasn't a clever criminal, or even a mild threat. It was just a fresh corpse on the beach, not far from the tide pools. He was lying in a circle of red sand, next to a broken bamboo raft. Apparently this guy had decided to take it out for a spin, maybe catch some nice fish. Instead he'd met up with Mr. Tiger. His left foot was gone, severed jaggedly at the ankle. He must have lost a lot of blood before he reached the shore. By the time he crawled out of the surf, it was too late. He was hemorrhaging, unable to stop the flow. Ribbons of flesh hung from the stump like pale fringe.

"Guess he won't be talking about his terrorist connections," Pepperdine said.

"Guess not," Logan replied, staring at the man's dead face.

Instead of launching a manhunt, they started processing the scene. The other two bodies were just as ugly. The Polynesian had crabs all over him. He was still pinned to the ground by the boulder, teeth bared in a death grimace. Graybeard had drifted into the recesses of the cave. He was harder to find than his red-haired friend.

When they dragged him out into the light, a sea krait emerged from his open mouth and wound around his fish-white neck.

His comrades made noises of disgust, shoving at each other.

Gonzales high-fived Logan for taking down two tangos and leaving a third for the shark. They all thought Logan's shark bite scar was pretty cool. They examined the camp at Shelter Bay like a group of boy scouts on a tropical vacation. Adult boy scouts, who ribbed him about how he'd spent his nights with Cady.

"Careful," he said. "That's my future wife you're talking about."

His teammates laughed at this, as if he was joking. But they shut up, just in case. They took pictures, bagged the bodies and loaded them up. Then they headed back to Nuku Hiva. Cady wasn't there, or in nearby Tahiti. Officer Sloan told Logan that she'd taken a late flight from Papeete to LAX.

"Your future wife left you," Gonzales said, smirking.

"Shut up, Gonzales," Pepperdine said.

Logan knew none of his buddies would rat him out about being in Cady's hotel room. They might tease him, but they'd have his back. He'd earned their respect. Whatever he did behind closed doors was his business.

It didn't matter, because he planned to be honest about their relationship. It wasn't a secret that he'd left the bar with Cady. He'd learned that there was no security footage from the hallway, due to a camera malfunction. Cruise ship officials had pieced together an explanation for their disappearance.

Logan found this story implausible, but it had a precedent. Drunk people had fallen over the railings of cruise ships before. Some jumped willingly, to commit suicide. Others did it in an attempt to save others. The chances of surviving such an accident were almost nil.

No one had even bothered looking for them.

Logan spent most of the day with Officer Sloan, going over the real story. Sloan didn't seem interested in the details of his relationship with Cady, so Logan didn't share them. They took an island-hopper to Papeete, and an afternoon flight from there to LAX. He wanted to call Cady as soon as the plane touched ground, but it was four in the morning. And he didn't actually know her number.

The closest naval base was an hour away, in the opposite direction of Long Beach, so he didn't go there. He booked a hotel near the airport and slept for a few hours, only to be jolted awake by ringing. He picked up the phone by his bed.

"Hello?"

"Petty Officer Starke?"

"Yeah."

"This is Commander Doheny. I'm sending a car to pick you up at eleven hundred. I need you and Miss Crenshaw to come downtown to the Intelligence Office. She's already been notified. Do you have dress blues?"

"I have service khakis," he said, sitting upright. He'd worn them on the plane.

"That's fine. Be ready, and try to look sharp."

"Yes, sir," he said, because that was the only response possible. Then he hung up and stared at the phone.

What was happening? Was he going to get interrogated? Reprimanded?

It was after ten already, and his khakis were in a wrinkled pile on the floor. Luckily, he was in a good hotel. He called the front desk to let them know he needed food and laundry services on the double. Someone came to pick up his khakis, promising to return within the hour. He shaved, showered and ate breakfast.

His car arrived two minutes early. It looked like a secret service limo, complete with an armed driver. Logan didn't ask questions. He just got in and went along for the ride. They went to a quiet-looking neighborhood in Long Beach.

Cady was standing on the front step in a daffodil-colored dress. Her hair was a cloud of ebony curls, soft and pretty. She was a natural beauty, and he'd liked her wild-island style, but all dolled up, she took his breath away.

He got out of the car to greet her parents. They were a mixed-race couple in their fifties. Cady got her good looks from her mother, who eyed Logan with a knowing smile. After Cady introduced them, her father shook his hand and thumped him on the back, thanking him profusely. Her mother just shook his hand.

Logan helped Cady into the limo and sat down beside her. He'd replayed their last conversation over and over again. He'd planned some things to say to her. Right now, he couldn't remember any of them. He just stared.

"You're a sight for sore eyes," he said.

"So are you," she admitted.

Straight up, like always.

"You told your mother about us. But not your dad."

"How do you know?"

"He was too friendly. He wasn't even eyeballing me."

"She'll probably tell him while we're gone."

"Is he a gun owner?"

She laughed at the question. "He is."

Logan didn't think he'd get quite as warm a reception the next time they met.

"Where are we going?" she asked.

"The NIO. Naval Intelligence Office."

"Why?"

"I'm not sure. They might want a second interview, with a sworn statement. They might want to tell us how to deal with the media."

She blinked in surprise. "The media?"

"This is the kind of story they like."

"I don't want to talk to the media."

"I'm with you on that," he said, glancing at her. He wanted to take her by the hand and kiss her knuckles. But he didn't reach out, because they weren't really alone, and this was official business.

"How did it go on the island?" she asked.

"It went fine."

"Did you capture him?"

"No. He'd…been bitten by a shark."

Her mouth dropped open. "Was he dead?"

Logan nodded, telling her a gentler version of the scene at Shelter Bay. "We wanted to take him alive for questioning, but there are other ways to get information. Other connections to investigate."

"When did you get here?"

"I flew in to LAX this morning, before dawn."

"Did you sleep?"

"A few hours."

They were quiet for the next twenty minutes. He studied her knee-length dress, admiring her smooth calves and stylish shoes. They were closed over the toe, with thin straps across the ankle and tiny little buckles. The look wasn't sexy, exactly. Maybe sexy librarian. She was dressed appropriately for…whatever they were doing.

"I like your outfit," he said.

"I like your uniform."

"This old thing? You should see me in my dress blues."

She smiled, looking away. "Modest, as always."

They arrived at the NIO, which was a distinguished brick building in downtown LA. Logan hadn't been there before. The driver escorted them to a quiet meeting room with a large table. Commander Doheny and some other bigwigs stood to greet him. There was a round of handshakes and introductions.

If Logan was in trouble, he was in *serious* trouble.

He sat down next to Cady, resisting the urge to tug at his collar. Was it hot in here? He needed a drink of water.

"Sorry for the mystery," Commander Doheny said. "This came together at the last minute. President O'Brien just flew in for a summit this afternoon in Rancho Mirage. He has a minute to say hello."

Logan drew a blank. "To who?"

The suits around the table laughed at his stupid question. "To you and Miss Crenshaw," Doheny explained.

Logan glanced at Cady. She looked terrified by the high-pressure situation. He tried to send calm vibes, but he didn't have any. There was no opportunity for the tension to build, because President O'Brien waltzed right in with a warm smile. Logan stood with Cady. He stayed close to her, in case she keeled over from shock.

O'Brien shook hands with Commander Doheny and the others. Logan couldn't believe he was in a room with the former president. O'Brien stepped forward to shake Cady's hand first. "Miss Crenshaw."

"It's an honor to meet you," she said, sounding stunned.

"Likewise," he replied, as if this was an important moment for him. He turned to Logan and shook his hand. "When I heard about what happened, I had to thank you in person. It could've been my daughter out there, lost at sea. The fact that you both survived is amazing. I'm told you're the reason, Petty Officer Starke."

Logan flushed at the praise. "We made a great team, actually."

O'Brien smiled again, his eyes crinkling at the corners. "I'm glad to hear it. Your commander says you'll be nominated for a bronze star."

That was news to Logan. He nodded, struck speechless.

"Maya asked me to give you this." O'Brien took an envelope out of his pocket for Cady. "She couldn't come with me, but she wanted to reach out."

"Thank you," Cady said, sniffling.

"If there's anything I can do for the two of you, let me know. You can call my office to get in touch."

They agreed dutifully. Then O'Brien had to leave. He walked out with his guards. Logan stared at the doorway, unable to process what had just happened.

"He shook my hand," Cady said.

"He gave you a letter," Logan added.

"He said you'd get a star!"

Logan was humbled by the moment. He'd been hoping he wouldn't get demoted for unbecoming conduct. A bronze star was beyond his wildest dreams. Commander Doheny returned to congratulate Logan on his nomination. His feet didn't hit the ground on the way to the limo.

"What does the letter say?"

Cady read it out loud. "I'm so sorry you were taken in my place. I'm glad you're okay. I'd love to hear the story of how you and Mr. Starke survived. Call or write me anytime. Best wishes, Maya."

He smiled as they climbed into the back seat. "Is there somewhere we can go to talk?"

She asked the driver to drop them off at a nearby botanical garden, which was perfect for what he intended. It was quiet and romantic. They strolled down the flower-lined path together, hand in hand.

"I always wanted to get married here," she said.

"Done."

She didn't laugh at his quick response. She let go of his hand, her brow furrowed.

Logan was serious about making things official, but maybe he was skipping a few steps. "You haven't forgiven me for going back to the island."

"It's not that."

"Am I moving too fast?"

She leaned her elbows against a wooden fence, contemplative. "I don't know if I can be the kind of woman you need."

"What kind is that?"

"Easy to leave. Quiet."

He did a double take. He had no idea where she'd gotten the impression that he preferred quiet, amenable women. "You think I need a lapdog?"

"I'm not calm or agreeable."

"I like that about you."

"We clash," she said. "I play it safe, and you take risks."

"We don't clash. We complement each other."

"We argue."

"So what? The only couples that don't argue are the ones who don't care. We disagree because we're passionate, not because we're wrong for each other. You're perfect. Calm women are boring."

She smiled at this overstatement.

He closed the distance between them and took her hand. He couldn't mess this up. She meant the world to him. "I understand why you were upset the morning I left. You said you weren't ready to make plans, and I didn't respect that. I wanted a commitment. I wanted to know how you felt. But I shouldn't have pushed you."

"Maybe I needed a little push."

He searched her gaze. "I don't want someone easy to leave. I want someone I can't wait to come home to."

Tears filled her eyes.

"And I don't need quiet. I need you. I love you just the way you are."

"I'm pregnant."

He wasn't sure he'd heard her correctly. He'd seen her lips move, but the words... "You're what?"

She pushed away from him. "I'm pregnant."

He raked his fingers through his hair, stunned by her announcement. Somewhere between the great escape and now, he'd stopped worrying about this possibility. He'd believed that thing she'd said about irregular periods. He'd convinced himself they were safe. "God," he said, imagining how this would've played out on the island. They'd have left on the raft and died. "We're lucky those kidnappers came back, aren't we?"

"You don't sound happy."

"Give me a minute. I'm still picking my heart up off the ground." He took a deep breath. "How do you feel?"

"Scared."

He nodded an acknowledgment. Parenthood was a scary prospect, full of challenges. "I'll take care of you."

"Will you have the baby for me?"

He chuckled, putting his arm around her. "I'll hold your hand, and rub your back."

She didn't pull away this time. "What if you're not there?"

"I'll be there. As soon as I know your due date, I'll request time off. I'll ask for short assignments from now until then. I'll do whatever it takes."

She rested her head against his chest. "Okay."

"Okay?"

"We can make it work."

"You'll marry me?"

"Yes."

"Are you sure?"

"Some risks are worth taking."

He wanted to shout across the rooftops, and do some victory laps around the gardens, but it was supposed to be a peaceful, meditative place. So he lifted her off her feet and carried her away from the path. She let out a little scream, clinging to his neck. He set her down underneath a willow tree, kissing her until they were both breathless.

They lingered beneath the weeping branches, enjoying the moment. He liked these gardens as a wedding venue. It was beautiful and intimate, with a bamboo forest that reminded him of Eiao.

"I guess I'll finally have to move out of my parents' house."

She laughed in agreement.

"My mother will be overjoyed. She's been telling me to settle down with a nice girl since I was twenty."

"Mine is already shopping for baby stuff."

"She knows?"

"She was with me at the appointment."

He gestured to a gazebo at the center of the garden. "I'm picturing a June wedding. You'll be adorably round. Flowers in your hair. What do you think?"

She didn't say no.

"Whatever you want to do. A small ceremony is fine with me. We could take a trip along the coast after, have a nice honeymoon…"

"Anything but a cruise."

"Agreed."

"I'd like a summer wedding," she said, looking up at him.

"Really?"

She nodded. "I love you."

He wrapped his arms around her, his throat tight with emotion. He couldn't believe his luck today. He'd met the president. He was getting nominated for a bronze star. He was going to be a father, and he'd won the woman of his dreams. It was overwhelming. "I can't promise that I'll never be in danger, or that I'll never leave."

"Will you do your best to come back to me?"

"Always," he said, kissing her lips. "I'll do whatever it takes. I love you so much, Cady. You won't be sorry you took a risk on me."

She threaded her fingers through his hair and kissed him back, as if she believed him. His heart pounded against hers, threatening to burst from happiness. They stayed under the tree for a long time, making plans. Then they strolled away from the gardens, hand in hand, and walked into their new life together.

\* \* \* \* \*

*Look for Logan's teammate's story
in the next Team Twelve novel
from Susan Cliff,
coming in early 2018!*

She was a quick learner and from the couch, Scrabble gave a
soft woof.

"Thanks, sweetie," Marie said to the dog, breaking the
lesson to go rub Scrabble's ears.

He stared at the two of them. "Choke hold."

Marie's eyebrows arched high as she gave him her attention.
"Really?"

He caught her hands and put them on his throat, immediately
regretting the contact. There was a warmth in her touch that left
him craving her hands on other parts of his body. To save his
sanity, he made her grip stronger. "Hold on. First, keep your
head."

"All right." Her eyes locked on his mouth and she licked
her lips.

A bolt of desire shot through his system. "Raise your arms
overhead and clasp your hands." He demonstrated and her gaze
drifted up his arms to his hands and back down to his biceps.

This was a bad idea. "Now sweep down and twist to one side." Gently, in slow motion, he showed her how to escape the hold.

"And run," she said for him when he was free of her.

"Your turn." He moved in front of her. "Ready?"

She gave an uncertain nod.

He wrapped his hands lightly around her throat, the blood in her veins fluttering under his hands. "This is practice," he reminded her as her eyes went wide and distant. Her hair was soft as silk against his knuckles. "Marie." He flexed his fingers, just enough to get her attention. "Keep your head."

He struggled to heed his own advice since everything inside him clamored to pull her into a much different embrace and discover if her lips were as soft as they looked.

"Uh-huh." Her arms came up, her hands clasped and she executed the motion perfectly, breaking his hold and dancing out of his reach.

"Well-done." He straightened his shirt and tucked it back into place.

"Thank you, Emiliano." She perched on the couch next to his dog. "That helps me feel better already."

Good news for one of them. Edgier than ever, he needed an escape. "I'll be in the study." He glanced at Scrabble, but she didn't budge from her place by Marie.

He left the room without another word. Her determination to be prepared and take care of herself made him want to lower his defenses and care for her. He couldn't afford that kind of mistake. His team was counting on him to do his part for the investigation and he would not let them down.

*Don't miss "Special Agent Cowboy"*
*by Regan Black in KILLER COLTON CHRISTMAS,*
*available December 2017 wherever*
*Harlequin® Romantic Suspense books and ebooks are sold.*

www.Harlequin.com

# Get 2 Free Books,

**HARLEQUIN**
ROMANTIC suspense

## Plus 2 Free Gifts—
just for trying the
## Reader Service!

HRS17R2

# *LOVE*
# Harlequin
# romance?

Join our Harlequin community to share your thoughts and connect with other romance readers!

Be the first to find out about promotions, news, and exclusive content!

Sign up for the Harlequin e-newsletter and download a free book from any series at

**www.TryHarlequin.com**

---

**CONNECT WITH US AT:**

Harlequin.com/Community

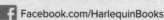 Facebook.com/HarlequinBooks

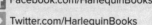 Twitter.com/HarlequinBooks

 Instagram.com/HarlequinBooks

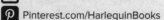 Pinterest.com/HarlequinBooks

ReaderService.com

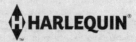 **HARLEQUIN**®

**ROMANCE WHEN
YOU NEED IT**

HSOCIAL2017